Miranda Writes

Gail Ward Olmsted

Black Rose Writing | Texas

First printing

This is a work of fiction. Names, characters, businesses, places, events, and incidents are either the products of the author's imagination or used in a fictitious manner. Any resemblance to actual persons, living or dead, or actual events is purely coincidental.

ISBN: 978-1-68513-023-7
PUBLISHED BY BLACK ROSE WRITING
www.blackrosewriting.com

Printed in the United States of America
Suggested Retail Price (SRP) $19.95

Miranda Writes is printed in Palatino Linotype

*As a planet-friendly publisher, Black Rose Writing does its best to eliminate unnecessary waste to reduce paper usage and energy costs, while never compromising the reading experience. As a result, the final word count vs. page count may not meet common expectations.

For Laurie, *toujours*

ACKNOWLEDGEMENTS

I wish to thank our niece Kim Early and her wife Sarah Kalka for helping me to understand the intricacies of the DCF (Department of Children and Families). Thank you to Amanda Dolan and Eliza Faris who clarified issues relating to the court system and the responsibilities of an Assistant State's Attorney. *Miranda Writes* is a work of fiction, but I wanted to include as much realistic detail as I could. I appreciate your interest, feedback and knowledge and if I got anything wrong, it's totally on me.

Thank you to editor-extraordinaire Anna Bennett. I love working with you. Thank you to Reagan and the BRW team for all of your support.

A final thank you to my husband Deane, who kept me well-fed and properly caffeinated during the writing of this book. You are the best person I know and I love you very much.

Miranda Rights

A legal requirement in the United States stating that suspects must be informed of their rights before they are interrogated. Based upon a 1966 case (Miranda v. Arizona) the U.S. Supreme Court ruled police must advise suspects in custody of their rights: the right to silence, the fact that any statement they make can be used against them, the right to counsel, access to counsel for indigent suspects and the assertion of rights at any time. The suspect must voluntarily waive their Miranda Rights before questioning can proceed. http://www.mirandarights.org/

Miranda Writes

A fictional blog and podcast written and narrated by Attorney Miranda Quinn, offering advice, interviews with experts and helpful information on all things legal.

Miranda
Writes

CHAPTER 1

Despite a brain still foggy from endless champagne toasts, I was feeling good. Yesterday had been a wonderful day. I finally had something to celebrate, following the demise of what had once promised to be a stellar legal career. My blog-turned-podcast, *Miranda Writes*, had recently garnered enough attention that the Sterling Broadcast Group had brought my closest supporters and me to New York in a limousine to sign a lucrative contract to host a daytime TV show. Things were looking up after a few tough years.

We had arrived back to Old Lyme, CT in the early evening and dropped off my dad and his girlfriend Sally, followed by my best friend Tracey and her husband Dale. Then, with help from the limo driver, I had carted all the floral arrangements and fruit baskets from future sponsors into my house. I was awestruck by the outpouring of support I had received. When I first started blogging, I had never imagined that it would lead to this. Honestly, back then I had been writing to maintain my sanity, nothing more.

The local network affiliate had already started airing promos of my upcoming show and I had stayed busy all night, fielding phone calls, texts and emails from friends, neighbors and former classmates. The calls stopped around 11:00 p.m., but I had lain awake for hours, my mind buzzing with topics for shows and names of legal experts I wanted to invite as guests. I had finally fallen asleep and was still in bed, debating the merits of a pot of home-brewed coffee and a slice of multigrain toast versus a drive-through latte and a cinnamon roll roughly the size of my head. My phone buzzed beside me. Probably a long-lost law school classmate or a childhood friend calling to congratulate me or to wish me well, I guessed. I checked the time as I found my phone. 5:45 a.m. Too early for a friendly call, I thought with a flicker of concern. *Hmmm*, unknown number.

"Hello."

"Um, hello. Is this Miss Quinn?" The voice was soft but familiar.

"Yes, this is Miranda. Can I help you?"

"Yes, ma'am. I need to talk to you, Miss Quinn. I don't know if you remember me—"

"Who is this?" I asked, barely masking my annoyance. I was rarely up for a game of twenty questions, and never before I had my coffee.

"It's, um. Becky. Becky Lewis." I sat bolt upright in bed, the chill I felt having nothing to do with the sudden loss of my down comforter. Becky Lewis? Yes, I certainly remembered her.

"Becky? Of course, I remember you. What's um, up?"

"I'm sorry, Miss Quinn. Really, I am. I saw you on TV last night and I thought I should get in touch with you about what happened." I was struggling to follow her. What had happened?

"What do you mean?"

"He did it again, Miss Quinn. He hurt that girl. Just like me and the other one." My heart sank. I knew who she meant. Of course, I did. Three years ago, I'd had the chance to put him away, and I had blown it. Now he had attacked another woman, and it was all my fault. This one was most definitely on me. But I still needed to ask. To be sure.

"Who, Becky? Who is *he*? What did he do?"

"Terry. Terry Kane. He raped another girl."

CHAPTER 2

I had worked for the New London District Court as an Assistant State's Attorney for nearly ten years when the Kane rape case was assigned to me. It was a weak case right from the start, but I had been determined to seek justice for the young victim. The police had brought nineteen-year-old Chelsea O'Hara to the emergency room at the New London Hospital on the morning of July 15. An anonymous tip about a young woman passed out in a public park had been called in. The responding officers noted she had been hit repeatedly in the face and her skirt was hiked up around her waist. She was barely conscious when the ambulance arrived, slurring her words and moaning. Upon examination and the processing of a rape kit, it was determined she had been brutally assaulted and raped in the early morning hours.

No witnesses had come forward in the following days, and Chelsea's recollection of her attacker was vague and slightly different each time she was questioned. According to her, he was white, tall—well, taller than her at 5'5"—possibly in his mid-twenties or even in his early thirties or maybe about her age. He was wearing jeans and a gray hoodie with a logo she didn't recognize, unless it was either a wolf or the mascot from her New London High School; a dog maybe? He had no tattoos or piercings, no facial hair. Well, maybe he had a goatee, but even with the hood on, she could tell his hair was a light color, so possibly his goatee would not have even been all that visible.

The assault had occurred when Chelsea was walking home from The Assembly, a blue-collar neighborhood bar at about midnight. She admitted to being maybe a little bit "wasted," but not that bad, as she could still walk, couldn't she? Her attacker had grabbed her as she passed the entrance to the park and dragged her into the bushes, where he punched her in the face while he pulled up her skirt and unbuckled his jeans. He forced himself on her, but since he used a condom, there was no semen to analyze. The rape kit examination revealed bruising and various abrasions. They found no discernible skin under her fingernails, although she thought she had fought back and was fairly certain she had scratched her attacker's face.

Chelsea recalled he had not exhibited even a trace of remorse when he was finished with her. She vaguely recalled him saying something like, "well, that ought to shut you up." According to her, he zipped up his jeans and adjusted his hoodie and as he left, he was humming to himself. After crawling out from the bushes, she passed out, coming to when the police and the ambulance arrived.

The police had combed the neighborhood, but were unsuccessful in locating any witnesses. They set up a tip line, and flyers featuring a sketch of a white guy in a hoodie were posted everywhere with a 'Have You Seen This Man?' headline. Traffic to the phone line was initially brisk, but although every call was taken seriously, it had soon become clear that the calls were essentially one of two types: some callers were eager to turn in their shifty neighbor or their creepy co-worker or one caller who claimed it could have been her ex-brother-in-law, who always had a 'funny way' about him. The other callers were seen as crank calls; Why was a girl walking alone? What had she done to attract attention? What had she been wearing? Was she high, drunk, or both? Was she just plain stupid? Was she a prostitute or a jilted girlfriend seeking revenge on her ex? After three weeks, the calls had essentially stopped coming in, until the night of August 8, when a timid girl's voice was recorded.

"Hello? I'm calling about that girl who got hurt in the park? I don't know his name, but some guy grabbed me near the park a few months ago. He hit me in the face and tried to drag me into the bushes, but I kicked him in the balls and got away. He was wearing a gray sweatshirt with the symbol from my high school. It was a bulldog, and I remember thinking it was weird cuz a guy I used to know had a bulldog named Rufus as a pet. So anyway, I hope you find the guy. Later ... um ... goodbye."

The next morning, the detectives assigned to the case had traced the call to a phone booth near the bus station. Many sets of fingerprints were visible, and luckily one of them matched a set already in the system. Six months ago, a young woman by the name of Rebecca Lewis was arrested for shoplifting. Her last known address was a shelter near the bus station. Officers found her there the next morning, and she agreed to come in and give a statement.

When they brought Becky in for questioning, an officer asked if maybe she should be accompanied by an adult, as she looked so young. But her ID showed her age as eighteen, so the questioning went ahead as planned. Becky's memory was sharper than Chelsea's and the detectives narrowed their search to a young white male in his late twenties who owned a gray hoodie bearing an image of New London High's mascot, the bulldog. The detectives assigned to the case went to work, narrowing their search to males in the system who met the general description and had attended NLHS.

Detectives then started scouring high school yearbooks for the years 2006-2010, looking for young men matching the attacker's description. Beginning with a list of nearly three hundred possible suspects, they narrowed their search to the twenty-seven who had a criminal record. A few days later, both

Becky and Chelsea identified high school photos of Terry Kane as their attacker, so they brought Kane in for questioning. Both girls picked Kane out in a lineup and claimed he had attacked them. Suddenly, the case was looking better.

When I met with Becky, I found her tearful account of the man who had dragged her into the bushes and tried to rape her was eerily consistent with that of Chelsea's, the victim in my case. Becky said, "he kept telling me to shut up, but that was weird cuz I was so scared I barely made a sound."

Kane's defense team had requested an expedited trial as their client was eager to put this all behind him. According to them, he wanted to "fight these baseless charges and restore his good name." I'd had no objection, as Chelsea's memory of the attack was fading almost as quickly as her bruises. The sooner I could get Becky to testify as a corroborating witness, the better it would be for our case.

When Becky disappeared from the motel where I had her stashed on the day she was to testify, the State's case against Kane fell apart. Tail between my legs, I slunk back to my office to host a pity party I assumed my colleagues would attend with me. I was wrong.

Word of my relationship with Adam Baxter reached my boss Rick Cooper, the State's Attorney for our district. I had never hidden the fact I was seeing another lawyer, but it wasn't exactly common knowledge either. Until it was. I was called into Cooper's office and questioned at length. Did I know my "lover" worked for the same law firm that had represented the defendant, Terry Kane? Did I ever divulge details about the case during "pillow talk"? Was I pressured to provide information that could be used in their case in defense of their client? I was adamant in my responses and vehemently defended my actions. Of course, I knew Adam worked for Schleyer, Houghton & Fogarty, the firm that had represented Kane. We had been dating nearly a year at the time of Kane's arrest. But Adam was not involved in this case and, as an associate, he was not privy to the strategies employed in cases other than his own. I had never divulged information about the case to Adam or anyone outside our department, I assured Rick. I chose not to tell my boss that after an evening in bed with Adam, I could barely put two words together, let alone have a meaningful conversation about my work.

But it was an election year and letting a suspected rapist go free did not look good for our office. They needed a scapegoat, so they asked me to leave. I received a paltry severance package and the assurance that they would keep the details of my sudden departure confidential. I had arrived back at the apartment Adam and I shared in nearby Mystic, feeling sad and angry and disappointed in myself. All that hard work. The eighty-hour work weeks, the promise of a bright future.

Vanished, just like Becky Lewis.

CHAPTER 3

Now I stared at the phone, picturing the girl on the other end. Becky had disappeared three years ago, and despite all my efforts to locate her, it seemed as if she had vanished into thin air. At some point, I had begun to believe she was dead. She was apparently waiting for me to say something, to tell her it would all be alright. I cleared my throat and took a deep breath. In my best lawyer's voice, I asked,

"How do you know this, Becky? How do you know it was Terry Kane?"

"I just know. They found that girl in the park. She told the police she had been raped. And I knew it. I just knew it. It was Kane."

"If you have evidence to support your claim, you should tell the police."

"It don't matter none, Miss Quinn. They got him already. They arrested him and this time they'll put him away. Locked up where he belongs." She didn't say the words aloud, but I could guess what she was thinking. *Please don't screw up the case and get him set free again.*

"Where did you hear this?"

"My sister told me about the girl in the park. And I just knew it was him. And then I saw you on TV. They said you're gonna be a celebrity or something. That you were going to host your own show. And I saw you and thought I should call you. You were nice to me. You believed in me and I let you down."

I *had* believed in Becky back then and I could still picture her so clearly. Such a tiny wisp of a girl. Slight build, long blonde hair, pretty when she smiled—which was not very often. Abusive home life, problems with drugs and alcohol since her early teens. Not the most credible witness I could have hoped for, but she was all I had in my efforts to get Kane convicted and sent to prison. I believed in his guilt as strongly as I believed in her account of the night when she had escaped Kane after he tried to assault her. And here she was, calling me three years later. Was she credible? Was she sober? Could I still believe her?

"Becky, I have to ask you—"

"I know Miss Quinn. I was high the night it happened and most of the days that followed. But I'm clean now. I swear I am. You can believe me."

"Where are you?"

"I'm back in New London," she admitted. "I was away for a while, but my sister needed me and I came back."

"Where are you right now? We need to talk."

She rattled off the address of the rooming house she was living in and I told her to sit tight. That I would see her soon. It was amazing how one phone call could change everything. Only yesterday, I had been out celebrating. *Miranda Writes* had filled a void in my life and resonated with readers, then listeners. With any luck, there would soon be viewers. I couldn't wait to get started on this next phase of my life.

But first, I had to get to Becky.

CHAPTER 4

I showered quickly and tried to recall all I could about Becky and the Kane case. Back then, I could not wrap my brain around the fact that she had bailed on me. Witnesses could be unreliable, but Becky had been so excited when I had brought her to the motel the afternoon before she was to testify. I assured her she would be safe and that I would order dinner to be delivered to her room that evening. "Don't leave the room," I had warned her, and she had looked at me, her blue eyes shining.

"I never want to leave this room," she had assured me, taking it all in. "It's the nicest place I've ever seen. I'm going to take a long hot bath, then watch TV in bed. Oooh, they have HBO," she had giggled. I looked around at the shabby room with its dated furnishings and tired bedspread. I was brought up on a beat cop's salary and while hardly the lap of luxury, my home growing up was opulent compared to the drab and rather dingy Ocean View Motel.

I left with instructions to listen for the knock around 8:00 p.m. when food would be delivered and reminded her to not open the door to anyone. I knew all this cloak and dagger stuff was probably nonsense, but I figured there was no good reason to take any chances. I spent the evening at home, preparing for trial the next day. Adam was also working late, arriving home around 10:00 p.m. We talked briefly before he kissed me and headed off to bed. I had kept at it, joining him a couple of hours later.

In the morning, I went to pick Becky up and found the bag of takeout food from the China Palace sitting untouched outside her door. Spidey senses tingling, I pounded on the door in vain before rushing to the front desk and demanding to be let into the room. I quickly realized my fear that she had gotten hold of drugs and OD'd was not the case. The room was empty and the full-to-the-top bathtub stood untouched, the suds long since gone and the water cold. A used towel lay in a heap on the floor. Her clothes were missing, and the bed had clearly not been slept in. I was both furious and scared shitless.

Had she gone off to score and forgotten about our arrangement? Gotten cold feet about testifying? I had known neither scenario made sense, recalling how enthusiastic she had been. Her plans for a bubble bath and a warm, cozy bed. And a hot meal. Even if she changed her mind about appearing in court, she would have taken advantage of some of the perks that had been offered. Wouldn't she?

I had assumed the worst. Someone had gotten to Becky and taken her against her will, probably only a short while after I had dropped her off yesterday afternoon. Unable to wait any longer, I had driven to the courthouse, praying that by some miracle, Becky would show up to testify. But she never did, and the case got thrown out and Terry Kane walked. And I lost my job.

It still haunted me, sometimes. Had I been followed? Had I inadvertently destroyed Becky's life the way I destroyed the case against Kane by losing her? She was never reported missing, and no one came to ask questions, so I had assumed that she'd left town and not looked back. I just didn't know if leaving had been her idea.

It looked like I might finally get some answers. I threw on a sweater and jeans, slipped my feet into a pair of ankle boots, and raced to my car.

CHAPTER 5

Driving through the familiar streets of downtown New London, I tried to put anxious thoughts aside, but I had my doubts. Had she been using this whole time? Having sex with strangers for cash or drugs? Three years was a long time, especially for someone living on the street. She had sounded good on the phone, but what could I expect when I saw her? This could be a wild goose chase. Worst-case scenario? An hour of my time wasted. But it might be a second chance to see Kane behind bars. A shot at reclaiming my reputation, maybe even a media boost to launch my new show? All the above? Cool your jets, hot stuff, I told myself. It's just a quick visit. But still.

There was light traffic this morning. I made a quick Dunkin drive-through stop and minutes later, arrived at the address Becky had given me. I sat and looked at the run-down structure with peeling paint and sagging porches. It had probably housed three separate families back in the day. Now it served as a transient boarding house of sorts.

I grabbed the box of donuts and the cardboard tray with two black coffees and a small bag of creamers and sugar packets. I approached the house warily. If Becky had told me her room number, I couldn't remember it, but before I even knocked, the door opened and a tiny blonde woman stood grinning up at me happily.

"You came, Miss Quinn. You really came." I was in awe at the change in Becky's appearance. Gone was the sallow, pockmarked skin, the limp blonde hair and the dull blue eyes. She had put on some much-needed weight, I noted, and her skin glowed. She went to hug me, but as I was loaded down with our breakfast, she settled for squeezing my arm, still grinning widely, showing off her lovely white teeth.

"Becky, my God. You look fabulous."

"You too, Miss Quinn. You haven't changed a bit."

"Please, it's Miranda. Well, Randi. That's what my friends call me."

"Randi? I like it and I'll try. I just think of you as Miss Quinn, you know? Well, come in. Where are my manners?"

I followed her through a dark vestibule and up a flight of stairs. As we approached her door, she turned to me. "I'm sorry. The place is kind of a mess. I haven't had time to—" I assured her it was no problem, that I was just glad to see her.

She pushed open the door, and we stepped into a bright, well-lit space: a large room with a bed pushed up along the far wall, a worn sofa, a tiny kitchenette and a crib. As I stared in surprise, the unmistakable sounds of a baby waking up filled the room. Becky crossed the room and scooped up a small child dressed in a yellow onesie.

"I'd like you to meet my son, Jesse. Jesse, this is Miss, um, Randi."

"Wow. A baby!" I hadn't seen that coming. I wiggled my fingers at him and he broke into a big grin.

"He's such a happy boy," said Becky. "Oooh, donuts!"

We drank our coffees and Becky wolfed down three donuts, all the while cuddling and cooing over the tiny human she had created since I had last seen her. He was a good-looking little fellow with a mass of dark brown hair and large brown eyes that seemed to see right through me. In between bites of jelly donuts and slurps of sweet, milky coffee, Becky shared that Jesse David Lewis was fourteen months old, had been born at Portland

General Hospital in Maine, currently weighed in at just over twenty pounds—which was amazing as his birth weight had been just five pounds—and his "best friend" was his two-year-old cousin Lucie, the daughter of Becky's sister Rachel. Becky did not divulge the identity of her baby's father, but given her background, it was certainly possible she didn't even know it. Her son looked well-cared for and appeared to be thriving. She was chattering away as I sipped at my coffee, watching her closely.

"We came back to New London a few months ago to help Rachel. She was separated from Eddie, Lucie's father, and she needed to work more hours. She's a hostess at the Indian Casino. So, Jesse and me moved in and I watched him and Lucie until last week. I found this place when Eddie returned. Rachel and I trade off babysitting so she can work and I can find a job." She sat back, apparently waiting for me to share something about my own life or ask her something. I had waited three years for this moment, but it was difficult to reconcile this glowing, healthy young woman with the scared, homeless waif I remembered. I had so many questions. Where to begin?

"Wow. That's a lot of information," I said. "But why did you disappear like that? You were all set to testify, and you just vanished." I couldn't hide the hurt I still felt over her betrayal. Becky's pretty face scrunched up in confusion.

"Why? He told me I needed to leave town. Said I was in danger. That you knew about it. That it was your idea," she protested. *My idea?* As if.

"Who told you that?" Becky looked surprised at my question.

"Adam."

CHAPTER 6

I sat back, shocked into silence. Adam? My former boyfriend, Adam? Adam Baxter had paid off the key witness in my case to make her disappear? The case that caused me to lose my job? The case that ruined my career? I had suspected Adam was hiding something back then, but I never actually thought he had been directly involved in Becky's disappearance. There had to be some sort of explanation. I took a deep breath before I responded, forcing myself to stay calm when all I wanted to do was scream.

"I'm sorry. I don't understand. Where did you meet Adam?"

"At the motel. He had your picture on his phone. Said you were gonna get married. He gave me five thousand dollars and brought me to the bus station. I went to Portland. In Maine. That's where I lived till a few months ago."

No, no, no, my inner voice begged. I squeezed my eyes shut, trying to block out an image of Adam paying Becky, forcing her to disappear. All to spite me. My heart racing, I gulped at air, trying to catch my breath. I needed to hear the entire story, and shouting at Becky would not help her trust me.

"What do you mean, Adam paid you five thousand dollars to leave town? What the f—hell are you talking about?" I asked, trying unsuccessfully to keep my tone even, calm. Becky placed her son back in his crib, returned to her seat, and grabbed another donut. With tears welling in her eyes, she broke the cruller into bite-sized pieces. Seeing her looking so miserable, I felt awful about my outburst.

"I'm sorry, Becky. I didn't mean to scare you. I'm just having a hard time believing Adam would do that."

Her blue eyes, now stormy, stared at me from out of her blotchy face as she struggled to regain her composure.

"I'm sorry Miss Randi. That was a bad time for me. I was using, and I was terrified. What if I went to court to testify against that Terry Kane and they arrested me for possession or prosti-, um, soliciting?"

"Is that why you didn't appear in court? Why you disappeared?"

"No, I told you. Your boyfriend Adam showed up and—"

"My former—never mind. Go on."

"Well, he knocked on the door and I ignored it, like you said. I was stepping into the tub and I thought he would just go away. But then he was shouting how you had sent him and you wanted him to get me somewhere safe. So now I'm like, 'what the hell? Maybe I should talk to this guy.' So, I peeked out and there's this big fella, all dressed sharp and looking good, you know? And he sees me looking, so he holds up his phone with this picture of the two of you: you and him all dressed up, looking like such a happy couple and all. And I'm thinking, 'well, maybe this dude's the real deal.' I put my T-shirt back on and wrapped a towel around me and I let him in. He was so nice, a proper gentleman. I've been in plenty of rooms with guys when I've been wearing a lot less than a towel, you know, but your um, Adam, made me feel comfortable, even though he said I was in danger. He told me to get dressed and grab my things, that he would take me some place safe." She took a breath, and I forced a smile and nodded gently. She continued.

"I said, 'should we just call Miss Quinn, you know, and ask her?' but he got all quiet and serious-like. He said it wasn't safe to call you and that he was my contact now. That you were having problems at work and were no longer assigned to the case. He told me to forget all about you. So, I got dressed and packed my things, including that pretty dress you got me for court. I still have it, the dress you know, but I can't wear it anymore. Since I got clean and then pregnant, I've been packing on the pounds."

"You look great, Becky," I assured her, eager to keep her on track. "Can we get back to that night? What happened when you left the motel?"

A puzzled look washed across her face, and she frowned at me, struggling to remember. "So, we got in his car and he wasn't talking much, like I had done something wrong. So, I said, 'what is it? Are you mad about something?' He just laughed and said, 'No, kid. I'm not mad, but listen, I gotta get you out of here, out of town, somewhere safe.' Then he drove me to the bus station, and he gave me a phone. He made me give him my phone. He told me they could track me and how I shouldn't call anyone, that he would call me when it was safe. We went inside and waited in a line and he bought a ticket. One-way and he gave it to me and told me I was traveling to Maine and that everything was gonna be okay and to lie low and not talk to anyone. He gave me an envelope full of cash and said to be careful and he patted me on the shoulder and said 'don't worry' and he walked me to the bus. He stood there and watched us drive away and I waved at him and he waved back. And I fell asleep and a few hours later, we were in Portland."

I sat spellbound, listening to her story, my mind racing. Think like a lawyer, not some vindictive ex-girlfriend, I told myself. If what she said was true, Adam was guilty of witness tampering at the very least. Probably obstruction of justice as well. But why? Had he been acting on his law firm's behalf? If so, why was Kane's legal team so hell-bent on getting him acquitted? I had to be certain Becky's account of that night was airtight if I was planning to take this sordid tale to the State's Attorney. I grabbed the pad I keep in my purse and a pen and sat forward, my eyes on hers.

"I appreciate your being honest with me, Becky. I need you to walk me through this one more time, and I'll be taking a few notes. You're not in any trouble, okay? Let's start with my leaving you at the motel. Tell me everything."

CHAPTER 7

Becky's second telling was consistent with her initial story. I
scribbled notes and asked for clarification on several points.
When we were finished, I felt confident I had what would be
required to get charges filed against Adam. I leaned back against
the sofa cushions and stretched. I felt no joy at the thought of
what Adam would face in court. If Becky's story were true, he
would be disbarred and probably face jail time. But I would be
redeemed in the process and could begin my new career with no
skeletons in my closet. And if Becky could testify and Kane spent
the rest of his life behind bars, it would provide Becky with the
closure she needed to move forward. Lost in thought, it took me
a moment to realize that Becky was still talking.

"I'm sorry. What did you say?"

"That's okay. I was just wondering about Kane's latest, um,
assault," she asked. "Can we find out more?"

"Sure. Let's check."

We searched for the police report on my phone. The details
were few and the name of the victim was being withheld. Kane
had been brought in for questioning last night and was
subsequently arrested on the charge of aggravated sexual
assault. He was being held in the New London jail pending
today's scheduled arraignment. I could only hope bail would be
denied and they could hold him until his trial.

We had run out of things to say, so I told Becky I would be in contact with her as soon as I knew anything. She thanked me for the donuts and hugged me with a fierceness that surprised me. I hugged her back and waved goodbye to Jesse, who was standing in his crib, a solemn look on his sweet face, his big brown eyes wide and curious. There was something so familiar about him.

***

As I walked to my car, I tried to recall everything I knew about Terence Thomas Kane. He had been raised by a single mother in one of New London's roughest neighborhoods. Then his mother married J. Blake Reis, a local business executive she had met while working at a gentleman's club. They moved across town to live with Reis in his large house in an upscale subdivision when Terry was eleven years old. That's when he had started cutting school and sneaking out at all hours. His step-father pulled some strings to get him into a private boarding school in order to separate him from the negative influences of his friends from the old neighborhood. But he never fit in with his well-heeled classmates and after just six months, they expelled him for fighting and stealing from the other boys. Returning home, his mother and step-father tried to keep him on a tight leash and threatened him with military school if he could not behave. He graduated from New London High School and, still living at home, returned to his old habits. He quickly progressed from prior arrests for loitering, shoplifting, and possession to criminal mischief and assault.

Three years ago, he was arrested on suspicion of the aggravated rape of Chelsea O'Hara, a teenager who lived only a few blocks from Kane's last known address.

Honestly, unless you were familiar with the details of Kane's shady past, upon meeting him, you would never take him for a career criminal and a sexual predator. He was of average height and build, no facial hair or piercings, and no visible tattoos. Put him in a pair of khaki pants and a polo shirt, and he was ready for casual Friday at an accounting firm. Totally unremarkable in every way, unless you had the misfortune of making eye contact with him. That's when you would experience an icy glare from a pair of glittering blue eyes. Positively chilling. When he had appeared in court three years ago, he was careful to avoid direct eye contact with the judge or the jury. But whenever I got up to speak or pose an objection, I would feel the impact of his cold blue stare.

Still sends chills down my spine today.

CHAPTER 8

I drove home from Becky's with the windows down, reveling in the breeze and the tangy salt air. It was a gorgeous day, already seventy-five degrees, but I couldn't free myself of the dark thoughts weighing me down, my mind cloudy with long-repressed memories and the horror of three years ago. Unable to focus on the road ahead of me, now clogged with beach goers, I pulled off into a deserted rest area to process what I now knew to be the truth about those first few weeks following the acquittal of Terry Kane.

That first night after I lost my job, Adam had brought home roses, wine and Thai food, and I'd drowned my sorrows in a bottle of Chardonnay. Later that night, he had held my hair back while I vomited up all I had consumed that day, wiped my face, and led me to bed. His soft promises that I would be fine, that we would get through this were gentle and reassuring. As I drifted off, he had whispered, "I'm so sorry, babe. I didn't think ... I'm really sorry." Now I finally understood what he had been sorry about, but back then, I was confused.

I recalled how I had woken several hours later, nauseous and dehydrated, and guzzled two glasses of cold water. Adam's last words had come back to me. What hadn't he thought? What did he have to apologize for?

I had rushed back to the bedroom and stopped, studying my sleeping boyfriend carefully. He was gorgeous: rumpled and sexy and if I hadn't been so curious to talk to him, I might have joined him in bed. I had loved this man and imagined a future with him. We had moved in together the year before, after dating for about a year, and we had been building a life together. I was in my mid-thirties, had spent the previous ten years focused on my career, and was ready to settle down. With Adam. He was a few years younger than me and was on the partner track at one of the biggest law firms in southern Connecticut. He was the best-looking guy I had ever laid eyes on, tall and well-built, with dark brown hair and big brown eyes I could lose myself in. When he didn't shave on weekends or on vacation, he was even hotter with all that stubble. Adam had an easy way about him and he literally charmed the pants off of everyone he met.

I was average looking with light brown hair I wore shoulder length, loose, or in a low ponytail. I credited my ability to stay fairly slim not with aerobic activity or a low-cal diet, but with a speedy metabolism I had inherited from both parents. I was a no fuss, low maintenance type, but whenever I dressed up or took a few extra minutes on my appearance, Adam always noticed and complimented me, frequently cutting short our nights out in order to get me home and ravish me. What can I say? We were a good couple, had great sex, made each other laugh and my dad approved of him. Life had been terrific.

I remembered perching on the edge of the bed and poking his shoulder. He had groaned and tried to roll away from me, but I had him pinned down and poked him again.

"Babe? Adam? Wake up. I need to talk to you. Why did you apologize to me? What was it you hadn't thought of?"

He had groaned again and, after a quick peek at me, squeezed his eyes shut.

"Jesus, Ran. What are you going on about?"

"Last night, babe. Right before I fell asleep you said—"

"C'mon. Let's not do this, okay? You suffered a setback at work and got sloshed. It happens. No need to rehash everything we—"

"A setback? That's how you would classify losing a high-profile case and watching my career circle the drain? A setback? It wasn't even my fault. My witness was a no-show. Who would have ever thought the entire case would collapse like that?"

Adam had struggled to sit up in bed and attempted to pull me close to him. I remained stiff and unyielding and he settled for patting me on the back.

"And that's what I said last night. I'm sorry it happened to you. It sucks, okay? That's all I said, so stop busting my balls, would you? If you're not coming back to bed, let me get in the shower, yeah? Some of us have a job to get to." He watched me stiffen visibly, before adding, "Wait too soon?"

"Fuck you, Adam. That was low."

He had tried again to pull me close. Tired of fighting, I slumped against him. He planted a kiss on my cheek and I kissed him back before struggling to my feet.

"I'll make coffee," I said, forcing a smile. "You go get ready for work." I watched him disappear into the bathroom and allowed myself an extra moment of self-pity before I headed back to the kitchen.

That was the beginning of the end for Adam and me. I had been disappointed in myself for sure and was liberally self-medicating with wine and ice cream. But for some reason I could not explain, I found myself angry with Adam. All the time. Whatever he said or did just pissed me off. His efforts to cheer me up were fruitless, and after a few days, he gave up. He took to working longer hours, rarely coming home until after I went to bed. I felt restless, and it was difficult to concentrate on the books I tried to read or the shows I tried to watch. I had less than zero interest in dusting off my resume. Finally tired of lounging around feeling sorry for myself, I was clearing off the clutter on the desk in my tiny home office when I saw it. There it was, clear as day.

The words 'Ocean View Motel' were outlined on the top page of a yellow legal pad. I had scribbled it down after making the arrangements for Becky, torn off the page, and shoved it in my bag. It never occurred to me I would leave traces of the name of the motel behind. The motel Becky had disappeared from only a week ago. I hadn't told a soul about it. Not even Adam. Adam, my boyfriend. The man I planned to marry someday. Adam, the ambitious criminal defense attorney who worked for the firm representing Terry Kane, the scumbag rapist who had gotten off when my only witness, a scared and damaged eighteen-year-old runaway, disappeared on the day she was to testify. I had cradled my throbbing head in my hands, trying to make sense of this new information. What had happened to Becky? Had Adam played some sort of role in her disappearing act? Now I knew he had.

Becky's story made sense to me now, but I hadn't wanted to believe it back then. That Adam could have been behind Becky's disappearance. That first day, I had told myself I was tired; I was hungover; I was upset. I had consoled myself with a pint of Ben and Jerry's Chunky Monkey ice cream, followed by a glass of white wine, then another. By the time Adam had gotten home that night, I was way past tipsy. I was drunk and itching for a fight. Oh, and I wanted answers.

He had entered the apartment with a cheery 'Honey, I'm home' greeting, but I was not some fifties housewife welcoming the man of the house and I was not in a playful mood in the least. I glared at him as he entered the living room. Adam was a genius at the art of social intelligence. He could read a room better than anyone I knew. And he didn't fail at the task today.

A wary look of apprehension morphed into one of loving concern before my eyes.

"Babe," he began as he crossed the room and perched on the sofa where I was reclining. "What's happening, Ran? Are you okay?"

"Did you know about the motel? Did you know where Becky was staying before the trial?"

"Becky? Oh, you mean your witness? Uh, no. I don't know where you had her stashed. I'm pretty sure you never told me."

"I know I never told you, Adam. My question was 'did you know which motel we had her at?' Answer the damn question." His attitude turned frosty as he looked at me, a frown on his face.

"Excuse me, counselor. I'm not on the witness stand, and I'm not in the mood to be interrogated." As I continued to glare at him, he stood and started to leave the room. He turned suddenly, still frowning at me.

"I shouldn't dignify that question with an answer, but I will. Just to be clear, I did not know where your druggie skank was staying and I had nothing to do with her disappearance. Get your shit together, babe, and get a grip, yeah? I know you would like nothing more than to hang the blame for your crap case on someone, anyone, but it sure as hell isn't gonna be me. Look in the mirror, would you? After you sober up some, that is. You look like hell and you're sounding like a crazy person."

I had watched him go to our bedroom and slam the door. Bile rising in my throat, I stumbled to the half bath in the hallway and vomited up wine, along with chunks of banana and chocolate. When I was done, I wiped my face on a hand towel and staggered back to the couch. I passed out and when I came to the next morning, Adam had already left for work. He hadn't made coffee and didn't leave a note, and I decided not to call him. What could I say, anyway? *Oh yeah, sorry about accusing you of witness tampering and all.* Whoops, my bad.

I had moped around our apartment all day and fell asleep in our king-sized bed when I finally realized he was still avoiding me. I heard him hours later, but it must have been his turn on the couch because I never saw him that night or the next morning.

The cold war between us lasted for several more days until one day, I realized I'd had enough. If this was the way we were going to handle conflict, well, that would not work for me. Also, I felt there was more to the story that Adam wasn't telling me, so I packed a bunch of jeans and sweaters and underwear, along with a few toiletries. I left him a note.

I'll send for my things. Over and out - R

I had loaded everything I could into my car and drove to my dad's house. Settled in my old room, I had taken up residence on the sofa and rarely left it for the next eight months.

Now I pulled myself together enough to get back on the road and head home. I turned into my driveway and, grabbing yesterday's mail, crossed my front porch and let myself into the house, feeling angry and out of sorts: the same emptiness I had felt during those first few months. The life I had thought I was meant to live had vanished—no job, no place of my own, and no Adam. At the time, I couldn't escape the feeling he had something to do with Becky's disappearance and apparently, if Becky could be believed, my suspicions had been right. What did it say about me and the choices I made?

If I could be so wrong in my assessment of someone that close to me, what else had I gotten wrong? *Damn.*

CHAPTER 9

It was later than I had thought, so I hurriedly searched in my closet for something work-appropriate. It had been years since I'd had to wear anything but jeans or shorts to work. Even when I interviewed guests for my podcast, I tended towards casual attire. But today, I planned to head back to New London before anyone left for lunch or started their weekend early, with a Friday afternoon off. By anyone, I meant two people in particular: my former boss, State's Attorney Rick Cooper and my former boyfriend, scumbag defense attorney Adam 'You Lying Bastard' Baxter. I figured my chances of catching one or the other in their office late on a Friday morning were pretty good.

I pulled my hair into a low ponytail and dressed in a lightweight navy pantsuit with a sleeveless green top, and low-heeled pumps. I knew the green matched my eyes and suited my pale complexion. Adam had always liked me in green. Fuck him, I thought, and almost changed into something else. But a glance at the clock told me that by the time I found parking, I wouldn't reach Cooper's office until just after eleven. 'Eat your heart out, jerk-face' I mumbled to myself and, grabbing an apple from the nearest fruit display, rushed to my car.

As I backed out of my driveway, I checked my phone. I had put it on silent since my call from Becky five hours earlier. *Crap!* Seventeen missed calls, at least a dozen text messages, and a shitload of emails. I returned my phone to my purse and concentrated on driving, certain there was nothing that couldn't wait until the afternoon. Reporting Adam's criminal behavior was tops on my list. Hopefully, I could get some info on the Kane case from Rick at the same time. Traffic was light and twenty-three minutes later, I was walking across the lobby of the New London District Courthouse. Passing through the metal detectors, I was given a visitor's pass and made my way to the bank of elevators. I got off the elevator on the sixth floor, anticipating a deserted lobby, and was surprised when I emerged to find a crowd of people milling about, excited chatter filling the air. I waved to a few people I actually recognized and was greeted with blank stares. 'It's only been three years, people,' I wanted to remind them, as I reached the reception desk.

Seated behind the desk was a young woman I didn't know in a severe black suit. She had black hair styled in a blunt cut, with one long streak of white grazing her cheek. I smiled in greeting when she ended the call she was on and looked at me.

"Hi, I'm Miranda Quinn," I had to shout as the noise in the crowded lobby had gotten even louder.

"How can I help you?"

"I was hoping for a minute with Rick Cooper. Is he in?" She frowned at me.

"He's not expecting you," she said. It was not a question. I backpedaled.

"No, he's not, but we're old friends and I just need a moment about a case. An old case, and maybe a recent case." I was babbling, but this woman's quiet, self-assured nature was freaking unnerving. So young and yet so composed. A deadly combination. I waited as she continued to appraise me coolly.

"I'm afraid," she said, just as the crowd suddenly grew still. You could literally hear a pin drop.

From the corner of my eye, I watched as my former boss strode into the center of the crowd. He was a small man, but he had a way about him that made you sit up and take notice. Many had learned the hard way, that they needed to hear what he had to say. He adjusted his dark-framed glasses, which were too large for his narrow face, and cleared his throat.

"Everyone quiet down, please. This is a place of business and we are here to serve the good people of our district," he began.

"What's up with Terry Kane?" someone shouted from the far edge of the throng of people. My ears perked up. What had happened? Cooper scanned the audience, perhaps to determine who had spoken up. When his eyes met mine ever so briefly, his face darkened, and his eyes flashed with barely controlled anger.

"If I may, I want to address the situation at hand. At approximately 5:30 last evening, they brought Terence Kane in for questioning at the New London police station. He surrendered without incident and after a relatively brief interrogation session and at the advice of Assistant State's Attorney Taylor and myself, he was arrested on the charge of aggravated sexual assault."

Cooper held up a hand to silence the verbal response he was expecting. "The victim's name is being withheld. The defendant's legal counsel was present. He is being represented by the law firm of Schleyer, Houghton & Fogarty. His attorney of record is Adam Baxter." My heart sank. *Adam was the lead on the case?*

"Please direct all calls and media inquiries directly to my office. My response will be that I cannot comment on a case actively being investigated. For now, I will ignore any mention of Kane's past charges. We were in no way at fault in his acquittal. Now please, let us get back to work and carry on with our day." He turned on his heel and left the lobby after a quick, whispered comment to one of his staff.

I stood there, not knowing what to do next. I needed to tell him about Adam and had important information to share about the case as well. But after the way Cooper had glared at me, I was fairly certain I would not be welcome in his office, even if I could get past Cruella de Vil at the reception desk. I was wrong. A tall guy in a dark suit approached me as the crowd thinned out.

"Miss Quinn, the State's Attorney would like a word," he said, before turning and heading in the same direction as his boss. I trotted briskly along behind him, grateful for my low heels and long legs. We stopped outside of Cooper's office and my unnamed escort rapped on the door. An older woman wearing a twinset and a strand of pearls, probably costing more than my car, greeted us. I recognized Louise at once and was about to say hello when she appraised me grimly, offering no sign of recognition.

"Attorney Cooper will see you now," she said and motioned me in. My escort left, and I silently followed her inside Cooper's office.

'Lou,' I wanted to say, 'it's me, Randi. We used to eat yogurt together in the break room and I brought you a slice of candy cane cheesecake from the Cheesecake Factory one Christmas. Remember?' But as soon as we entered Cooper's inner office, she turned and walked away, leaving me alone with my former boss.

"Hi Rick," I began and approached his desk. I wish I could say he did not fit the stereotype of the short man in power who sits in elevated chairs and looks down on those with lower chairs to appear dominant, but I can't say that. It would be a lie, and I rarely lie unless it is absolutely imperative. I remembered well his wood paneled office with its smell of cedar and pipe smoke, decorated with Currier and Ives prints featuring hunters, anglers and spotted dogs. I was fairly certain that Rick neither hunted, fished nor smoked a pipe, but I gave him props for creating an office with an uber-masculine vibe screaming money, success and, mostly, power.

He watched me silently and I willed myself not to trip as I continued to walk towards him. I reached his desk and stood awkwardly in front of him. Damnit, I was a successful legal spokesperson about to launch a TV show I expected millions of viewers would tune in to. This pompous ass had no sway ...

"Sit," he said, and I immediately perched on the edge of one of the large leather chairs facing his desk. It was as low slung as I recalled, but I let out a little sound of surprise in the split-second delay before my butt actually made contact with the seat.

"How are you?" I began, but he silenced me with one of his signature hand gestures.

"I can only assume you came here today to talk about the case against Terry Kane," he said.

"Unless, of course, you are now working for the defense, that is." I laughed nervously.

"Oh yeah, sure, me a defense attorney," I said.

"Well, Ms. Quinn, certainly you can understand my confusion. You were sleeping with the enemy when you destroyed our case against Mr. Kane. Your gross negligence was—"

"Excuse me, but you just told your minions we did nothing wrong. Am I not part of we?" At his cold silent stare, I tried again. "Are you saying there's no 'I' in 'we'?" I quipped.

"Ah, there it is. That snappy sarcasm that serves as the foundation for your schtick. It should work well for you on daytime television." So he knew about my new career. That crack about switching sides was just meant to rattle me. I smiled at him.

"Well, I certainly hope I can count on you to watch my show. The first episode should ... "

"Please, let's cut to the chase, Ms. Quinn. Because of your ineptitude, the State of Connecticut will go through the expensive and time-consuming process of prosecuting Mr. Kane for a second time."

"And, of course, the senseless, brutal rape of another defenseless young woman?" I was incredulous. Was it all just dollars and headlines for this guy?

"Well, of course, that is why we are here. Jennifer Ramos, AKA the victim. We have been able to keep word of your transgression from the media until this point. But I'm wondering if that would serve in our favor if it were to be made public. We failed the first time, but now with a qualified attorney leading the charge, this time we will triumph and justice will be served."

My breath caught in my throat as I tried to assess the damage a claim like that made by this office would cause, right as my show was being launched. It would destroy my reputation and possibly provide reason for Sterling Broadcast Group to revoke the contract I had signed only yesterday.

"Unless you have something else to say, this is a good time to say our goodbyes." Rick's tone was brusque, dismissive. Not so fast, Ricky-boy, I thought.

"Actually, I do. I have important information about the current Kane case, but first I need to fill you in on a case of witness tampering from his first trial." That got his attention. He motioned for me to continue, and I told him everything I knew about Adam's role in Becky's disappearance and how he must have learned where she was staying. He sat spellbound, listening as I unraveled the mystery that had plagued us both for years. While I was the one who lost her job, Rick had taken his share of blame for the acquittal as well. When I finished, I sat back, a sense of relief washing over me. Rick was one of the smartest lawyers I had ever worked with. Surely, he —

"I agree with you. It is unlikely that Baxter acted on his own." He frowned at me. "Is your Ms. Lewis willing to testify to these charges?" he asked.

"Yes, I'm sure she is," I assured him.

"Will she be a credible witness?" I pictured Becky as I had seen her just a few hours earlier and nodded.

"Yes, she will." I felt confident about this.

Rick told me his office would set up a time for Becky and me to come in to make a formal statement. He stood, and I knew it was time to leave. I thanked him and left his office, walking right past Louise without a single word. I nodded briefly at Cruella, who was back on the phone, and once inside the elevator, I sagged against its steel wall and tried to catch my breath. I had just opened up a giant can of worms by reporting Adam and revealing Becky's return to the area. I could only imagine the lengths Adam and his partners might go to in order to hide evidence of their crime. I had to consider some sort of security measures for Becky and Jesse.

I would keep them safe, no matter what happened next.

CHAPTER 10

While paying what seemed like an exorbitant amount to rescue my car from the parking lot next to the courthouse, I realized I had been inside for less than an hour. It had felt much longer. As it was close to noon, I figured I would grab some lunch before paying a visit to my least favorite scumbag defense attorney, the dis-honorable Adam Baxter, Esquire, lead council for the accused Mr. Terry Kane.

Satisfied with how the day had gone so far, I decided to splurge and treat myself to a steaming bowl of lobster bisque and a couple of cheddar bay biscuits. I drove down to the harbor to Nemo's. I had beaten the lunch crowd, and I snagged princess parking right near the entrance. I hustled inside, planning to get my food and eat at one of the picnic tables on the waterfront dock.

The smell of fried seafood and Old Bay seasoning was so welcoming, I almost swooned. After a brief wait, I placed my order and was given one of those little table placards and told my food would be delivered to me. Number twenty-three, my lucky number!

My luck held out as I chose a prime spot and received my order promptly. The bisque was heavenly, thick and rich and dotted with chunks of fresh lobster and fragrant with a generous splash of sherry. I was about to dive into my second biscuit when my view of the water was obscured by a large shape hunkering smack in front of me. I couldn't believe my eyes. HIM! I gulped down some water before I found my voice. I would be cool, professional, detached. *Or not.*

"What the fuck do you want, you kidnapping pervert?" I hissed at my former boyfriend. So much for cool.

Adam's face broke into a wide smile. The years had been kind to him. Only three years, but still. He was lean and tan. His smile was dazzling. His eyes were the same chocolate brown as I remembered. I used to lose myself in those eyes, I recalled with a sharp pang. His wavy dark brown hair was trimmed short and there were a few silver threads making their appearance. The same sort of silver threads I had been coloring out of my hair for years. Men can get away with so much, I thought. It's not fair. Adam's eyes were bright and he let out a low chuckle.

"That's a mighty wild accusation you're tossing about there, counselor. Are you still actually practicing law or just 'Judge Judy-ing' your way into the hearts and minds of the American public?" I seethed with barely controlled anger.

"I am still licensed to practice law in both Connecticut and Rhode Island, Adam. How about you? Finally made partner, I hear. Who did you have to?" I mimicked giving oral sex when Adam leaned across the table and grabbed my arm to stop me. I pulled back in surprise and he let go. We both stared at each other for a long moment.

"What do you want?" I asked slowly, enunciating every word. "You can't just come here and—"

He chuckled again and reached over for my biscuit. My last biscuit. He took a large bite and crumbled the remains into tiny bits. I glared at him.

"You owe me a biscuit, you jerk." As well as a witness, I almost added, but kept silent. It was possible he didn't know about my early morning meeting with Becky. But of course, he knew.

"How's Miss Lewis keeping these days?" he asked genially. "Is she still on the pipe?" He mimicked what I could only imagine was the smoking of methamphetamine. I scoffed at his faulty characterization of Becky.

"She's great," I assured him. "No worries there. Clean and sober and such interesting stories to tell. But why do you care?"

"I don't care. Just a little chitchat between friends is all."

"You're not my friend, Adam. And when you're found guilty of obstruction of justice and witness tampering, I am certain I won't be yours," I vowed.

"Good luck proving any of that," Adam said, but he had clearly lost some of his usual swagger. I should probably quit while I was marginally ahead. Scooting my chair back noisily, I stood to leave.

"Well, this has just been a little slice of heaven," I announced airily, with a cheerfulness I was not feeling. "See you in court, counselor. Bye for now," I called over my shoulder and made my way to my car on shaky legs that somehow supported me. I drove home in a daze, my mind numbed with fear, worry, and confusion. Adam knew I had met with Becky this morning. But how? Was he tracking her phone? Having me followed? I needed to let Rick know this and enlist his help in protecting Becky ASAP.

Becky, Rick and Adam: three ghosts from my past coming back to haunt me on the very same day. I pulled into my driveway, certain of only one thing.

I needed get in front of this disaster in the making before it destroyed everything.

CHAPTER 11

Rick was not available when I called him, so I left a message for him to call me back. Minutes later, I got a call from his office, but it was to confirm a time for Becky to make a formal statement so they could charge Adam. I agreed to accompany Becky to the courthouse the next day at 9:00 a.m. and immediately texted her with the details. I stared at my phone for a while, waiting for a return text and finally, tired of wasting time, I got to work.

I spent the afternoon returning phone calls and emails and trading texts with Brian, my agent, and Robin, the network liaison. Launching my blog and then a podcast seemed ridiculously simple compared to the complexities of creating a TV series. Although I felt comfortable with the team that the network had assembled, it appeared they required my input on just about every decision, from the color of the rug on the set to the font style being used for the signage. I seriously doubted any of my guests would care about the carpet and as long as *Miranda Writes* was legible, I was on board. But I dutifully responded to these types of requests and mimicked the type of behavior that was apparently expected of a lawyer-turned-TV-host. My primary interests were actually quite straightforward: what guests were lined up and what brand of coffee would be served to the cast and crew. I had already submitted my guest wish list and I would lobby for Green Mountain Coffee if they included me in the decision. Other than that, I really had no preferences to share.

Miranda Writes is a legal advice column in the form of a blog and an accompanying podcast. I post articles, interview notable experts and answer questions about the law- everything from tenant's rights, to shared-custody arrangements to property transfers, trusts and wills. I started blogging just over two years ago, seeking a haven while I healed from my humiliating fall from grace. I had been camped out on my father's couch for months after losing my job, my credibility and my boyfriend all in the same week. Hiding out in Old Lyme made sense, and it really was the perfect place to recover. But you can only spend mornings walking on the beach and the balance of the day curled up on the couch, eating ice cream and drinking wine for just so long. Even I knew that.

My dad, a retired cop, gave me plenty of space and let me "be me," but I could sense his relief when I shared my plan to create a blog. Unfortunately, it did not last long. After I explained the precious little that I actually knew about developing a blog, he got suspicious.

"What's it pay?" he had asked me.

"Um, nothing."

"Oh, well," he'd said, barely masking his obvious disappointment. "As long as you know what you're doing." I loved him for that and I knew it hadn't been easy for him to watch me wallow. I had been fairly certain my presence was cramping his style, but he never complained.

The idea for the blog had been planted when I helped a neighbor with a problem she was having with her landlord. He refused to replace the faulty furnace in the house she was renting, and she had vowed to not pay her rent until he did. He had threatened to evict her and in desperation, she reached out to me for help, as I was the only lawyer she knew. I did some research, and I found Kathy had every right to stop paying rent as the landlord's action had caused a 'reasonable fear of harm' by failing to provide standard services such as heat and hot water. I wrote the landlord a letter to that effect and… problem solved. A new furnace was installed the very next day. Kathy was so grateful that she had brought fresh-baked cookies and muffins every day for a week.

"You're so smart," she had said. "You're like a Dear Abby, but for legal stuff."

Helping her reminded me of how much I loved the law and why I became a lawyer. I thoroughly enjoyed helping people! And I loved to write. So, I wrote up what had happened and how I had identified the solution to Kathy's problem, omitting any names or identifying information and posted it online. After too much wine one night, my best friend Tracey had muttered, "Well, wouldja look at that? Miranda writes." And it stuck.

My first few blog entries got very little attention. My seventh-grade English teacher had commented on every post and reminded me she had predicted I would become a writer someday. She also corrected my grammar, sentence structure and frequent use of the passive tense. Then, a few friends got wind of it and my dad told everyone he knew in town, and soon each successive post was getting an increasing number of views. The first post that was seen by one hundred viewers was around week six. I was thrilled.

Month after month, the number of viewers grew as word spread about my quippy, occasionally snarky legal advice column. I had 63,000 subscribers to my blog at the end of the first year. Granted, they were free subscriptions, but still. Realizing I could not survive without an income for much longer, I started a half-hearted job search. But deep down? I wanted to keep writing and knew I needed to figure out a way to monetize my efforts. After some research, I began offering premium blog posts to paid subscribers. Acting on the advice of a friend of a friend who was a self-proclaimed social media expert, I started a weekly podcast I recorded in the basement of the Old Lyme Town Hall in the studio that once housed the local Public Access channel. A sixteen-year-old neighbor kid named Skip Hansen served as a sound engineer and editor. I paid him twenty-five dollars an hour to record and edit my hour-long podcast, which equated to an expense of roughly one hundred dollars per week. I told my dad I was doing a podcast now as well.

"What's it pay?" he had asked.

"Um, it's costing me a hundred dollars a week," I had admitted.

"Well, as long as you know what you're doing," he had mumbled as he walked away, shaking his head. I'm certain he was wondering if I was ever going to move out and make something of myself, but he kept his opinions to himself. A few months later, my marketing friend landed me a paid sponsor, then another. Soon I was generating actual income from my efforts, but chose to keep my overhead low and maintain my shared space in the basement. But I gave my dad a break and moved into a tiny house in nearby Niantic. I was on a monthly lease with an option to buy. If I had the money for a down payment in six months, I would plunk it down and buy my first house. I could run my little media empire from wherever I wanted and being close to Pop and Tracey was my preference.

Miranda Writes continued to grow, and I hired Skip's eighteen-year-old sister Sarah as my part-time assistant. She collected mail from my postal box and sorted it into piles: potential topics to develop, general comments and fan mail and, finally, crank mail, which included everything from threats from ambulance-chasing attorneys to marriage proposals and dick pics from ardent fans. Poor Sarah had been so embarrassed the first time we received an explicit photo. After that, we laughed and filed them away as evidence in the off chance I was ever kidnapped or attacked in public. She posted the tweets I wrote and kept my Facebook page updated several times a week. I was feeling confident about the future, certain that I could make this work.

The free content on the blog needed to be updated regularly and shared on social media in order to drive traffic and paid subscriptions to my premium posts and podcasts. I spent most of my time on the latter and after listening to my first couple of audio efforts, which were cringe-worthy, with one subscriber commenting that listening to my voice was even more boring than watching paint dry, I loosened up and let my personality come through. I had fun with it, especially when interviewing passionate and intelligent legal experts. My love of the law and all things legal kept the focus on the complex issues facing so many of us and I left the paternity reveals and cheating spouse exposés to someone else.

When I first got word that the Sterling Broadcast Group was considering me to host a legal talk show they were planning, I had tried to remain cautiously optimistic. Opportunities like this did not happen to people like me. But it did and now, here I was looking at carpet samples for my own show. What a rush! It was a dream come true to move forward and close the door on my past, once and for all.

Since Rick hadn't called me by 6:00 p.m., I figured I would not hear from him until tomorrow. I decided to call Becky. I had delayed making the call earlier, as I did not know Jesse's nap schedule and hadn't wanted to disturb them. She wasn't returning my texts and after the phone rang a couple dozen times, I finally realized she would not answer. Given no option to leave a message, I hung up the phone. I texted her again.

Hey Becky- so good to see you and meet Jesse. You have my number. Pls call me when you can. We need to talk about next steps. Miranda/Randi.

I inserted a heart emoji, then thought better of it and sent the message.

Suddenly at loose ends, I debated ordering a pizza and binge-watching whatever looked good on Netflix, but remembered how the network stylist had harped on me about my weight as the camera supposedly added ten pounds and—according to her—I was already carrying a few extra pounds. I decided pizza was a bad idea. Unless I could get someone to share a medium buffalo chicken pie with me. I called Pop, and he answered on the first ring.

"Hello, this is Dez Quinn," he shouted into the phone.

"Hey Pop, it's—"

"How's my girl?" he practically bellowed, and I resolved once more to take him in for a hearing test really soon.

"I'm good. Hey, have you eaten?" I asked.

"Nope, but there's a square of lasagna with my name on it in the fridge. I mean it. The waiter at Mario's put my name on it the other night so Sally and I wouldn't get confused. She had chicken parm, and ... "

"Wow, your own name. What are they, Starbucks?"

Silence. He didn't get my little joke. I was fairly certain my father had never paid more than a buck for a cup of coffee in his life, the police stereotype of living on coffee and donuts notwithstanding. That I thought nothing of dropping five dollars for a cup drove him absolutely crazy. But we were getting sidetracked.

"Anyhoo," I began. "How does splitting a buffalo chicken pizza with your daughter sound?"

"Will you hog all the blue cheese dressing?" he asked suspiciously. I assured him I would request extra blue cheese and that I would arrive at his home at about the same time as the delivery. I ordered our dinner and jumped in the shower. It had been a long day, and I was hoping it would revive me.

As I hurriedly toweled off and pulled on a pair of jeans and a reasonably clean T-shirt, I pictured my dad and smiled. Desmond Thomas Quinn was a recently retired cop and at sixty-eight years old, he had the energy level of a man half his age. He enjoyed fishing and playing a weekly game of poker with a bunch of his cronies, and he had recently begun dating again. His gal-pal Sally was a perky, trim sixty-three-year-old divorcée with two grown children. They had met through mutual friends and seemed to enjoy each other's company. She was nice, but I had to admit that even though it had been twenty years since my mom had passed away, it was weird seeing Pop with another woman.

I waited as the delivery van backed out of the driveway, then pulled in and locked my car. I walked into the kitchen, the same one I spent many happy hours in, eating meals with my folks or baking cookies with my mom. Harvest gold appliances and trivets hanging off the faded avocado tiled backsplash, I kid you not. My dad greeted me with a big smile.

"Hello, my girl." I put down my bag and gave him a quick hug.

"Pop, what can I get you to drink?" I peered into the fridge. There was the aforementioned foil-wrapped square of lasagna, DEZ scrawled across it with a big black marker.

"I'm all set. I popped a cold one after you called," he assured me. "Help yourself to whatever." I saw a couple stray cans of Bud and a 2-liter bottle of Mountain Dew in the fridge that was mainly full of condiments and a half loaf of bread. "Sally and I are hitting Costco tomorrow. And I know what you're thinking. That I need to eat better so ... "

"Wrong-o Mister. I was busy trying to count how many jars of mustard a bachelor needs is all. I stopped at six."

"I don't hear you complaining when I make you one of my sandwich creations at lunchtime," he retorted. "The Dijon is for ham, the yellow for corned beef and the horseradish one is for roast beef."

I bit my tongue to stop myself from commenting on the lack of low-fat turkey or chicken. Based upon my own dietary choices, I was in no position to judge anyone.

"C'mon, let's go sit out on the porch and catch the sunset. And eat this while it's hot." He nodded and grabbed the pizza box and carried it out to the round metal table that had graced the tiny space for as long as I could remember. I collected napkins, a container of grated cheese, and, after pouring myself a glass of tap water, followed him out. I sank down in a chair and gratefully accepted the slice of pizza Pop held out. Too hungry to tear the corner off a packet of blue cheese dressing to drizzle over it, I wolfed it down, wiping the grease from my fingers and lips with a napkin. Domenic's made the best pizza on the entire Connecticut coastline, in my humble opinion, but all that cheese made for a high grease count. I noticed my dad was looking at me with a puzzled expression on his face.

I grabbed another slice and, before I began shoving it in my mouth, asked him, "What's up?"

"You tell me." What was on his mind? I tried to guess.

"No clue but—"

"Terry Kane. Name ring any bells?" He studied me closely, as if my answer was of supreme importance to him. *Of course.* A retired cop, Pop spent a portion of his day chatting with his old crew from the force. Terry Kane's arrest must have been today's chief topic of conversation.

"Were you trying to keep this from me?" he asked, a worried look on his face. "How're you handling the news?"

I took a huge bite of pizza and chewed reflexively for a moment. Do I tell him about seeing Becky or my meeting with Rick or how I had run into Adam at lunch?

"Yeah, you heard about Kane then, huh?" I asked. He almost sputtered his angry response.

"This time that dirtbag had better prepare himself for a guilty verdict. He managed to skate once before, but ... " Yeah, I thought, but your darling daughter messed up and his defense team got lucky. This time, it would be Adam calling the shots, I remembered. My stomach clenched as I recalled our angry exchange earlier today. How long would it take to get charges filed against him? I wondered. At the very least, I expected they would suspend him while the investigation was ongoing.

"Pop. About Adam?"

"What about Adam?" he growled.

"Do you remember me mentioning to you back then I had more or less accused him of being involved in my witness going missing?"

His brow furrowed, and he seemed to choose his words carefully. "I remember. But I blamed it on the wine you were guzzling." I had the grace to look embarrassed, and he went on. "Why? Do you still think Adam was involved?"

I filled my dad in on my conversations with Becky and Rick from that morning. His rigid posture and clenched fists spoke volumes, but he let me continue. I ended with my run-in with Adam on the deck at Nemo's.

"Sonofabitch," he thundered. "That dirty bastard. And now I hear he's running the defense team for Kane." Nobody objected more vigorously to a criminal going free than a prosecutor or a cop.

I tried to placate him. I was exhausted, and I wanted to be certain the evening ended on a positive note. "With any luck, Adam will be off the case soon. And this time, I'll be certain Becky stays safe and sound. If I have to, I'll drive her to court myself."

My dad looked skeptical. "You know you're no longer part of the DA's office, right?"

"Of course, I know that." I knew that, didn't I? "But I can offer to help, to do what I can. I'm waiting to hear from Rick about how we might offer Becky some protection. I am supposed to bring her in tomorrow to make a statement about Adam's role in her disappearance and then I hope she'll still agree to testify in the Kane trial." Pop looked pensive, so I gave him a minute to collect his thoughts.

"Where does Becky live?" he asked, and I read him off the address from my phone.

"Why? What are you thinking?"

"I know a bunch of over-the-hill guys like me. All former cops put out to pasture. Maybe I could arrange for twenty-four-hour stakeouts on her place. We could work in shifts, park on her street and watch for any suspicious activity." His eyes bright with excitement, he asked me, "what do you think?"

"I think it's a great idea," I said. "Do you think they'll go for it?"

"Most of them will jump at the chance, but we may have to sweeten the deal with a few six-packs and some takeout."

"That's on me," I assured him. "Keep me posted, okay? I'll need to let Becky know so she doesn't get paranoid about strangers guarding her house." I checked my phone again. No response from Becky and it didn't appear she had even read my last messages. That was odd. Wasn't every young twenty-something perpetually glued to their phones? "Let's start right away, yeah?" He agreed, but it seemed he had more to say. "What is it, Pop?"

"I just don't want to see you hurt again. The last case you worked on tore you apart."

"I'll be careful," I said. "I won't get too involved as long as Becky is safe and Adam gets charged." Please let that be true, I thought.

"Good to hear. And anyway, you're gonna be the next star of daytime TV. You'll be moving on, moving up," he said proudly.

"So how cool was that trip to New York?" I asked. It was only yesterday, I realized. It felt like it was years ago that we were drinking champagne and riding in a limo.

"I never lost faith in you, Randi."

"Not even when I went for a year without a paycheck?" I asked with a wink, trying to play off the surge of pride at his words.

"Not even then," he assured me.

I wrapped the remaining slices of pizza in aluminum foil and stuck them in the fridge. "Your lunch tomorrow?" I suggested.

"We'll be at Costco at lunchtime tomorrow. Sally loves their hotdogs. Anything you need me to pick up for you?"

I reminded him that as a single woman; I had no actual need for a jumbo pack of sixteen rolls of paper towels or a gallon-sized jar of peanut butter. The only thing I would consider buying in bulk were those mini fun-sized chocolate bars they sell in bags of one hundred or more. But that would not be in keeping with the nutritional needs of a soon to be TV host and besides, Halloween was months away.

"Thanks, but I'm fine. Tell Sally I said hello. Love you," I said, looking over at my shoulder at him. He was sitting at the kitchen table in the same chair he'd been inhabiting for nearly forty years. I felt a lump in my throat. God, I loved this man. He was the one true constant in my life.

"Love you more," he called out, and thoughts of our lovely evening kept me feeling all sorts of warm and cozy during my twenty-minute drive.

It lasted all the way to my front door, which was strangely ajar. Spidey sense tingling, I peeked in, already calling 911. As the phone rang, I surveyed the broken glass, the overturned bookshelf and the couch cushions zig zagged with slashes. The remains of several fruit baskets were scattered everywhere, and a mixture of colorful flower petals carpeted the floor. As realization hit me, I stumbled back a step, gripping the stair rail to keep myself upright and struggling to breathe. Was someone still in the house? As I staggered back toward my car, my call was answered.

"What's your emergency?" the operator asked.

"I'm at 51 Walnut Street. They broke into my house," I spoke with a numbness that threatened to paralyze my vocal cords. I got back into my car and locked the doors. I closed my eyes to get rid of the image of my home, invaded and no longer safe, and waited for the police to arrive. I took a few deep breaths, trying to dispel the tightness that had lodged in my chest. What were the facts? I had met with Becky, then Rick, and had run into Adam. What was the link in this chain? I knew it was not some random break-in. Someone was trying to send me a message, to scare me off my efforts to help Becky, to see Adam charged and to put Terry Kane away for good. What would prosecutor-me have advised?

Stay the course.

Watch your back.

Yelp for help.

All the above.

CHAPTER 12

Two patrol officers showed up in a matter of minutes and, after making certain my house was vacant, they ushered me inside. "Don't touch anything," the younger one, a female officer named Grey, warned. I barely heard her as I took in the extent of the damage. It was even worse than it appeared when I had first peeked in. Furniture was overturned and my kitchen looked as if a tornado had hit it. Full canisters of flour, sugar and tea bags had been upended and the refrigerator door was propped open with a roll of paper towels. I opened the door all the way and peered inside. Everything still looked cold, so the vandals had probably left within the last hour or so.

"What part of 'don't touch anything' do you not understand?" asked Officer Grey.

"Sorry, I'm just a little, well, you know ... " She nodded sympathetically and patted my hand.

I turned down the hall and entered my bedroom. The older cop, an Officer Jamison, was right behind me as I surveyed the room.

"Not much going on in here," he stated flatly, and I looked at him for some sign of humor in his remark, but found none. I had to agree with him. The messy bed and the pile of clothes were the fault of yours truly. And sadly, he was right about the apparent lack of recent activity. My sex life was circling the drain.

"You have to see this," Officer Grey called down to us, so we headed up the narrow staircase to the second floor. There were two tiny bedrooms separated by a short hallway. I used one as my office and the other as a guestroom and storage area. The sense of dread I had been feeling since I got home threatened to explode when I peeked into my office. This was apparently the intended target of my vandal/intruder. The desk drawers and file cabinet gaped open, paper files and office supplies strewn everywhere.

The evidence was clear. Someone tied to Kane was trying to get information and send me a message. This break-in was not random, nor carried out by a would-be thief. I tried to think about what could have been found. I jumped when Grey spoke, spooked by my grim thoughts.

"What do you keep in here?" she asked.

"Um, mainly print outs of my blog posts, tax returns, old cases ... "

"Cases?"

"Yeah, I was with the State's Attorney's office until—"

"Ah crap," the older cop said. "You're Dez Quinn's kid then? The one who ... " He didn't finish his thought, but I saw the look the two exchanged.

"That's me," I said as I bent to look at the files at my feet. Officer Grey was quick to protest.

"Don't—"

"Yeah, yeah. Don't touch anything," I said.

"No computer or tablet?" Jamison asked as he looked around.

For the first time since I'd gotten home, I felt a wave of relief. My laptop was in my briefcase in the car. Unless someone had broken into it in the last fifteen minutes, it was safe. I stored duplicates of most of my paper files on my computer, including notes and ideas for my upcoming show. My file labeled "Kane, T" was on my hard drive. I had left the dog-eared paper files in my office the day they fired me. As far as I knew, my electronic copy was the only one that existed outside of the office. I was certain the Kane file was what the intruder had been searching for. All the other mayhem was designed to throw me off, to make it look like a regular burglary.

A short while later, I left my home, now festooned with yellow crime tape, and drove back to my father's house. I let myself in with the spare key I always carried and, after deciding my dad was probably asleep, went to my bedroom. I got undressed, finding an oversized T-shirt in one of my drawers. Forgoing my nightly ritual of flossing and brushing my teeth and moisturizing my face and neck, I crawled in under the covers and lay on my back, staring at the ceiling. Why would anyone think I had held onto evidence implicating Terry Kane? Was Adam somehow involved in the break in? Was Becky okay? Were she and Jesse safe?

I lay awake for hours, finally falling asleep just as the first streaky rays of sunlight filtered through the curtains.

CHAPTER 13

I woke slowly and looked around, confused at first by my surroundings. Although I spent a lot of time with Pop, I hadn't slept in this room since I moved out nearly two years ago. Sunlight flooded the bedroom, as I began to recall the events of the day before. What a mess, both literally and figuratively. I stared at the picture on my nightstand. It was me with my parents at my high school graduation. I had been valedictorian, class of 1998, at Old Lyme High School. God, I looked so young, standing there in my maroon polyester gown, wedged between my folks. My mom, Nora Brennan Quinn, was beautiful with her red hair and sparkling green eyes and my dad looked quite handsome, beaming with pride as he posed with his girls. That's what he always called me and my mom. *His girls.* My eyes filled with tears as I imagined all my poor mom had missed out on, dying at forty-four after a quick and merciless bout with lung cancer. Never smoked a day in her life, my dad had said nearly a million times in the past twenty years. Each time, shaking his head in disbelief. *Never a day in her life.*

I heard noises from the kitchen, so I pulled on my ratty blue robe, grabbed a scrunchie, and fashioned my hair into a messy bun as I padded barefoot down the hall. I could smell the fresh coffee before I reached the kitchen and watched my dad empty a bag of donuts onto a plate and place it on the table.

"You went to Francesca's," I called out by way of a greeting. I received a harrumph and opted to wait until we both had cups of coffee in front of us before attempting further conversation. Neither of us were particularly 'morning people' and we'd had dinner together just last night. Not too much to say.

"When were you going to tell me?" my dad asked. He was not a tall man and only slightly built, but had a way of sizing up a suspect in a way that made all but the most hardened of criminals go weak in the knees. Just like he was looking at me right now. I stalled for time by grabbing a couple of mugs from the cabinet and filling them both.

"Black, yeah?" I asked him, although I already knew the answer and, without waiting for a response, deposited his mug on the table. Cradling the other in my hands, I breathed in the bitter steam and tried to collect my thoughts. My dad was still in touch with his former colleagues, some retired and others working up and down the Connecticut coastline. A break-in at his daughter's house only a town away would surely have reached him hours ago. I took a seat and pretended to survey the display of donuts. Dad had driven across town to Francesca's, because he knew how much I loved their donuts.

"What happened Miranda?" I put down my cup and shook my head sadly.

"I don't know. I drove home from your house—"

"Did you go straight home?"

"Yes, Pop. I did. I got home and my front door was open. I peeked in—"

"You dialed 911 right away, yeah?"

"Of course. And I waited in my car till they showed up."

"It was Jamie and someone else. I don't know her."

"Officer Grey. Yeah, they were great. We walked through the house and it looked like a normal break in."

"But you don't think it was?"

"No, I don't. It's just too much of a coincidence, you know? The same day I see Becky, meet with Rick and run into that jerk face Adam ... that's the day someone randomly breaks into my house? It didn't seem like they took anything. I'm just not buying it." Pop's face darkened.

"What did you tell them?"

"About the Kane case and Adam and Becky? Nothing. Not one word."

"I'll make a call."

"You don't need to do that—" He cut me off angrily.

"I'll not be standing by twiddling my thumbs while the hump who broke into your house is still out there."

"They were looking for my laptop, Pop. The Kane file. I'm sure of it. But it's safe, here with me." I pointed in the general direction of my bedroom. He jumped up suddenly, all systems go.

"I've got a spare flash drive. Download everything from the case and transfer it to the drive. Wipe it off your computer. Then we'll store it in my safe, with my guns."

"Look at you," I teased. "Downloads and flash drives. Whoever said you can't teach an old dog?"

"I could really impress you if I told you to store it on the cloud." He said it with a grin, his first of the morning.

"In the cloud," I interjected gently, but I was impressed. Who had taught him about the cloud? Sally?

"Whatever. Let's take a run to your place and pick up your things."

"Huh, what things?"

"Surely you'll be staying here for a bit."

"No way, Pop. The last time I hunkered down on your couch, I didn't leave for nearly a year. I will not get scared out of my home." We argued back and forth before he finally threw up his hands.

"You're the most stubborn ... "

"Where does that come from, you suppose? Now eat a donut, would you? Start acting like a cop, yeah?" I helped myself to a Boston cream and gobbled it down. As I started to grab a second donut, my mind flashed on a very irritated Robin, so I poured myself more coffee instead.

"You're a million miles away," my dad said. "Where're you at?"

"I'm just thinking about the show. Do you believe it? Little old me, on daytime TV."

"I always knew you were destined for great things, Miranda. Your mom would be so proud."

I leaned over and squeezed his hand. With a lump forming in my throat, I managed a feeble,

"I know. I wish ... "

"Yeah, me too," he said, ending our pointless wishing before we really began. "I'll go get that flash drive." As he was leaving, he turned to me with an impish grin on his weathered face.

"It's Friday. Maybe my rich and famous daughter would treat her old man to the fish and chips special at Brennan's, heh?" I groaned at the thought of fried food for lunch after eating donuts. Robin would kill me. Still ...

"You betcha. Let's transfer the files and then I'll grab a shower."

After copying the files making up the entire State of Connecticut vs. Terence Thomas Kane case I had managed to "borrow" three years earlier, I gave the flash drive to Pop and deleted them from my computer. I felt a chill, recalling how the only person besides Pop who knew of my sneaky tendency to hang onto case files was ... Adam. Was he following me? Was he somehow listening in on my phone calls or was my house bugged? I felt better knowing my files were safe and by the time I emerged from a long, steamy shower, I had convinced myself I was being ridiculous. Nemo's was a very popular spot in New London and hell, Adam and I had enjoyed a meal or cocktails there more times than I could count. It was probably one of those freak coincidences. Nonetheless, I vowed to stay alert to anything out of the ordinary. I could not afford to drop any of the balls I was currently attempting to juggle. There was way too much at stake with the Kane case and Adam's witness tampering, plus everything I needed to do to prepare for my TV show.

On the drive over to the neighborhood tavern, I remembered something.

"You were supposed to have lunch with Sally today, Pop," I reminded him.

"I called her earlier. I told her what happened, and she insisted I spend the time with you."

That was nice of her. *Maybe?*

"Why don't I call her and ask her to meet us, yeah? Do you think she'd agree?"

Pop assured me she would, so I found her number and texted her the details. I ended with;

I hope you can join us- Randi. I added a heart emoji and sent it, then tapped out a quick text to Becky asking her to call me and this time, I added a heart. I tried to recall what else was on my list.

Leaning back into the comfy upholstered passenger's seat in my dad's ancient Jeep Wagoneer, I typed in a reminder on my phone to schedule a spa day courtesy of my new employer: mani, pedi, massage and facial—the works! There was an incoming text from Sally, and I skimmed it quickly.

"Cool. Sally's gonna meet us. Nice of her to be so flexible." He took his eyes off the road for a split second and grinned in my direction.

"She gets it. When one of her kids calls, she cancels on me and whatever she's doing to get to them. That's how it is when you have family responsibilities."

"She has a son who lives nearby and a daughter up near Hartford, right?" I asked. Pop nodded.

"Her daughter Julie just got married last year. Nice guy named Brad. Her son Jake and his wife Meg have been having some problems starting a family. Sally is champing at the bit. She wants to be a grandma in the worst way."

My dad was far too evolved to ask me when I would get around to providing him with grandparent status. That ship had sailed as far as I could see. I would turn forty in just over a year and the chances of me making him a grandpa were practically nil. I have never been confident I would have made a good mother, but Desmond Quinn would totally rock the role of grandfather. Sorry, Pop. It's just not in the cards.

We spent a companionable afternoon enjoying the lively atmosphere and the delicious meal. Sally looked lovely in a light blue sundress and a cute denim jacket. Sitting across the booth from her and my dad, I thought she looked a decade younger than her sixty-three years. She was a lot of fun, and Pop looked at her like he just won the lottery or something. They were an adorably cute couple.

I switched to water after two sodas and witnessed once more how much everyone loved my dad, as countless friends popped over to our booth. I got my share of hugs, well wishes and congratulations as well. We walked Sally to her car, a baby blue hybrid sedan, and by the time we got back to the house, I was beat and turned down my dad's offer of coffee. I knew I should get back to my house and clean up the mess made by last night's intruder. I hugged him and drove home, relaxed from a wonderful visit and only mildly concerned about what I would find when I got there. My bigger worry was Becky. Why hadn't she called me, or at least sent a quick text? If I hadn't heard from her by the morning, I would drive to her house.

I spent the evening straightening up the mess, then collapsed on my sofa, after flipping the cushions to hide the slashes to the fabric. Since I had consumed half of my body weight in fried fish just hours earlier, I made do with a carton of only recently expired raspberry yogurt and a Diet Coke for my dinner. Sipping my drink, I flipped through channels absentmindedly, trying to recall what series I had been watching recently. It wasn't coming up in my 'Continue Watching' feed, so what the hell was it? My phone rang as I was about to turn off the TV and head off to bed. An unknown number, *déjà vu*.

I answered with a guarded 'hello'. The sound of sobbing filled my ears, and I heard the voice of Becky Lewis calling me for only the second time in three years.

"Miss Quinn? Randi? You have to help me. I'm in jail and they took Jesse."

CHAPTER 14

The next several hours passed by in a blur. As if on auto-pilot, I drove to the police station in New London, wondering what the hell had happened. Just yesterday, Becky had been happy, devoted to her son and confident in her ability to take part in the worthy cause of seeing Terry Kane finally brought to justice. How did everything go so wrong? I found out quickly.

On my way to the station, I called one of the few department contacts I had left. Allie Reynolds had just finished her shift on patrol at 11:00 p.m., and didn't know what had transpired, but promised to call me right back. After I parked my car and walked up the steps, my phone rang.

"Hey Allie," I spoke in a low voice. "Were you able to find out anything?"

She said an anonymous tip had been received earlier that evening. The caller was a young male who had identified himself as a neighbor living in Becky's rooming house. He reported he had been hearing the sounds of an infant crying for hours. He had rambled on during a call lasting a full two minutes. *Could that nice young girl on the second floor have gone off without her baby, possibly with one of the questionable young men who seemed to come and go at all hours, day and night? Was it possible that the young mother had once again succumbed to the lure of drugs? The ones she had previously kept in a box on the top of her fridge?*

"Wait, you're telling me he was familiar with the location of her drugs but not friendly enough to knock on her door to see if she needed help?" Whatever happened to love thy neighbor?

"Hey, I'm just the mess—" Allie began. I had to cut her off as I approached the desk.

"Thanks Al," I said. "I owe you one."

Twenty minutes later, I was sitting in a tiny, windowless room when a uniformed officer led Becky in. Compared to the radiant young woman I had reconnected with only yesterday, Becky definitely looked the worse for wear. There were dark circles under her eyes and her blonde hair was a tangled mess. Her overall appearance was marred even further by her oversized T-shirt featuring Metallica and a pair of faded leggings.

I hugged her and she collapsed against me, sobbing incoherently. I doubted we were being taped or watched, but I didn't want to take any chances. I made her sit with her back to the large two-way window and told her to keep her voice low. I finally got the story out of her. Two officers had arrived at her address at 9:00 p.m. She had been sleeping next to Jesse and woke to the sounds of her baby crying and a loud banging on her door. She had tried to comfort him as he struggled in her arms while attempting to reassure the officers there was nothing wrong. Her nervousness and disheveled appearance, combined with the crying infant, must have confirmed the tip that brought the officers to the house. She nodded in assent when they had suggested they look around, and she followed them into the tiny kitchen. She was ready to apologize for its relatively bare state as the younger of the officers walked over to the fridge. She was surprised when, instead of opening the door, he reached up and grabbed the cardboard shoe box from the top.

"What's in here?" he had barked.

"Um, just some photos and things. There's not a lot of storage," she had said. When they asked to search the box, she had consented, but had gasped when she saw the glass pipe and a baggie full of white powder on top of the pile of photographs. She had started to cry.

"They're not mine. I swear. I'm a good mother. I would never..."

She had been handcuffed and read her rights as they arrested her for possession of a controlled substance with intent to sell. The police had asked if there was anyone to care for the baby and she had said there wasn't. Her sister Rachel was working the night shift at the casino without access to her phone, and Lucie was with her dad. Becky had called her brother-in-law Eddie several times, but he never picked up.

The Department of Children and Families was called and in less than twenty minutes, the on-call social worker arrived and took custody of Jesse. They led Becky into the awaiting police car as Jesse screamed for her and the last Becky had seen of him was through the rear window of the police car as they drove away. Upon arrival at the police station, she had been fingerprinted and processed. Allowed her one phone call, she had chosen me.

"Please help me," she begged, her body wracked with sobs. I told her I would represent her, confident a case this flimsy would never go to trial. I felt the evidence was circumstantial and that I could get it thrown out. I could feel her start to relax when a fresh round of worry hit her.

"You need to call Rachel. I am supposed to be at her house tomorrow to watch Lucie. She'll be worried and mad at me for making her miss her lunch shift at the casino."

I wanted to impress upon Becky that skipping out on child care duties was the least of her worries, but I didn't want to upset her any more than she already was. I told her I would and studied her. We needed to talk. As soon as her teeth stopped chattering, I cut to the chase. I was uncertain how much time they would allow us, and there were things I needed to know.

"Becky, is there any chance the drugs are yours?" I asked. That resulted in another round of tears and denials. I waited a couple of minutes for her to calm down. "I need you to listen to me. This is important." That must have come across sharper than I planned, as she sat up straight and shook her head at me.

"No way. I've been clean since I found out I was pregnant. Almost two years," she said, shaking her head for emphasis. I told her about the 911 call that had been made.

"Do you know of any reason drugs would be found, or why an anonymous tip would have been called in?" She was dumbstruck.

"I don't know why anyone would do this to me. I swear Jesse made barely a peep all day until he woke up crying. And by then, the cops were already there." Saying her little boy's name out loud brought forth a fresh round of tears. Once again incoherent, the only words I could make out were Jesse, my baby and Pennywise. *Pennywise?*

"It's his stuffed clown doll. It's his favorite. I call him Pennywise after the clown in that movie, you know? It was just a joke, but it stuck."

I assured her I would go to her apartment first thing in the morning, locate Pennywise and deliver him to DCF. After they arraigned Becky in Superior Court, I would arrange for her bail. Together, we would set the process in motion to get Jesse released into her care. Because Becky's arrest had happened over the weekend, I assumed DCF would recommend a ninety-six-hour administrative hold, since that would not require formal permission from the courts. As a single parent out on bail, I doubted they would return Jesse to her immediately, but kept that thought to myself. The poor girl sat in a daze on the cracked vinyl chair and that news would destroy her chances of getting any rest that night.

I hugged her and after they led her back to her cell; I hurried out the door to my car. Gulping fresh air, I called Rachel on her cell and she answered on the first ring. It was close to 2:00 a.m. and she was on her way home. I introduced myself and filled her in on what had transpired that evening. She sucked in a long breath.

"Oh, that's awful. How can I help?" she asked.

I shared my concern that until Becky was acquitted and they deemed the home safe; it was unlikely Jesse would be returned to his mother.

"I can take him," she said. "He can stay with me." I told Rachel I would call her in the morning with an update and drove home. I saw I had several missed calls from earlier in the evening, two from Brian alone. I hadn't been checking in, but how important were carpet samples when an innocent young mother was in jail? But it was an ungodly time of night to call anyone. I told myself everything would look better in the morning.

I set the alarm on my phone to wake me at 7:00 a.m., then flopped down on my unmade bed after pushing the mattress back onto the bedframe.

I fell asleep, my slumber marred by jarring dreams of evil clowns rocking out to the sounds of Metallica.

CHAPTER 15

"You need to take my calls, Miranda. I can't help you if you won't talk to me." My agent Brian's tone was just short of menacing. I felt the need to defend myself.

"I'm sorry. But you can't imagine how crazy everything is here," I protested. "The last few days have been—" Brian cut me off, his voice dripping with sarcasm.

"Yes, I'm certain as I navigate the sidewalks of Times Square replete with rabid tourists, pissed-off locals and street people, I have no clue how wild and crazy the sleepy burbs can be. What's happening in West Lyme, anyway? Hey, watch it asshole," he shouted. "Christ, these people can be ... "

"It's Old Lyme, Brian, and I live in Niantic, but anyhoo. Did you call just to yell at me or was there something you needed?" I was rushing out to my car, clutching my briefcase, my purse, a travel mug full to the brim with coffee and an armful of reusable shopping bags. Reaching for my car keys, I felt the mug slip out of my hand, spewing hot black coffee everywhere and as I watched, the bags fell into the largest of the puddles. *Aaarrgghh*. Brian had been talking, and I'd missed whatever he'd had to say.

"I'm sorry. What were you saying?"

"Excuse my French, but you need to get your shit together. The network wants to set up a schedule to film those promos. Affiliates from the top fifty markets are coming in and they need you to commit to a day and time." Brian spoke with practiced patience, as if he was used to dealing with wacko clients. I pictured his earnest pink-cheeked face scowling at the phone.

"Any day is fine. You pick and I'll be there," I assured him. I dumped my briefcase on the back seat and tossed the empty mug in, too. I picked up the soggy shopping bags and fanned them on the floor mats to dry out. I sank down into the seat, and closing the door, started my car. "Brian? Does that work for you?" I asked as I adjusted the mirrors and buckled my seatbelt.

"Just book your treatments and meet with the wardrobe consultant first." *Crap.* I had forgotten to schedule my beauty treatments and I wasn't even sure I could locate the contact info for the consultant. "And how's the diet going?"

"Um, well, I got broken into the other night. My place is a train wreck right now. And I spent most of last night in jail. Well, not in jail, but at the jail. Can you text me the name of the salon and the details for the wardrobe, um, place?" I heard a sharp intake of breath as Brian took in what I had said. My few texts to him over the past three days had been work-related, and I had shared none of the more sordid details of my messed-up existence with him.

"Jesus, are you okay? What do you mean, you got broken into? What's going on? And why the hell were you in jail?"

As I drove towards to New London, I filled Brian in on the situation with Becky's reappearance. I did not share the news of Adam's betrayal but concluded with, "Now I've got to go to Becky's and pick up a stuffed clown, bring it to DCF, then stand up at Becky's arraignment and find a bail bondsman and get her out of lockup." There was a long pause as I found street parking near Becky's rooming house. I nodded at a couple of guys sitting in a parked car across the street. Pop's surveillance team had begun this morning at 6:00 a.m., nine hours after Becky had been arrested.

"Isn't there someone else?" Brian asked.

"Well, I guess I could ask her sister to get Pennywise, but I'm already at her place and court doesn't start till—"

"I meant to represent her. Isn't there someone else? A public defender or whatever? I'm uncertain you should be one standing up in court defending some drug dealer right now. The Sterling folks will flip out."

His voice trailed off as I hurried along the sidewalk. Becky had said to knock on the landlord's door and I struggled to remember the number of his unit. It was 8:00 a.m. and my day was already proving itself to be way more challenging than I could handle. Especially without coffee.

"There's no one else, Brian. I have to help this girl. I'm the reason she's in this mess."

"I'm just saying the network won't like it if there is anything that can harm them or you. Drug dealing? Rape? That's not good for your brand, Miranda." I tamped down on the anger I was feeling and drew in a breath. Time to take back control of this conversation.

"I'm Teflon, okay? Nothing will stick to me, I promise. I'll get this drug possession case dropped and find a family lawyer for Becky to help her get Jesse back. Text me the contact info for the salon and the image person and let me know what day to be at the studio and I'll work backwards. Yeah? We good?" I raced up the steps to the rooming house, eager to end the call.

"Okay. I'll keep you posted then. But you never answered me. How's the diet going? Are you watching your weight?"

"I'm doing great, you'll see. Gotta go," I said and disconnected the call. I hadn't lied, I reassured myself. I hadn't had a drink since the champagne a few days earlier except for one beer and my stress eating habits had been under control for the most part.

But there were a couple of Dunkin's on the way to the courthouse, so maybe I shouldn't pat myself on the back just yet.

CHAPTER 16

I hurried up the stairs of the New London District Courthouse, feeling ill-prepared and looking downright disheveled. I had yet to shower, and I had pulled my hair back in the messiest of buns. I tightened the belt on my lightweight black trench coat and hoped it would be the only element of my otherwise sloppy ensemble the judge would notice. I had rushed out the door that morning with my mind on locating Pennywise the clown and delivering him to Jesse's caretakers. The thought I would appear in court on behalf of my client had just now registered with me. If my new stylist/wardrobe consultant could see me now.

I wiped a trace of powdered sugar from my left sleeve and made my way through the crowded lobby. I showed my ID at the front desk and asked which courtroom Rebecca Lewis was being arraigned in. I nodded when I was told it was Courtroom 203, second floor. I hustled in and was among the first to enter the nearly empty room. I hurried down to the front and, after eyeing the two tables placed in front of the judge's podium, slipped into a chair at the table on the left side. It had been a minute, and I hoped this was where the defense team was expected to set up camp. I pulled a thin file from my bag and, placing it on the table in front of me, sat back to wait.

A few minutes later, a couple of uniformed guards trooped in with Becky between them. I saw she was handcuffed and made a mental note to protest this unnecessary precaution. She looked thin, but that could have been because of her oversized orange jumpsuit. I tried to give some sign of encouragement, but she kept her eyes looking down at her feet as she stumbled along between them.

The arraignment went fairly smoothly as the judge informed Becky of her Constitutional rights, before formally reading the charges against her: criminal possession of a controlled substance with intent to sell and reckless endangerment of a minor child. At my direction, Becky pleaded 'not guilty' to all charges.

I asked that she be released on bail as she was neither a flight risk nor a danger to the community and bail was set at ten thousand dollars. I considered the balance in my checking account before telling Becky I would make the arrangements with a bail bondsman and that I would see her back at the station shortly. She appeared to hear me, but gave no sign of actually understanding. She was nearly catatonic.

My phone buzzed with a new text message. I had texted Becky's sister Rachel while I waited in the drive-through for my breakfast. I could not locate the landlord and had not gained access to Becky's apartment. I had asked Rachel to get Jesse's favorite stuffed toy and plan to meet me later this morning. **Got it. Where 2 meet?**

No mention of Becky or her arraignment, but I saw it as a positive sign. If things went the way I believed they would, Rachel could help us in supporting Becky's plea to regain custody of her son. She was a couple of years older than her sister, married and had a good-paying job. I looked at my watch. It was just after ten o'clock. Having no clue how long it would take to arrange for her bail, I gave myself a bit of a cushion. I recalled Becky telling me where her sister lived and I knew it was an area full of fast-food restaurants. I fired off a quick text.

Mc D's near you. 12:30? Three dots appeared instantly.

We will b there came her speedy reply. For a moment, I wondered about her choice of 'we' but quickly realized that naturally she would have her daughter Lucie with her. I texted back a thumbs-up emoji and hopped in my car. I drove right past a couple of bail bond offices closest to the courthouse, their parking lots already full. I finally found one that looked like they might accommodate me quickly and after paying the ten percent fee of one thousand dollars, I secured bail for Becky. If they could process her quickly, we could meet Rachel together.

I hurried to the police station and miraculously, Becky's bail was sorted out and she was released into my custody. I may have let it slip to the desk sergeant I was Dez Quinn's daughter, which definitely moved things along. Soon I was accompanying Becky to my car. I wished I had taken a few minutes to grab her a clean T-shirt, but her stained and faded heavy metal shirt would just have to do.

At 12:40 p.m., we pulled into the restaurant parking lot. Becky, who had been silent for the entire ride, sighed loudly as she unbuckled her seatbelt and opened the door.

"You okay?" I asked her. She nodded and looked away from me, but not before I saw her blue eyes well up with tears. We walked across the parking lot and into the restaurant, which was fairly empty. There were a few couples sitting in booths and a cluster of young mothers watching their children play in the adjacent bounce house. I heard Rachel before I saw her.

"Becky," she called out. "Over here." We saw a young woman waving wildly from a booth in the corner. A baby stroller was parked next to the booth and an adorable little girl holding a stuffed clown started calling out, "Bexy, Bexy." We hurried over to them and Becky introduced me to her sister. Seeing her family seemed to have energized her a bit.

"Rach, this is Miranda Quinn. Remember the lawyer I told you about? This is my sister Rachel. And my favorite niece, Miss Lucie DaSilva," she finished proudly.

Rachel and I smiled at each other and I settled in the booth across from them. Although the two women had different fathers, there was no mistaking the fact they were related. Rachel was a couple of inches taller and much huskier than her younger sister, but both had the same straight blonde hair, huge blue eyes and pert upturned noses. The women hugged each other, both crying. I glanced over at the little girl.

"Hello, you," I said in a bright voice. I never knew how to talk to kids without feeling foolish. She stared at me before breaking into a wide, toothy grin. *Well, okay then.*

The two sisters were gabbing away, and neither was very specific when I asked what they wanted, so I stood online and ordered three combo meals, a chicken nugget kids' meal and three chocolate shakes. While I waited for our food, I looked over at them sitting side by side, deep in conversation. I never had a sibling, and I felt a pang of something hit me. Sadness? Loneliness? Just fatigue, I decided, and studied the menu on the large marquee. Who knew a Big Mac meal was close to a thousand calories? Probably something I should have seen before ordering, but what can you do? A few minutes later, I returned to our booth with a tray piled high and deposited the food on the table.

For several minutes, we busied ourselves inhaling our lunch. I pushed the image of Brian's face from my mind, knowing how much he would disapprove of my choices. I would stop on the way home to buy the makings for a salad for dinner, mentally adding a trip to the grocery store to my long to-do list for the day. Becky's latest predicament had come out of nowhere. I had been on the go for hours but had completed nothing even remotely related to my blog, podcast or upcoming show.

My priority needed to be making some serious headway in restoring my home. If I wanted to get any work done, I needed to focus on my home office. I had to write next week's blog posts and outline the script for my next podcast as well. I hoped Sarah would be available to help me later and sent her a quick text while I thought of it.

Lost in thought, I realized Rachel had been trying to get my attention.

"Sorry, I missed what you said," I apologized. Rachel took a huge slurp of her shake and studied me closely.

"I was just wondering what's next for my little sister here," she asked, a frown on her pretty face. "What do we need to do to get Jesse back?" Little Lucie starting cooing "Jesse, Jesse," which gave me a moment to collect my thoughts. Becky studied her hands and let out a long breath as I began.

"I have a call in to a friend from law school. She's terrific, specializes in family law. I'll tell her—"

"I want you," Becky interjected. "Why can't you help me?" The poor girl seemed about ready to burst into tears. She reached across the table and grasped my hand in her tiny ones. "Please Randi."

I explained what I knew about the process of returning a child to its home following an arrest and I hoped I had them convinced it would be in their best interests to have someone knowledgeable in family law working on their behalf. I assured them I would focus my efforts on getting the charges against Becky dropped.

Becky looked uncomfortable and couldn't seem to make eye contact with me. She was anxiously shredding a paper napkin as she stared down at the growing pile in front of her. Her voice was shaky when she finally spoke.

"But what about, you know? The—" Rachel cut her off.

"What she's trying to ask is how much is this going to cost exactly? Two lawyers to pay, not to mention all the shifts I'm missing from work." Becky nodded miserably and finally looked directly at me, her eyes red and swollen. I wanted to reassure her we would work something out, but I hadn't even talked to Lisa and had no clue how the firm where she was employed as a junior partner felt about pro bono work. *Oh hell!*

"I won't charge you anything," I assured them. "And Lisa's firm will let her represent you *pro bono*, that's—"

"Charity," Rachel said with a knowing smirk.

"For the public good," I corrected her. If I was wrong, I would pay Lisa's fee myself. Feeling one hundred percent responsible for this mess, I would work for free and cover any additional charges as well. I pictured a civil suit against Adam and his partners I could file on Becky's behalf, but that was way down the road. I did not know the amount of Rachel's lost wages, but figured I could help.

"Why don't you keep track of how many shifts you miss while we are sorting things out? I might be able to help. How much do you figure you earn each shift?" Rachel appeared deep in thought before she responded brightly.

"Probs about three hundred dollars each shift," she said with a hopeful expression on her face. *How much?* Becky choked on her last French fry at that and Rachel, perhaps realizing she had exaggerated a bit, revised her estimate. "Well yeah, but usually closer to um, two hundred?" I wanted to give the classic 'are you asking me or telling me?' response, but just nodded.

"Well, I'll see what we can do," I said, and she leaned over to Lucie, wiping her ketchup-stained face with a wadded-up napkin. I winked in Becky's direction and she smiled at me.

"Thank you," she mouthed silently,

Rachel busied herself collecting the remains of our midday feast, and after loading up a tray, she crossed the dining area towards the trash bins near the exit.

"Miss ... Randi," Becky whispered. "I can't thank you enough for everything."

"You know I am glad to help you in any way I can," I assured her.

"Rachel's just upset because she thinks that—"

"What do I think, Becky?" Rachel interrupted us with a frown. Becky stayed silent, so she continued. "I need to get this one in for her nap. Am I dropping you off?" she asked her sister, who nodded. "Then you need to be at my place by four thirty so I can get to work on time. I switched shifts today so I could be here for you." She glanced over at me, a knowing look in her eyes. "Unless your lawyer can cover the—"

"I'll be there," Becky assured her. "The bus will drop me off on your corner, and without Jesse in his stroller, it will be a lot easier. It's usually such a—" She looked at us in amazement, her chin quivering. "What's the matter with me? Did I just complain having my baby with me is an inconvenience? That I'd be better off without him? God, what kind of mother am I?" I was about to reassure her she was a wonderful mother and she'd have Jesse home soon, but Rachel beat me to it.

"Compared to freaking Cindy, you're like Mother of the Year." Turning to me, she said, "Did Bex ever tell you about Cindy? Our mom?" I shook my head. "Well, let me tell you, she was the worst. No Department of Children and Families protecting me and my baby sister, that's for sure. One time, she brought us to a booty call in the middle of the night. I was maybe six and this little squirt here was about four." She grinned at her sister, who looked like she was about to cry again. "Anyway, we hightailed it down to some crap motel a couple blocks from the dump we lived in and while Cindy is trading her ass for a bump of rock, we sat outside on a couple of those metal chairs motels always have. You know the ones?" I nodded mutely, clearly picturing the chairs. "So dear old mom must have been out cold, cuz we fell asleep in the chairs and when we woke up, the dude she was with gives us a couple of dollars to get some donuts."

"That's terrible," I said. Rachel grinned wickedly at me.

"Nah, it wasn't that bad. The motel had free donuts in the lobby and we got to keep the cash anyway," she boasted.

"C'mon Bex. Let's get going so I can get Lucie-Lu in for her nap."
I hugged Becky and smiled at Rachel.

"Alright then. I'll be in touch and don't forget my friend Lisa will be calling. If you don't hear from her in the next day or two, call me, yeah?" Becky promised she would, and I watched them walk over to Rachel's beat-up VW bug. I brushed back the tears that welled up, and I knew I had to do everything in my power to get Becky reunited with her little boy. She had been manipulated and abused her entire life and while there was nothing I could do to make up for her horrible childhood, the very least I could do would be to ensure she could provide a happy home for her son.

Adam and his partners would need to pay to make that possible, and I would make that happen, no matter what it took.

CHAPTER 17

I drove to the grocery store, a vague feeling of unease clouding my thoughts. I was confident I could get the possession with intent to sell charge against Becky dropped. As a former prosecutor, I knew a weak case when I saw it and the case against her was positively anemic. An anonymous tipster who just happened to know where the drugs might be? A weak-ass excuse to enter the home, probable cause be damned? *Puh-leeze.* Any judge would see the whole thing for the ridiculous stunt that it was. But there was more.

Based on recent developments, I had asked Rick to postpone Becky's visit to make an official complaint against Adam. I realized it was a top priority, and I hoped a brief delay wouldn't affect the case. I felt it was way more than Becky could deal with right now.

The most pressing challenge, as I saw it, was how to get Jesse returned home quickly. That would take some doing. Becky was extremely fragile and she would require a lot of TLC in order to deal with all that she was up against. I would speak with Lisa today to get her started on the process. And the specter of the Terry Kane trial loomed large. Was Becky strong enough to testify against Kane, assuming the State's Attorney would call on her? I thought so, but something else was bothering me. Becky's current situation was dire, and while I blamed myself, I thought Rachel could help more. And those lost wages? If she was earning anywhere near that much, why was Becky shlepping across town by bus to watch her niece several times a week? Was Rachel paying her? Where was Rachel's husband Eddie in all of this? How was Becky surviving? Adam's five fucking thousand dollars had to have disappeared ages ago. Had he ever contacted her again? Had his firm given her more money to stay gone? I needed answers, and soon. Becky was my client, after all. I had a right to this information; the next time I saw her, without Rachel, I would dig deeper.

An hour and a half later, I was back home, my fridge full of healthy food and my office nearly back to rights. I got hold of Lisa, who assured me she would represent Becky at no charge. I asked about Becky's chances for gaining back custody of her son, and there was a prolonged pause on Lisa's end. *Uh-oh.* Until then, I had never actually considered Becky could lose custody permanently.

"It's hard to say, Randi. I gotta be honest with you. Based on what you told me, from the court's point of view, we've got a single mother, barely out of her teens, no work history, no permanent address, arrested on possession with intent—"

"I'm gonna get those charges dropped. And she's a lovely young woman and a terrific mom." Please be true, I thought. "You'll see for yourself."

"And you'll make a wonderful character witness on her behalf, if it comes to that," Lisa assured me. "But let's consider the facts as you told them to me. Becky has no education, no means of supporting herself, let alone a child, and a history of problems with drugs and alcohol. If her past as a sex worker is brought to light, well, let me just say that under these circumstances, I think the most we can hope for is supervised visitation. Just until the court feels confident that it is in the best interests of the minor child to be returned to the home." An awkward silence followed, ending with a sigh. "Let's just take this one step at a time, okay? I'll meet with Becky tomorrow. You focus on getting the charges dropped. That will go a long way in assuring the court of Becky's ability to raise her son."

I assured Lisa that I would do just that. I spent the next few hours researching insufficient evidence, taking copious notes and citing several cases that appeared similar. I told myself that I might use this in a segment of *Miranda Writes*, so I wasn't abandoning all of my current work. I was deep in thought when the doorbell rang.

It was Tracey. I had forgotten our long-standing date, and she knew it as soon as I swung the door open.

"You forgot tonight's *The Bachelor*," she said. I didn't even try to deny it. I hugged my friend, the best friend a woman could hope for. She had been with me through all my life's challenges and triumphs. As I'd once phrased it to Adam, she knew where all the bodies were buried.

"I'm so sorry T," I said. "You know how much our evenings together mean to me. Was Dale able to watch the boys?" She grinned.

"Yeah, I told him all the overtime in the world didn't matter. The kids ran me ragged all day and have you ever had to convince two thirteen-year-old boys to do their homework and pick up their sweaty gym clothes? Believe me, getting out of the house tonight was a blessing all around. Things would have gotten ugly."

I had to laugh at that. Tracey was the gentlest, most even-tempered person I knew. She enjoyed her job, running a daycare center out of her home, and she was a terrific mom to her twin sons.

"I really am sorry. I got caught up working on something for Becky. I told you I ran into her, right?"

She nodded as I tried to pinpoint when I had last updated her. With a smile that said she knew it was more than a run-in,

Tracey crossed her arms across her chest and shook her head, brown eyes twinkling.

"Oh, you bleeding heart do-gooders are all alike," she said with mock severity. "The pizza will be here in twenty. How's about you grab a quick shower and I'll tidy this place up a bit. At least clear a pathway to the TV." God, I loved this woman.

"Thank you. Sounds like a plan," I said as I hustled off to the bathroom. "Grab some money out of my bag, yeah? The least I can do is treat you to a pizza." Tracey was quick to concur.

"Oh yeah, I'm pretty certain I'll never pay for another thing again when I'm with you, Ms. Moneybags," she assured me. "Now scoot, cuz someone is getting sent home tonight and I don't want to miss a thing."

"I love you," I called out just before I closed the door behind me. "Ditch that loser you're with and marry me instead. It's now legal, you know." I turned on the shower, grinning as I heard her hooting with laughter.

**

After we watched a horribly disjointed group date filmed at a hipster-style bowling alley, the roses were handed out and one girl, a petite redhead from Dallas, was sent home. Be glad you got out, I thought. This season's bachelor was even douchier than his predecessors. I turned off the TV and studied the three slices of pizza remaining in the box.

"Why don't you take this home for Dale? I need to watch my weight, you know?" Tracey scoffed at that.

"You weigh the same as you did in high school, for Christ's sake. How many women our age can say that?" Tracey pinched at her ever-so-slight tummy bulge and grinned at me. "Hell, and I pushed out nearly fourteen pounds of boy babies, so I guess I'm doing okay in the weight department, too."

"I know you're right, but the camera adds ten pounds and besides, it's all that salt. My face is so puffy. I should look into a juice cleanse."

"America is gonna love you, Randi. You'll be the darling of daytime. Mark my words." I forced a smile at that, but she wasn't buying it. Her eyes narrowed, she persisted. "What is it? You've been kind of out of it all night. Spill it, would you please? It's got to be more interesting than my boring little life. I'm up to my eyeballs in middle-school drama and daycare shenanigans."

"And your hubby, Dale," I said in a sing-song voice. She blushed slightly, and I grinned at her.

"What's your secret? You two have been hot and heavy since you were, what, twelve?"

"I was sixteen," she answered primly. "You were the only one who knew the first time we had sex."

"Yeah, you called me from your bathroom right afterwards, if I recall. You dragged your princess phone in with you and were all, 'Oh Randi, I love him. He's sooo dreamy.'" She swatted at me, but missed. "Then remember, after his freshman year at UCONN, you two came out to everyone as a couple? I thought your brother was gonna beat the shit out of him." She shook her head, a faraway look in her eyes.

"It took him awhile, but he eventually got used to the idea."

"See, if you'd have married me, we could have avoided all that drama." Tracey laughed, but suddenly turned serious.

"Yeah, okay. It was a lovely stroll down memory lane, but you changed the subject. We were talking about you. What's going on?" I rotated my head around, feeling tension in my neck and shoulders. I needed a massage, but would have to settle for another hot shower.

"It's just this nonsense trying to get ready for the show. They want me to jump through all these hoops, you know? Hair, nails, wardrobe, makeup." I rattled off my to-do list. Seeing Tracey respond with a motion that looked like someone playing the world's smallest violin, I hurried on. "And I told you about Adam, yeah? I can't believe he paid Becky to disappear. Totally derailed my career. What a bastard." I was still in shock over his betrayal. It was unforgivable. How could I have misjudged him so?

"Don't get me started again on that ass wipe," Tracey snarled. "Well, you'll beat him in court this time for sure."

"It won't be me in the courtroom, T. I don't know who Coop is going to assign the case to. I'm out of the loop unless they call me as a witness. But that's unlikely because if I told what I knew about the case from three years ago, that could prejudice the jury." Tracey rolled her eyes.

"Oooh, it would be soooo horrible if the truth was exposed in a court of law," she said. I ignored her sarcasm.

"Meanwhile, I've got to get the drug charges dropped and return Jesse home to his mother. And find out how my break-in fits in." Someone from the Kane defense team was trying to scare me, but so far, I would not cave. "I have to help her," I said with a shrug. "I'm all she has."

Tracey nodded in agreement as she wrapped up the pizza in a large square of aluminum foil. "And don't forget your blog and your podcast. They're still your bread and butter." I groaned at that. This evening had been fun, but I had to get to work first thing in the morning.

We hugged goodbye, and I promised to be in touch soon. I watched her drive off, feeling the fatigue threatening me all night overtake me. I put the empty pizza box and our soda cans in the recycling bin, turned off the lights, and made sure both doors were locked tight. After checking in with Pop's cop network and hearing all was quiet at Becky's, I took the hottest shower I could stand, directing the spray to my aching neck and shoulders. Then I trundled off to bed and slept like a rock for nine solid hours. It was divine.

CHAPTER 18

Waking rested for a change, I fought back the urge to go out for donuts by scrambling some eggs and toasting a slice of only slightly stale multigrain bread. While I waited for my coffee to brew, I made notes of what had to get done today. I took my breakfast out to the back porch and enjoyed the smell of the coffee and the warmth of the mug I grasped in my hands. I ate quickly and after I poured a second cup, I left my dishes in the sink and grabbed my phone. The first notification I read informed me my screen time was up this week by a whopping thirty-seven percent. Well, no shit, Sherlock, I thought as I dialed the State's Attorney's office in New London.

I still had a former colleague or two who would take my calls and in just a few minutes, I had the information I needed. Becky's drug possession case had been assigned to a relative newbie in the office. Ben Thomas had started shortly after they let me go and from what I knew, he was a solid performer. Decent record in court, nothing showy or dramatic. He was just an able-bodied public servant, dedicated to keeping criminals off the streets. I dialed his direct extension, and he answered after the first ring. We spoke only briefly, but I sensed compassion in his tone and he agreed to meet with me this morning at eleven to discuss Becky's case.

I quickly showered and pulled my still wet hair into a low ponytail. This would have to do. I had to make a few more calls in the half hour I had left before leaving the house. Sleeping in had been great, but man, it really killed the morning. I found the number for the stylist and made an appointment for later in the week. I scheduled all my beauty treatments next, and before I knew it, the rest of my week was chock full of must-dos. Brian will be so proud of me, I thought. I made a mental note to text him later in the day and grabbed my purse, and walked to my car. Correction. What was left of my car.

I stood in the driveway, staring in shock. All four tires were slashed, and they had hit the windshield with a hammer or something like it, resulting in an intricate web of cracks. Someone had spray painted a message in red paint on the windows. **IT ALONE LEAVE** I read as I circled the car. *WTF?* Leave it alone, I read, retracing my route. Obviously, someone wanted me to back off Becky's case. Could it have been Adam? Was his firm involved? Would they stoop to such depths to keep Becky from testifying against Terry Kane? That was a rhetorical question. Of course, they would.

I was deep in thought when one of my neighbors approached to view the damage up close. Within a few minutes, I was surrounded by a group of well-meaning men and women, most of whom I barely knew other than to nod to or smile at in passing. *Yes, it was a shock. No, I didn't think it was the beginning of a crime wave in our little cul-de-sac. Yes, it probably would have been better to park in my garage last night.* The bottom line? No one had heard or seen anything. I brushed off their concerns and assured everyone I was fine, just fine, and after reporting the incident to 911, I called the State's Attorney's office. I explained I was delayed and Ben agreed to meet me at 1:00 p.m. instead. While I waited for the patrol car, I called Pop. No surprise, but he had heard the news on his scanner and had been just about to drive over to my house.

"Pop, no," I argued. "It's just some neighborhood kids pulling a prank and besides, I need to be in New London soon. I'll keep you posted, I promise," I said and disconnected the call. I had not informed the 911 operator that the red spray paint had been a message, a warning, and was relieved my father did not seem to know about it. Nothing would stop him from showing up if he thought I was in any kind of danger.

I studied the damage and read the message again, even as I saw a patrol car heading towards me. The paint had dripped, but now appeared to be bone dry. I knew enough not to touch anything, hoping to preserve any evidence left behind. It was now 11:00 a.m., twelve and a half hours since Tracey had left. I would have seen the damage as I waved goodbye from the porch, so the vandalism must have taken place in the wee hours.

I sighed and walked over to greet the officers who were getting out of the car. Grey and Jamison, the same ones who had investigated the break-in a couple of days earlier. Pasting a smile on my face, I greeted them.

"We have to stop meeting like this," I protested cheerfully.

They photographed the many signs of damage to my car and I gave my statement. I responded honestly to their questions. Had I noticed anything suspicious in my neighborhood? No, not since the other night. Had I heard anything strange last night? No, not a thing. Did I know who might want to scare me? No, I did not. I was being honest. Did I *know* who it could have been? No, not with any degree of certainty. But I certainly had my suspicions, and I needed to find out just what was going on and who was responsible before something else happened. It had to be tied to Terry Kane, that scumbag. I kept my thoughts to myself, tuning back in to the conversation about my upcoming show.

"I'm going to tape every episode and watch them after shift," Officer Grey promised, and I thanked her gratefully. If I could just get Becky cleared and put an end to all this craziness, I could enjoy my current level of celebrity. If my show bombed, it wouldn't last too long.

At just past noon, Jamison and Grey dropped me at Tim's Garage, which doubled as the only car rental place in town, and minutes later I was driving a pearl gray minivan towards New London.

***

Ben Thomas smiled shyly as I entered his office precisely at one o'clock and gestured for me to take a seat. "They call you 'Quinn for the Win'," he said. I groaned inwardly at the nickname. I hadn't heard it spoken aloud in over three years.

"Don't believe everything you hear," I advised only half-jokingly and, pulling a pad and pen out of my bag, I sat back in a brown leather chair facing his desk. I decided to cut to the chase and jump right in. "Thank you for seeing me today, Ben. I apologize for the delay and I appreciate your flexibility in accommodating me." He nodded, and I continued, trying to channel the dozens of times a defense attorney had sat in front of me asking that I cut their client some slack and pleading for a reduced charge or the dropping of all charges. Now it was my turn, sitting on the other side of the desk, asking for ... what? Understanding? Compassion? A lucky break?

"As you know, I'm representing Rebecca Lewis and I'm here today asking that the court drop the charges of drug possession with intent and child endangerment. Ms. Lewis is a single mother and I can testify she is no longer using drugs and has never been engaged in the selling of drugs." I sure hoped that last part was true. "She is the sole provider for her infant son and is employed as a care provider for her sister Rachel's daughter. I can attest to the fact she has gotten her life in order and I can prove beyond a shadow of a doubt that the planting of drugs in her home was a desperate ploy by Terry Kane's legal team to discredit her as a witness in his upcoming trial. I ask that all charges be dropped, and that they return the minor child to his home." There, I had said my piece. I was compiling arguments to refute whatever defensive statements he might make, but listened in surprise as Ben spoke up.

"I wholeheartedly concur with you, Ms. Quinn, and the paperwork is already on its way to the New London Police department. As well as to DCF," Ben said, and I studied him in amazement, my mouth agape. *Seriously?* I collected myself and tried not to look surprised at his pronouncement.

"Well, that is good news. My client will be so relieved. But, um, can I ask what factors you considered in your decision?" I knew I should probably leave well enough alone, but I could count on both hands the number of times in my career when I had dropped all charges this early in the case. How had we gotten so lucky? He shrugged, looking sheepish.

"Apparently, the drugs in question were nothing but baking soda. There is no evidence of illegal drugs being found in the home. There was a glassine pipe, but it had not been used, and no drug remains were found. Just someone's idea of a joke, it would appear," he said.

"Yeah, hilarious. Those crazy kids will do anything for a laugh, am I right?" I tried to sound flippant, but inside I was seething. Becky had gone through hell and the only thing of which I was certain was that it had not been anyone's idea of a joke.

I gathered my things, preparing to leave, when Ben stopped me.

"My wife and I are looking forward to your show, Miranda. It is all anyone talks about around here these days. I'll be setting up my DVR so as not to miss a single episode," he said. I thanked him profusely, relieved to hear the gossip surrounding me these days was positive for a change.

"Maybe you and your wife would like to attend one of the live shows," I began. "I can arrange for tickets."

"That would be wonderful. Diane will not believe I met you today. I can't wait—" I cut him off and shook his hand vigorously.

"I can't wait to share this with my client," I assured him. "Thank you, Ben. I'll be in touch about the tickets." I felt like jumping up and clicking my heels as I scurried down the hall.

I knew Becky would be thrilled, and I dialed her number as I tried in vain to remember where I had parked my rented minivan. The good news was she would get Jesse back. The bad news? There was still a target on our backs and the stakes were higher than ever. *See what we can do to you?* That was their message, and I had received it, loud and clear. The closer we got to the truth, the more exposed we were. I would have to inform Rick about this latest incident and figure out how to keep Becky safe.

Pop's Cop Squad, as I had taken to calling the group of ex-cops, was helpful, but I imagined any potential threat against Becky would only increase over the next couple of weeks.

CHAPTER 19

Closing my eyes, I drew in a breath as I stepped on the scale, hoping it would not expose the junk food binge I had engaged in last night. When I had left Ben yesterday, I had been feeling mostly optimistic about Becky's situation. Since then, however, everything had gone to hell and, in my typical fashion, I had eaten my feelings with a pint of ice cream and half a tube of refrigerated cookie dough. Contrary to my understanding, Jesse had not been returned to his home. Although the DCF acknowledged the drug charges had been dropped, their brief visit on the night of the arrest had revealed several less-than-ideal red flags in the current living arrangements. Follow-up visits would be scheduled and, meanwhile, Jesse Lewis remained in foster care. I was seriously worried about my client's mental state and planned to be present for as many of the visits as I could. But today, all the focus was on me. *Oh boy!*

The attendant tsked slightly and wrote something on her chart. I opened my eyes to see the number that flashed before me as I hopped off the scale. *Damn.* Not as bad as it could have been, but not good either. Salad tonight, I told myself.

"I'm just one stomach bug away from my ideal weight," I quipped. The young woman whose name tag identified her as Tasha barely stopped herself from rolling her eyes and beckoned me to follow her down the hall. I was at the image consultant's offices today for a series of appointments. So far it had resembled a high-end private medical practice, but as we passed through a large sunny solarium, I revised my judgement. It was looking more like a luxury spa and I silently wished I was on my way to a lovely massage or a relaxing facial instead of the real reason I was here. I had taken the train to Stamford this morning and then it was only a quick cab ride to the high-rise complex housing the offices of Mirror Image, Inc.

Silently, I followed Tasha into one of the small rooms clustered at the edge of the marble lobby. She started pointing and barking orders at me. "Remove your clothes and place them in the bin. Leave on your bra and panties and sit over there. Grab a towel first. No, from that pile," she corrected me, a bit too harshly in my opinion. I grabbed a towel from the appropriate pile, which were dead ringers for the towels in the inappropriate pile, and started unbuttoning my shirt.

I had worn jeans and a striped button down today and it wasn't until I had sat in a crowded waiting room with women dressed to the nines, that I realized I should have taken a bit more care with my wardrobe when visiting a wardrobe consultant. I was about to add that I generally stripped down only to music, but Tasha was ignoring me, studying her clipboard as if the secrets to the universe were written there.

I slipped off my shirt and stuffed it in the bin provided, then unzipped my jeans, relieved as I noted my underwear was both clean and none too shabby. I know lots of women who enjoy buying and wearing expensive lingerie, but I was not one of them. My panties came in a package of three and my bras were more sporty than sexy. I perched on the only chair, clutching my towel around me, waiting for Tasha to instruct me on what to do next. She turned to look at me, motioning with her free hand.

"Up," she commanded and, like an obedient dog, I hopped up and stood before her. Wearing what I viewed as a rather malicious grin, she measured every inch of me. Bust, waist, hips, inseam, arm length and so on. As she did so, she rattled off her findings aloud and jotted them down on her clipboard. And there were plenty more tsks as well. I studied my tormentor as she finished her report on me. Couldn't be much more than twenty, stood an inch or two taller than my 5'8" frame and probably weighed thirty pounds less, with big boobs and a tiny waist. Sort of a medium-sized Barbie doll, with the demeanor of a prison matron. What a charmer!

"You can take a seat. Belinda will join you in shortly. No," she said as I went to retrieve my clothes. "Put on the robe," she said, pointing to a terry-cloth robe hanging on the hook of the door. Wrapped in plastic and hermetically sealed, I guessed. "And there are flip-flops too," she said, indicating a canvas bag with plastic-wrapped pairs of sandals.

"Thank you, Tasha," I said as she left the room. She softened slightly and smiled.

"You're welcome, Miss Quinn. Good luck," she said, and with a wave, left me alone, closing the door behind her. I find most people are fairly pleasant if you treat them with respect. Except for unrepentant assholes and career criminals like Terry Kane and jerk face fucktards like Adam Baxter, that is.

***

The next couple of hours flew by. I sipped peppermint tea and listened to Enya while dishing with the elegantly attired Belinda about my upcoming show, checking my phone every few minutes to see if Becky had reached out. I tried to answer truthfully as Belinda rattled off a series of questions.

How did I want to be seen by the American viewing public?

Knowledgeable. Authentic.

What was the image I was seeking?

Hmmm. Knowledgeable? Authentic?

Sexy or professional?

Professional, of course. But sexy too. 70/30 or maybe 60/40?

Joan Lunden or Meredith Vieira?

Who?

Tyra or Ellen?

Seriously?

Warm or frosty?

A little of both, depending on the guest or the topic.

By the time the session ended, I finally figured out who I wanted to be: a 'girl next door' Katie Couric with Ellen's wit, Kelly Ripa's enthusiasm and Dr. Oz's credibility. That was a tall order, but I was certain Belinda and her team of magicians at Mirror Image Inc. were up to the challenge. I hoped I was too.

According to Belinda, all the clothing in my on-air wardrobe would be chosen specifically to accentuate my height and relatively narrow shoulders, augment my meager bust, and minimize my child-bearing hips. Black was determined to be too severe for my pale complexion, so my palette would be navy and charcoal gray with touches of color in my favorite teals and corals. Jackets would be structured, left unbuttoned, and I voted to wear fitted slim pants instead of pencil skirts. The last thing I wanted to worry about was showing too much leg, and pantyhose was a deal breaker. Nothing frilly or lacey, which suited me just fine. Jewelry would be simple, either gold or silver small hoop earrings and a delicate chain with a pendant. I refused to wear pearls (shades of Judge Judy) or anything chunky and was delighted by the persona I was picturing.

It was a satisfying morning, and I left the offices feeling accomplished and upbeat. If I hadn't been so worried about Becky and Jesse, I might have wanted to celebrate. *Miranda Writes* would be a classy, informative hour of television and viewers would turn in daily, or at least set their DVRs to gain useful knowledge about the legal matters that touched their lives. According to the latest text from Brian, the Sterling folks expected me to head into the city tomorrow to begin the process of set design at the studio. I had been sent a series of staged photos featuring a variety of low sofas, armchairs in muted tones and coffee tables made of every material imaginable: recycled barn board, shabby-chic wicker, elegant teak wood and a sleek metal one I liked with a tile top. Decisions, decisions! I should have stayed in the city tonight, but I figured I could use the time on the train to review the set designs more carefully and make some notes to prepare for the meeting. This was actually happening!

Certain I had done all I could for the show for now, I shifted my focus back to Becky. I had spoken with Rick earlier, catching him before he went to court. He had expressed concern about the damage to my car and the message left by the vandals, but I told him I was more worried about Becky and the threat posed to her by Adam and his law firm. He had offered to arrange temporary housing for her and her son, and I said I would keep him posted. The short-term solution we had in place was working, for now.

I swung by Pop's house on my way home. As I had hoped, he and several of his retired cop friends were sitting in the kitchen, writing on a big poster board. They were fine-tuning the schedule for the upcoming week to provide round-the-clock security for Becky. I made them promise they would call the "real" police if they saw anything, and I got smirks and grins in response.

"This is the most excitement these jokers will have this year," Pop said with a chuckle. "Present company included." I thanked them and assured them that on-duty takeout food and off-duty beer would continue to arrive. Sally had graciously offered to coordinate the food and Pop was handling the beer, and both had my credit cards to cover the costs.

"How about your place, Randi?" Pop's friend Ron asked. "Should we put together a schedule for you, too?" I assured them I was fine, but I saw a look pass between him and Pop. I wouldn't be surprised to see a strange car on my street from time to time for the next few weeks.

And I was okay with that.

CHAPTER 20

The next day, I drove home from the New Haven train station in the mid-afternoon. The set design meeting had gone surprisingly well. The group consensus was to keep the furniture neutral in shades of taupe and beige, highlighted with colorful pillows and fresh flowers. We chose a teak coffee table and end tables. We all agreed the overall look would be fabulous: fresh and elegant, warm and inviting. I decided to return some calls while sitting on the back porch with a water bottle and a bag of baby carrots. I tried not to think about the veggie burrito I had consumed on the train. I checked in with Pop and agreed to meet him and Sally for dinner later in the week. Tracey was in the pickup line for the twins and couldn't talk, but said we would catch up soon.

I sent Becky a quick text. **Just checking in. How're u doin? R**

I had called her repeatedly last evening and finally reached her by dialing her sister's phone. She had explained that her phone had died and her charging cord was at home, where she didn't want to go as it reminded her of Jesse. Rachel and her husband both had iPhones, so Becky and her flip phone were out of luck. I told her it was important she be accessible for me, as well as her lawyer Lisa, and the DCF staff. I instructed her to go buy a spare charging cord at the bodega on the corner and said

I would reimburse her when I saw her. I had not heard from her today and I was beginning to worry. Just a little.

Then I called Lisa. She had excellent news to share. Based upon the formal dropping of all charges and a personal call from State's Attorney Cooper, DCF had reversed their earlier decision and would return Jesse home within the next day or two, barring any difficulties. There would be a few visits to the home in the weeks that followed, but all in all, it was great news. I was thrilled! I thanked Lisa, and on a whim, offered to buy her dinner. We agreed to meet at six at a little sushi joint in Mystic. Lisa lived nearby and said it would be quiet this early in the week. It was near the loft where I had lived with Adam. I assumed he still lived there, but it was possible he had moved. I thought the odds of running into him were slim to none. It was the perfect place for a celebratory dinner and it would be an early night.

I added to Becky's text. **Heard the good news. Call me when you can. Congrats. R**

An hour later, I left to meet Lisa. The parking lot was nearly full, and I hoped the happy hour crowd would soon depart so we could talk. Lisa had snagged a corner booth, and I rushed over to her. After we hugged, I thanked her again for all she had done for Becky. We ordered a variety of sushi and sashimi and it arrived on an enormous platter. As we ate, Lisa shared news of her job as a family attorney and we gossiped about friends and acquaintances that we had in common. I brought her up to speed on all that had transpired as *Miranda Writes* evolved from blog to podcast to TV show. I told her about my visits with the wardrobe consultant and the set designers, and she responded enthusiastically.

"It all sounds great. I'm so proud of you and I can say 'I knew you when.' I can't wait for the show to air!" Lisa's phone rang and after a quick look at the screen, said "I gotta take this," and walked towards the exit. I was debating ordering dessert, a plate of those delightful little green tea flavored mochi ice creams, when I felt someone approaching on my right. I looked up quickly to see Adam looming over me. *What the hell?*

"Fancy meeting you here." He spoke in a low tone, obviously trying to sound suave and sexy.

"What do you want?" I snapped. "Are you following me? Do I need to take out a restraining order?" His large brown eyes twinkled gaily.

"What's this now? You're into restraints these days? I don't remember that level of kink from you back in the day," he teased. "But if you're game," he leaned in to whisper in my ear, "I am sure we can arrange something." I held back a shudder of pure disgust. What had I ever seen in this smug bastard?

I kept my tone low, smiling at him sweetly. "Fuck off, you piece of shit kidnapper. Get out of my sight or you'll wish you did," I warned him. He studied me, shaking his head sadly.

"All work and no play Ran. What's become of you?"

Just as Lisa returned to our booth, Adam smiled and waved a quick farewell. "Lovely running into you, Miranda. Can't wait for your new show." And he left. Lisa slipped into her seat looking mystified.

"Who was that good-looking male specimen and why did you let him get away?" she asked, eyebrows raised. Lisa and I had lost touch several years back, and she had never met Adam when we were a couple. I had less than no desire to explain the horrific train wreck our relationship had become. I studied my shaking hands as I responded.

"Just a blast from the past. So, are you up for some of those little green tea mochis?"

***

It was just after 4:00 a.m. when my phone started buzzing. I ignored it for as long as I could, but considering some of the other middle-of-the-night calls I'd received lately, I rolled over onto my back and grabbed it. What on earth was going on? I wondered as I started scrolling through several recent posts. *Oh no!*

The headlines said it all. My favorite was, "Legal Lovers Linger". What you didn't get from the alliterative text, the grainy photo provided all the sleazy commentary that anyone needed. There I was, ensconced in a booth at last night's sushi dinner, with Adam so close to me the camera exhibited too many points of contact to count. He was leaning in, looking like he was about to kiss me, and I appeared ready to kiss him back.

I read the article, my sense of dread rising with every word. Wait just a damned minute now. *Married?* Adam had gotten married? I tried to process what I was reading. They spelled our names correctly, but had me at thirty-nine and Adam at thirty-three. We were actually thirty-eight and thirty-four, but whatever. They described me as an overnight media sensation and the fresh face of daytime TV. Adam was portrayed as recently married and the very successful law partner about to represent defendant Terry Kane in his upcoming trial. Adam's wife's name was not given, and the article described our breakup of three years earlier as volatile. Adam was married?

I tried to imagine the scene from the restaurant last night. Had Adam manufactured the whole thing, trying to publicly embarrass me? But why would he do that, as he looked just as guilty as me? More than likely, a nearby diner had recognized me and when they saw me with a good-looking guy, figured it was worth snapping a photo. Adam would have been fairly easy to identify.

I studied the photo more carefully. Based on where Lisa and I had been sitting, it had to have been taken from outside on the sidewalk, through the window. The glare from the glass made certain aspects of the setting nearly unrecognizable. But what was easy to see? A handsome man with his lips on my ear and me with a smile on my face. I flopped back down on my bed and pulled the covers over me. *Take me,* I begged silently of the malevolent spirits clearly inhabiting my space, intent on ruining my life. *There's nothing left for me here.* I tossed and turned for another half hour and finally gave up any semblance of sleeping.

My phone rang at six. I had been up for an hour and consumed an entire pot of coffee. I picked up. It was Brian.

"Good morning, Brian."

"How're things in Peyton Place? Breakup any marriages lately?" *Grrrrrr.*

"I didn't know he was married."

"What the hell, Miranda? Are you trying to create a disaster? Isn't it bad enough you're consorting with drug dealers and prostitutes?"

"Becky is neither of those things and did you actually just say 'consorting'?"

"That's not the point. What in the hell is going on?"

"It was a simple dinner with a friend. I did not know I would run into my—Adam. He just came over to my table to say hello. Nothing happened. And again, I did not know he had a wife."

"Her name is Kimberly Nolan Baxter. She's from Vermont, twenty-eight years young and a paralegal at his firm. They have been married for nearly a year. You're welcome." *Wow!* Brian had sure done his homework. The news that Adam had married someone ten years younger than me hurt more than I wanted to admit.

"Well, I'm certainly not the first woman to have been photographed with a married ex," I said.

"You are the first woman who is going to star in her own TV show and who is my client," he countered. "And you're supposed to be this honorable, ethical, legal expert and not some floozy. Think of the sponsors."

First consorting, now floozy? For a millennial, Brian sounded positively geriatric at times.

"Feel free to issue a statement that Adam and I are old friends and that's that." Brian hung up on me and I headed to my bedroom. *Rude.*

I took a long shower and then talked briefly to Pop. Sally had seen the photo on Facebook and shared it with him. I assured him I was not getting involved with Adam again.

"I guess that's the price of celebrity," he harrumphed and I had to agree. I tried Tracey, but she was in the middle of morning share-time and promised to call back later.

A new text came in from Becky. **Are you back with him?**

I hurriedly typed a response. **Adam? No. Just ran into him.** No return text.

U OK? I bet you're thrilled to get Jesse back.
Yeah. TTYL

Maybe she was in a hurry, or just stressed out. I had been expecting a bit more enthusiasm, but it was early, and she'd had quite an eventful week. She had gratefully accepted the news that a bunch of retired cops were going to be watching over her, and I hoped it would help her feel safe. I would reach out to her later and offer to bring over lunch in a day or two.

A run on the beach was in order to work off this nervous energy and hopefully sweat out some caffeine. I drove the two blocks, found street parking and began my 'run', which was actually 50% fast walking and 50% limping. Even in my prime, I was never much of an athlete. But it was a beautiful morning, and the beach was nearly deserted, so I focused on my breathing and tried to clear my head of thoughts of Adam, his young bride, and whatever was going on with Becky.

I had a lot to catch up on today for my next blog post and weekly podcast taping and I looked forward to experiencing the feeling of satisfaction hard work nearly always delivered.

CHAPTER 21

Refreshed after my "run," I changed into leggings and a UCONN sweatshirt and settled down to work. I mapped out my blog posts scheduled for the next several weeks and then logged into LexisNexis and did a bit of background research for my post on determining visitation rights and calculating child support. I emailed Skip to confirm he was planning on taping the upcoming podcasts with me on Wednesday morning and reviewed the scripts for each one. I set up a meeting with Sarah to go over the mail that had probably been flooding my postal box. I knew I had to put in hours of hard work in advance, realizing that things would change considerably for me once the new show was on the air. After emailing each of the three guests to remind them of the day and time of the podcast taping, I sat back and stretched.

It was late in the day. While I had been working, the sun had disappeared and dark rain clouds dotted the sky. I was glad I had worked out before the quickly approaching storm. I was about to pour myself a chilled glass of whatever wine was open in the fridge and draw a hot bath when the doorbell rang. I wasn't expecting anyone, so I figured it was a neighbor stopping by to stay hello or maybe congratulate me on my show.

I hustled over and pulled the door open and found ... no one. The porch was unoccupied, but I saw a small package on the top step. I bent to grab it, then straightened up, looking both ways at the empty street. A chill ran through me, not solely from the wind whipping around the nearby trees. I took the package inside and closed the door behind me, taking care to turn the deadbolt. The small package was deceptively heavy and wrapped in brown paper, tied with a piece of twine. I turned it over in my hands. I looked for some sort of marking, but found none. This was odd, I thought. I pulled at the twine and unwrapped the layers of paper. It was a rock, just a plain stone about four inches in diameter. Confused, I sifted through the pile of wrapping and found a square of paper that looked like someone had ripped it off the bottom of a pad. I read the message crudely written in what appeared to be a black Sharpie. *leave it alone or nex time this wil go threw a window*

Stunned, I sat on the edge of the couch and tried to think. Essentially, the same 'Leave it alone' message that had been spray-painted on my car, just dumbed down a little. Clearly, whatever I was doing had someone more than a little concerned. Maybe a bunch of someones. But what exactly had I done? Gotten the bogus drug charges against Becky dropped, offered a bit of support to return Jesse to the home and met with the State's Attorney. That was it. Since Becky's first call, there had been the break in, the vandalism to my car and now a threat of violence, not to mention running into Adam twice in a week. It all added up to one giant cluster-fuck designed to keep Becky and me from aiding in the case against Kane and/or getting charges filed against Adam. But like the proverbial dog with a bone, I was a cop's kid and had been a kick-ass prosecutor. I was more determined than ever to seek justice for Becky and watch both Adam and Kane get put away for a long time. Surely the Sterling folks would see more value in an actual attorney doing her job than a vapid mouthpiece.

I stared at the rock and racked my brain. For now, I was ruling out Adam, at least for the vandalism to my home and my car. I just could not see him in that way. Likes to keep his hands clean. He might have paid someone to do his dirty work, but who and again, why? Clearly, he had moved on with his life after we broke up. He had been made a partner and assigned to the high-profile Kane case. And, thanks to Brian, I now knew he married a perky blonde paralegal named Kimberly. I had searched on Facebook and found Kim Nolan Baxter's page. Precious few pictures of Adam, but then he had eschewed all forms of social media except LinkedIn, back when we were together. "Who cares what I ate for dinner or how many steps I took today? No one, that's who," he had countered whenever I suggested he post something.

There was a wedding photo of the two of them. Adam looking resplendent in a charcoal gray bespoke suit and a crisp white shirt, open at the neck. No tie. His hair was cropped short and his brown eyes sparkled in his tanned face as he gazed adoringly at his young bride. She wore a simple white sleeveless dress, cut just above the knee, and her blond hair looked effortlessly chic in a rolled chignon. She, too, was beaming. I hated to admit it, but they were a very good-looking couple.

I debated calling Officers Grey and Jamison to come over to check out the rock for themselves, but watching out the window at the rain now coming down in sheets, I decided I would hold off. What good would it do? I checked the lock on the kitchen door and certain I was safe and my home was secure; I surveyed my relatively empty kitchen cabinets. I had missed lunch and was now starving. Yesterday, I had loaded my fridge with fresh produce and vegetables plus a couple of salmon filets. None of it sounded in the least bit appealing. I saw a few cans of soup and a boxed rice mix but figured I would need to check expiration dates—and soon—before I resorted to anything in that cupboard.

The next cupboard yielded a family size box of sugar-sweetened cereal I had bought when Tracey's twin boys had spent the night last month. I grabbed the box, poured the remaining portion into a soup bowl, and splashed nonfat milk over it. Grabbing a banana from one of the deconstructed fruit baskets, I took my dinner into the bedroom and made myself comfortable propped up on my bed. I pointed the remote control at my TV and saw the storm had knocked out the cable. At least I still have electricity, I consoled myself only seconds before the lamp on my bedside table flickered and then died. *Crap!*

I would have to get through the storm on my own and in the dark, so I held my Kindle with its lighted screen in one hand and, balancing my dinner on my lap, got caught up in the latest Elin Hilderbrand novel while alternately slurping cereal and munching on a banana. Livin' the life, I thought to myself. I read for a while before realizing I had skimmed the same paragraph three times. Thoroughly exhausted, I put my empty bowl on the nightstand and pulled the covers up to my chin.

I awoke with a start just after four in the morning. The power was back; my TV blared loudly, my digital clock radio was blinking furiously and all the lights in the house were on. I knew I wouldn't fall back to sleep, so I got up and brewed a pot of coffee and reviewed the scripts for my upcoming podcast tapings one more time. I kept flashing back to Adam, to Becky, and to Terry Kane. What was the link that I was overlooking? I had been drawn into a career in law, thrilled by its logical sense of right and wrong, of black and white.

But from where I sat in the pre-dawn hours, everything in my world was a cloudy shade of gray.

CHAPTER 22

Rick Cooper's administrative assistant called shortly before 8:00 a.m. She said Rick wanted to see me and that both Becky and Assistant State's Attorney Thomas Shea would join us. I offered to reach out to Becky myself, but Louise said she already had contacted her and asked me if 10:00 a.m. would be convenient. I agreed and after a shower, I ate an apple and a pear, passing on more coffee. My nerves were jangling from all I had already consumed. I texted Becky.

See you soon. U good? R

I watched my phone to see if she had read it and I waited for a response. Nothing. This was crazy, I told myself. I pulled my hair back into a low ponytail, applied mascara, blush, and lip gloss and slipped into a black sheath dress that was positively ancient, but always came through for me. I slipped into a pair of low-heeled sandals and a blue cardigan and raced out the door.

Although not on my way, I drove over to Tracey's. I knew she would be up to her ears with kids at her daycare, but hoped she could spare a few minutes to talk. I felt nervous and out of sorts. Why was Becky ghosting me? Could the newspaper article have spooked her that much?

I found street parking a couple of houses down from Tracey and Dale's ranch home. They had converted the two-car garage into a large playroom with a bathroom, small kitchenette and plenty of open shelving for games, toys and puzzles. They had covered the floor in a colorful patchwork of rug squares I had helped to install and decorated the walls with murals of flowers and unicorns. Just behind the garage was a large fenced-in yard where Tracey kept her tiny humans on nice days such as these. I scooted around the back, hoping to find her.

I lucked out as Tracey and her assistant, an older woman named Helen, had just handed out the morning's snack: cartons of low-fat milk, a graham cracker and a sliced banana. As the eight children munched happily away, I shared all that had been going on over the last couple of days. Her eyes bugged out when I told her about last night's rock incident.

"What do the police say?"

"I haven't actually contacted the police."

"Are you nuts? You could be in real danger, Randi."

"It's probably just a—"

"Coincidence? Is that what you were going to say?"

"I'm just—"

"Bullshit," she said, and two of the little ones sitting several feet away giggled.

"Ooh, Miss Tracey said a bad word," one of them said in a sing-song voice, reminding me once more why I was never having kids.

"No one likes a tattletale, Chrissy," Tracey responded tartly. She pulled at my arm and we left the play area and started walking towards the front of the house.

"Randi, I am your oldest friend and your best friend, and I know you better than anyone. You're in denial if you can't face that Adam is behind this." I protested, but she cut me off. "When it comes to the law, you have all the answers, but this is different. It's not all nice and neat like everything in your textbooks. It's real, and it's messy and you could get badly hurt here. Look at the facts. Adam lied to you. He tricked your witness, gave her money and sent her away all to tank your case. He followed you, threatened you in two public places, broke into your home, vandalized your car and now he's the lead on that scumbag Kane's case. Someone planted drugs in that poor girl's apartment, caused her to lose custody of her kid. Don't you see? It's all connected."

"Damn girl, don't hold back. Tell me what you really think," I protested weakly. She continued to watch me closely until I shrugged and agreed with her.

"You're right. I'm sure you are. I'm just so tired. It's all such a mess and I can't see my way out of it."

"I get it, believe me. But you're the smartest woman I know. Take it step by step. One day at a time. Keep your eye on the prize." But what was the prize, exactly? Before Becky's first call, my primary focus had been getting my TV show up and running and regaining the credibility I had lost. But now? Getting Becky's son back? Seeking monetary damages to help her start over? Seeing Adam face charges? Ensuring Kane was found guilty? All the above? I sniffed loudly and wiped my nose with the crushed tissue Tracey produced from her pocket. It looked more than a little used.

"Ugh, kid snot."

"Comes with the territory. Woman up, girlfriend. So where are you off to?"

"I'm meeting with Cooper at the office. Becky's going to join us. He'll have a couple of New London Police detectives take her statement about Adam and he'll want to go over her testimony to get ready for the trial. Then I figured I would take Becky out for lunch to celebrate. They are bringing Jesse back to her later on today." Tracey groaned in response.

"Go somewhere nice, yeah? With cloth napkins and real silverware? Think of me while you're dining on oysters and chateaubriand. I'll be here, hunched over a kid on the potty while I try to eat a smushed PB&J with no crusts."

"I was thinking of unlimited soup, salad and breadsticks at the OG, but I hear ya. Then I'll head over to the police station to file a report on the rock incident."

We were standing on the sidewalk and Tracey looked up and down the street.

"Which one is yours?" she asked, and I pointed to the minivan.

"I have to call the shop later on to find out when my car will be ready."

"Tell me you're going to look for something flashy when things settle down, please? Stop being such a tight ass. We can't have the new queen of daytime tooling around town in a beater like yours." I shrugged noncommittally and hugged her. A new car was way down on my list of priorities. With a wave, I hopped in and headed to New London.

I arrived at my former place of employment a few minutes before my scheduled appointment time. They gave me a visitor's badge and escorted me to the elevators, which I took to the sixth floor and approached the reception desk. Cruella was back on duty and she watched as I approached.

"Good morning," I said cheerily. "I have a ten o'clock with Rick."

She nodded in greeting, then buzzed me in to the main office. I walked to the back of the large open space and saw Louise walking towards me. I greeted her warmly and asked,

"Is Becky here yet?"

CHAPTER 23

Louise frowned at me and left me standing in Rick's doorway. I looked in and found the cavernous office empty. As I stepped inside, the door to Rick's private bathroom opened and he walked out, drying his hands on a paper towel.

"We meet again," I declared in as cheery a tone as I could muster. "Am I the first one to arrive?"

He did not respond, and I knew something was up. Now what? "Rick, I—"

"She's not coming." His tone was flat, and he watched me closely as I struggled to understand.

"Who? Becky? I thought that ... "

"I thought you had this situation under control, Miranda. We were counting on you."

"Um, but everything was all set," I stammered. What was it about this man? I turned into a stuttering fool when I was around him. Why? He had no power over me. There was nothing he could do to me.

"I'm contacting the State Bar Association," he announced as he sat in his chair and swiveled to face me. "Sit." Oh man, this was getting old. I sat and waited for him to continue. And waited.

"The State Bar," I prompted.

"Yes, to start the investigation of a case of witness tampering."

"Against Adam? Can you do that without Becky's sworn statement?"

"Against you, Ms. Quinn," he announced. I was momentarily speechless.

"M-Me? What are you talking about?"

"Ms. Lewis is the one witness we have who can connect Kane to this recent charge and apparently, she is unwilling to come forward. She had agreed to join us this morning, but we got a text from her a half hour ago canceling our meeting. Then I received an email from her stating you coerced her into disappearing three years ago and when she agreed to testify this time, you threatened her and had drugs planted in her apartment, so she lost custody of her child. She claims Adam was not involved and blames it all solely on you."

"What the hell? Rick, that's bullshit. All of it. What reason would I have to threaten a potential witness? Isn't that something Kane's legal team might try to pull?"

"It is a serious breach of ethics, Ms. Quinn."

"What's with the 'Ms. Quinn' Rick? You've known me forever. We've had our difficulties, but Christ. You can't imagine I would deliberately sabotage your case like that."

"Ms. Lewis claims you approached her the other day and asked her to not testify against Kane. She said you told her if Kane were convicted, it would point the finger back at you as you had botched the original case against him. That you couldn't risk that coming to light, what with your new show and all."

I sat in stunned silence. How had all this gotten so turned around? And by whom? Becky had dropped out of school at sixteen. Although she was fairly articulate, I doubted she possessed the sort of intellect needed to invent an argument like that and to think so strategically.

"Adam," I said simply and dropped forward, cradling my head in my hands. "This is all Adam's doing."

"Ah yes, Adam Baxter, the lead attorney on the Kane defense team. Your 'ex' yes? You two looked awfully cozy the other night," he said, as he pushed a copy of the *New London Day* towards me. There it was on the front page, right below the fold. The grainy low-quality image of yours truly in a secluded booth looking like I was about to suck face with my married former boyfriend. The headline had been updated: "Quinn Hooks Up with Kane's Legal Team."

I tried to protest, but Rick held up his hand to stop me.

"You should really have an attorney present."

"This is crazy. Where is all of this coming from? It was Adam. He's the one who paid her, he's the one who got her out of town. I knew nothing about it until a few days ago. I reported to you what I found out as soon as I had heard. I swear it. What reason would I have to tank my own case, to ruin my reputation?" I tried to slow my breathing, conscious of the sweat now soaking my armpits and pooling between my breasts. This could not be happening!

Rick's eyes shone with anger through the thick frames of his eyeglasses. "That will be up to the prosecutor assigned to your case to determine. That you were sleeping with a member of the defense team back then suggests that you were unduly influenced, perhaps to please your lover. And with this latest ..." he said, gesturing at the newspaper. "It's a disaster in the making."

"You honestly think I did this on purpose? I hid out on my father's couch for almost a year. I lost everything when Kane got set free. You know that. Adam and I broke up right afterwards."

"That is not my concern. Perhaps it was a last-ditch effort to hold on to him. That you broke up so soon after suggests your relationship was already on the skids when you conspired to ... "

Suddenly, I couldn't breathe. The stress of the past week caught up with me as I gasped and sputtered. After everything I had gone through three years ago, I had worked hard and been rewarded with the promise of a lucrative career. Since then, I had been threatened, my home and car vandalized, my reputation tarnished and my credibility questioned. Becky had been arrested, lost custody of her child and was being watched twenty-four hours a day by a bunch of retired cops.

"Water," I begged, and Rick leaped up to pour me a glass from the pitcher on his sideboard. He bent down next to me and I took the glass from him. I took a long swallow and tried to collect my thoughts. He studied me closely, a frown on his face.

"As a former colleague, I advise you to seek legal representation. These accusations are—"

"Utterly without merit and ridiculous," I said, and he silenced me with a look. He straightened and walked back around his desk. Sitting again, he picked up his signature ballpoint pen and grabbed a file. He adjusted his glasses and looked at me one last time.

"Find yourself a lawyer, Miranda. You'll probably still be disbarred, but if you cooperate, you might not have to do any real time." He turned his attention to his paperwork, and I stumbled out of his office.

If I were disbarred, I could not help Becky seek civil damages from Adam and company and, of course, they would cancel my show. I would lose everything. If I went to jail? A former prosecutor? The daughter of a cop?

Oh man, I was so screwed.

CHAPTER 24

You know when you're watching your favorite show or an old movie and the main character goes to do something really stupid, like try to reason with a knife-carrying murderer or climb the stairs in an abandoned house to the attic where the monster is hiding? You're saying to yourself, "Hey dumb ass, get out of there. Run. Call the police. Stop what you are doing and think!"

Yeah, well, those warnings were going through my head even as I left increasingly angry voicemail messages on Becky's phone. I went from "Please pick up the phone Becky, we need to talk" to "What the fuck are you doing to me?" over the course of four or five calls. I knew it was more evidence of witness tampering or intimidation and would only add fuel to the fire that would eventually burn my sorry ass, but I was livid. Had Adam and his law firm bribed Becky to turn on me? To get her to refuse to testify, so I would need to call her as a hostile, and therefore significantly less reliable witness? All I had ever done for Becky was to help her. Granted, three years ago, one could argue I had been using her, bribing her with a night in a motel and twenty dollars' worth of lo mein and pot-stickers. But I knew from my ten years as a prosecutor how empowering it could be for a witness or a victim to stand up in a courtroom and face the accused.

It would have been a win-win. I would have maintained a relationship with Becky afterwards. Helped her get clean, found her a safe place to live. But she disappeared for three years and showed up out of the blue with a baby and a wild story about being bribed and hidden away. And now she was accusing me of being involved all along. Whatever happened next, I was guaranteed to lose my show. I knew the network could break our contract based on the morality clause and even sue me for damages, as my actions resulted in monetary losses for them. My career comeback would be over before it even began.

I located my minivan, got in, buckled up and drove home in a fog. I left the car in the driveway and let myself into my house. Tossing my keys on the side table, I headed for my bedroom. I stripped down to my undies and after putting my phone on silent, climbed onto the unmade bed and burrowed in. With any luck, I would pass out from sheer exhaustion and get some much-needed sleep. I would have to notify Brian, of course, as well as Pop and—

Stop it, I told myself. Shut your brain down and get some rest. Things would look better after ...

***

I woke to the noise of someone banging on my door. I hopped up, totally out of it, and slipped into my robe. I saw it was ten minutes past five. I had slept for several hours, but still felt sluggish as I hurried to the door.

"I'm coming," I hollered as I peeked through the glass. It was Tracey, looking totally freaked out. "Hold your horses," I cautioned her as I pulled the door open. Then I saw the reason for her panic. There were several news vans idling on my street, and my small front yard was overrun with reporters and cameramen milling about. The din grew louder as they spotted me and I pulled Tracey inside and closed the door behind her.

"What the actual fuck is going on?" I asked her. "Has my so-called date with Adam taken on a whole new life? That's so yesterday, isn't it?" Tracey stared at me in amazement.

"You haven't been answering your phone. Do you have any idea what kind of three-ring circus is going on? It's the media shit show starring Miranda Quinn," she announced dramatically. I grabbed my phone and started scrolling. *Oh no.* The press had indeed moved on from my rendezvous with Adam. The juicy news story of the hour was "Legal Lover Locked Up!" There was a photo of Adam being hustled into what looked like the New London Police Department, escorted by two burly patrolmen. It was a brief article, just a summary of how it had come to light that an over-zealous attorney had bribed a witness and kept her out of sight in order to get the case against his client thrown out of court. It described the payoff and the ensuing cover-up as an attempt to bolster Baxter's fledgling career and end the once-promising future of his former girlfriend, Assistant States Attorney Miranda Quinn. The unnamed source at his law firm, who preferred to remain anonymous, reported that Baxter had acted without the knowledge or support of his employer and that his actions were both scandalous and not in keeping with the high standards of the firm. Baxter had been suspended without pay and was being charged with witness tampering, perverting the course of justice and bribery. The article said that he had been arrested without incident at his home earlier in the day and would be arraigned in New London District Court tomorrow at 9:00 a.m.

The report concluded by stating it was unclear whether formal charges would be filed against Ms. Quinn, who may have been part of the plan to destroy her former employer's case against Terence Kane. The last line sent chills down my spine. "Officials at the Sterling Broadcast Group who are producing a daytime talk show starring Quinn could not be reached for comment."

I sat back, trying to digest what I had just read. Becky had never made a formal complaint against Adam, instead shifting all the blame towards me. Had someone from his firm thrown Adam under the bus, accusing him of masterminding the whole thing? But why would Adam pay Becky out of his own pocket? He hadn't even been assigned to the Kane case back then. It made no sense whatsoever. Did he really despise me that much? Tears welled in my eyes and I wiped them on my sleeve. *Motherfucker*. Even Rick believed Adam hadn't acted alone. Was my ex the sacrificial lamb this time around?

I squared my shoulders and started for the kitchen. Tracey called after me.

"How can you be so calm? I thought I would find you freaking out." In response, I yawned and wrapped my robe tighter around me.

"Coffee?" I asked. Tracey followed close behind me and stood watching as I bustled about getting coffee beans from the freezer, measuring and grinding them, the familiar whirring sound temporarily halting our conversation. "Get some mugs, yeah?" I asked and breathed in the familiar slightly spicy aroma. Heavenly.

"Who are you and what have you done with my best friend?" Tracey demanded, whirling around and placing two mugs in front of me. I frowned in her general direction as I watched the coffee's progress and, minutes later, poured us both a cup.

"C'mon let's sit in here," I said and led the way back to the living room. It was a beautiful day, and it was feeling stuffy inside the house, but with reporters and cameras everywhere, I figured we should play it safe and stay out of sight. Once we settled on the couch and I had drained my first cup, I sat forward, facing Tracey.

"The only way I can make sense out of this, it to fall back on my training as a prosecutor. My personal feelings towards Adam and even Becky have to take a back seat." I began counting off on my fingers. "Let's look at the facts. First, we have a call from the missing Becky after three years of silence." Tracey interrupted me.

"Back up a bit. What about you? Suddenly you're the *It Girl* of daytime TV and your name and face are everywhere. Isn't that what prompted Becky to reach out in the first place?"

"When you're right, you're right," I admitted. "Okay, so first I get my name in the news. Next, Becky calls me to tell me Adam paid her off."

"Which she thought you had authorized," Tracey said.

"Okay, that's true. Then I run into Adam at Nemo's for the first time in three years. Can't be a coincidence, yeah?" Tracey shook her head, and I continued. "And before I run into Adam, I meet with Rick and he wants to bring Becky in to make a statement so Adam can be charged."

"But at the start of it all, Terry Kane gets arrested for rape," Tracey said, before she added. "Again." I shook my head in protest.

"I think I'm out of fingers and if this continues, we are going to need something with a bit more of a kick than coffee, babe."

***

Four hours and two bottles of wine later, I texted Dale to please come and pick up his wife. While I waited, I looked outside and was relieved that the media circus had moved on. When Dale showed up a short while later, I tried to apologize.

"I'm sorry. We didn't mean ... " He was silent, but I could tell he was miffed.

"Just ... never mind," he said.

"No, what Dale? What is it?" He started to respond, then stopped himself shaking his head, before he blurted out,

"It's just that Tracey has, I mean we have, a good thing going, you know? The boys are doing well in school and Tracey has a yearlong waiting list for spots at her daycare center." I eyed him suspiciously.

"What does that have to do with me?" I asked.

"I love you, Randi, you know that. But this newfound fame of yours? It's big, and this town is small. People talk."

"And what are they saying? These people who talk?"

"Tracey isn't like you, okay? You can ignore the rumors and the comments. You're tough, you've got a thick skin. Tracey couldn't handle it if she thought people were judging her."

"Judging her for what?" My head was throbbing. I was clueless.

"Because of you. Her friendship with you. You're drunk on your dad's couch one minute and the next you're sipping champagne in a limo."

"I seem to recall you sipping some of that champagne too, my friend."

"I know. I did, and it was a great day. But since then, you're bailing out drug dealers, hooking up with your married ex, getting your name in the paper. Your house gets broken into, your car gets trashed and you're threatened with a rock. Then Adam gets arrested and now I have to come out in the middle of the night to find my wife three sheets to the wind and barely able to stand up."

"I can stand," Tracey piped up. As if to prove it, she tried to stand on her own, but failed. "Or not," she said as she slumped back against her husband.

I couldn't tell if I was sad Dale thought so little of me or mad that I was being accused of things completely beyond my control. I went with mad.

"First off, it's ten fifteen, Grandpa, so cool your jets. I am a lawyer and if my client is arrested, I will bail them out. That is my job. I did not hook up with Adam. I didn't know he was married, or that he had bribed Becky. I have no clue why he did that, but I am fairly sure he was pressured into it. I'm sorry if vandalism and threats against me are worrying you and I'm sorry you had to drive over here tonight. I'm sorry," I repeated. "Really, I am."

"I just don't want my family caught up in your mess, Randi. I'm sorry too. I know it's harsh, but you'll be whooping it up with your sponsors in mid-town Manhattan when this blows over. But the collateral damage to Tracey's reputation could last a long time." Dale looked miserable as he stood there, hanging on to his very drunk wife. "Please don't drag her down with you."

I felt so tired and the future, one without my dearest friend by my side, stretched ahead of me, flat and bleak. I couldn't imagine a world without her.

"I understand. I'll be more careful, you'll see. I'll distance myself from Adam, get Becky straightened out and go to work on my show. Just please don't take Tracey ... " I started to sob. I couldn't finish. His face crumpled.

"Oh Ran, you know I would never do anything to break you two up. I'm her husband, but you're her soul mate. Just be a little more careful, okay? That's all I am asking."

I wiped my eyes and nodded. He swept me up in a one-armed hug and, for a moment, I closed my eyes, letting myself be comforted. Then he pulled away and kissed the top of my head. He scooped Tracey up in his arms and headed for the door.

"Lock this behind me," he warned. "We'll get her car in the morning. G'night. Get some sleep."

I watched them drive away before turning off the outside lights and locking the door, slipping the safety chain into place. I turned off the lamp in the living room and padded barefoot down the hall. For just a minute, I allowed myself to enjoy the fantasy I had someone waiting for me. Someone who loved me the way Dale loved my best friend. But all I had was a scumbag ex who would probably end up in prison and a pissed-off agent who had to rue the day he had signed me. I was an unqualified hack with a magnetic attraction for trouble. I drew it in like oxygen. I would never be successful.

As I collapsed in bed, my last thoughts were of Tracey. I could hear her assuring me, loud and clear.

"Not with that attitude you won't."

CHAPTER 25

I woke early, feeling well-rested and ready to seize the day or whatever. It was overcast and looked like rain, so I postponed my run. While my coffee brewed, I took a shower and when I emerged from my steamy bathroom wrapped in my robe; I looked out at the front of my house. It appeared as if the coast was clear, not a news van in sight, so I brought my cup out to the front porch and settled into one of the wicker chairs. Sitting quietly, I let the steam rise over my face. I took a few sips, feeling better, more in control. The panic from the previous night had all but dissipated and I was firm in my resolve to clear my name, especially in light of Adam's arrest. I needed to reach Becky and find out what had caused her about-face. Maybe getting Jesse back would be what she needed to focus on and motivate her to help with Kane's prosecution.

I had lots to do regarding my show, but took a moment to send my lightweight bestie a quick text.

T- My best wishes for a speedy recovery this morning. Have I told you lately how much I love you & your big bear of a husband? R

I drank more coffee and my thoughts turned to Adam. He was being arraigned shortly and I wondered if they would release him on bail. It's not like he was a threat to society or anything. Did he have that much cash sitting around? No one from his firm would help, that was certain, since they denied having anything to do with the payoff three years ago. But if not them, then who? Adam didn't hate me that much that he would pay to get me discredited. In the light of day, I truly believed that. But who else wanted Kane to be released? Just him and his family, I imagined. It was hurting my brain. And besides, I had my own issues to deal with.

Provided no new fires ignited, I felt confident I could resolve everything that was pending or up in the air. I would check in with Lisa to ensure all was secure on Becky's end, and that she would get Jesse back today. Assuming I would have good news to deliver, I would try to get Becky to open up. In only a day or two, I went from being her savior to the person trying to ruin her life. I hoped she would talk to me. I received a text from Rick telling me that all was clear and I took it to mean that Adam's arrest would trump Becky's email and that he would not report me to the bar. Good news, but I would call him later to confirm.

It was time to get to work. I had to review my podcast scripts and get Sarah in to sort through the mail after collecting it from the post office box. I owed Brian a call to let him know his favorite client was back on track and raring to go. Maybe we could schedule the time for promo spots with the broadcast affiliates. A day in the city away from all this craziness sounded terrific. Maybe I could ask Tracey to ... No, I thought as I remembered my promise to Dale. I would travel on my own and have some one-on-one time with Brian to reassure him I could beat this image problem I had been having.

I grabbed my phone just as it rang. Without glancing at the caller ID, I answered with a cheery,

"Good morning." Pop's booming voice was clear and strong.

"Good morning to you as well. I was just thinking that I hadn't made you a sandwich in a long time. I've got roast beef and—"

"You had me at sandwich, Pop. How's twelve?"

"See you then, my girl," he shouted. I put down my phone and grabbed my coffee mug. I had roughly four hours to do some damage control and complete two days' worth of work. I had to get moving.

***

"This is mmm, so delicious." I groaned loudly and took another bite. "How on earth—" I somehow got the words out, despite a mouthful of bread and meat.

"Can you be so awesome? Have the physique of a Greek god?" My dad puffed out his chest and grinned broadly as I pretended to cover my eyes.

"Eww. No, I was going to say come up with so many amazing sandwich creations?" I asked. "Don't get carried away, yeah?" I studied him as I chewed and swallowed. He did look great. Younger? More virile maybe? He had never carried any extra weight on his compact frame, but his chest looked broader, his shoulders wider. But it was more than his physical appearance that had changed. He looked ... happy! He caught my stare and folded his arms in front of him.

"What's on your mind?" he asked. "Something you want to say?"

"Are you happy, Pop?"

"Am I happy? What kind of question is that?"

"It's a yes or no kind of question. Don't overthink it."

"Okay then, yes. Sure, I'm happy. Do you want to know why?" I nodded, and he continued. "I woke up this morning with the usual aches and pains, but no new ones developed overnight. At my age, that's a blessing. My pension checks come in regular, I paid this house off and I still have some savings to fall back on if I need to," he said with a touch of pride. "And I have a superstar daughter who will take care of her old man if need be."

"But what about, you know, other people in your life?"

"I am still not sure what you're getting at, but okay. I'll play along. I consider myself a lucky guy. I have friends I enjoy spending time with. Then there's my ... well, there's Sally." I leaned forward. Yes, there was Sally. His eyes narrowed.

"You know, if you want to know more about Sally, all you have to do is ask." I let out a breath.

"I'm glad you have her in your life. I really am. I was just looking at you and I realized how good you seem. Younger than ever and fit. Is that what the love of a good woman does to you?"

"I guess so. Sure. I'm crazy about Sally. She's a terrific woman. We have fun together."

"Do you want it to be more?" He was now thoroughly confused.

"More?"

"Am I cramping your style? I'm always in and out, always calling you and stopping by. Am I keeping you from something more serious?" Pop looked thoughtful for a minute, before shaking his head slowly.

"Your mother, my beautiful Nora, was the love of my life. She was it for me and I have missed her every day of the past twenty years. Sally knows that. She knows how I feel. And she's fine with it. Her marriage wasn't all that great, I guess. Ended in divorce. But we're happy. Just taking it day by day."

"But what if I wasn't in the picture?" His look of confusion morphed into one of alarm.

"Why would you not be in the picture?"

"I'm just speculating. You know, what if I didn't live one town over? What if I got my shit—I mean my life together — and I wasn't calling you every day? Would you and Sally be ready to take things to the next level?" At his blank look, I continued. "Living together? Marriage?" He looked about ready to protest before he sat back and threw up his hands.

"I honestly don't know. Okay? Maybe we would be further along. But what is the point of playing the 'what if' game? We're happy to go out for dinner, catch a movie or stay in and watch TV together. We both have our own spaces and we value our privacy. Why mess with success? Doesn't that sound like the best of both worlds?"

"It sounds great," I agreed enthusiastically. "I just wish ... "

"I wish you would meet someone, Randi. I know you're focused on your career right now. And I couldn't be prouder. But don't get so caught up in your ambition you neglect yourself." He paused, looking as if he might have gone too far.

"I have a life outside of *Miranda Writes*," I said, but the words sounded hollow as I spoke them aloud. My personal life was clearly on life support. "You're right." I admitted.

"What about that Brian fellow?"

"Huh? Brian? My agent Brian?" I sputtered.

"Last I looked, he is gainfully employed, I guess, although I am not at all sure what his actual job is. He's tall, what maybe 5'11", 190 pounds. No facial tats or piercings, that I could see." My dad, the cop.

"Wow Pop. Way to set the bar really low. He's also a registered voter, and he speaks highly of his mother too, don't forget."

"What else are you looking for?"

Hmmm. A sense of humor? Okay, Brian had one. Sarcastic, but still. A physical attraction? Nooo—Brian was arguably attractive, in a way. Not my type, but where had falling for guys who were ruggedly sexy with a bad boy vibe gotten me? Single with zero prospects and very close to turning forty. But honestly, Brian? I pictured him briefly, thinking how often he was displeased with me or disappointed in who I was or all that I wasn't. I frowned and shook my head.

"He works for me. That would be too creepy."

"Yeah," he said drily. "You wouldn't want to mix business with pleasure." *Ouch.* "But I'm just saying I don't want you to end up alone, okay? I won't be around forever. None of us knows how long we've got. Sometimes you just have to take a leap of faith."

"Pot meet kettle," I said. "If you actually took your own advice, what is stopping you from moving forward?" He shrugged and drew his hands skyward.

"I don't know. I honestly don't. I can't picture my life without Sally in it, but I'm not sure I'm ready for anything more. And that is the truth. I'm sorry, but that's who I am." I leaned over and took his hand and brought it up to my cheek.

"As long as you still make me sandwiches, yeah?" I took another bite. It was fantastic.

"It's the horseradish," he announced proudly. "I make my own sauce with mayo, minced garlic and just the right amount of grated horseradish. Fresh, not that stuff from a jar."

"Mmm ... " I was too busy chewing to do anything but nod.

"Hey before I forget, what's that Becky's brother-in-law's name?" I swallowed before I answered him. I had grown accustomed to his habit of abruptly changing the subject, but what had prompted this question?

"Um, Eddie. Eddie something. Why?" He frowned at me.

"It's probably nothing. His name just came up in relation to hers. The other day, we were playing cards. The usual guys—Red, Bill and Ronny." Now I was puzzled.

"What does your weekly poker game have to do with Becky or Eddie?"

"We were talking about the surveillance of Becky's place. Kane's name came up and Bill asked me if you were gonna be part of the trial. We all want to get that scumbag off the streets for good, yeah?"

"Of course. But what does that have to do with—"

"That's what I'm trying to tell you. I said that you would probably be involved one way or another. And Bill said they got word her brother-in-law's name came up as part of an investigation. DaSilva, yeah that's it. Eddie DaSilva." I drew in a deep breath before asking for details.

"What sort of investigation?"

"The guys from Vice are trying to bust up this big gambling ring. Illegal betting, stolen lottery tickets. The thing is huge. Started out in Bridgeport, but looks like it's made its way here."

"What are you saying? That Eddie is running it?"

"No, that's not it. Bill says they got someone on the inside. Looks like Eddie was into them for thousands. Made a bunch of lousy bets. Owed fifteen thousand or more. They were gonna take him out, make an example out of him. And suddenly, he comes waltzing in and pays off his whole debt. Just like that." He snapped his fingers, and I felt my stomach plummet.

How the hell had Eddie gotten his hands on so much cash? Was there a connection to all that was happening with the Kane case? I needed to find Becky, and fast. I didn't want to get my dad suspicious, so I tried to hide my concerns. I grabbed my purse and gave him a quick kiss on the cheek.

"Wow, that is some story. Keep me posted if you hear anything more. But meanwhile ... will you promise to at least think about what I said? Maybe step it up with Sally when you think you're ready?"

"I will if you will," he countered, and I promised him I would. I rushed out to my car. She wasn't taking my calls or returning my texts, but I could be at Becky's in less than a half hour at this time of day.

If I pounded on her door long enough, she would have to talk to me.

CHAPTER 26

My mind was on Becky as I drove through town towards I-95. Nothing about her sudden change of heart made any sense. She had texted Rick's office to cancel a meeting, and she sent an email exposing the bribe and came right out and blamed me for the whole thing. It just didn't add up. Was she hiding out, too embarrassed to see me? As far as I knew, Adam was still in jail, so she wouldn't be worried about him. And the surveillance team outside her place was still in place. What had her so rattled? Rachel didn't seem to have a clue what was happening and Eddie suddenly shows up with fifteen grand. My Spidey senses were tingling as I drove east towards New London.

I found a parking place in front of Becky's rooming house and ran to the door. She came down to let me in only a minute after I knocked. She was fresh from the shower, her blonde hair still wet and combed back to reveal her glowing complexion. She was a sight for sore eyes.

"Hey Randi," she greeted me with a hug. "Jesse is coming home today and you're here, too. I was wondering when you were going to get back." *What?*

"Back from where? I haven't gone anywhere."

"What do you mean? Rachel told me you had to fly out to L.A. for your show. That you would be gone for several days. That's why we had to cancel the appointment with your boss, right? You were going to be out of town." Warning bells went off in my head. The pieces of the disjointed puzzle were starting to fit, and everything was falling into place. I would try to be casual, play it cool, as I tried to sort it all out.

"Hmmm ... " I said noncommittally. "What else did Rachel tell you?"

"Ummm, I dunno. That's about it, I guess. I lost my phone the other day, so she told me you called her and you canceled the appointment. And Eddie got me this new phone. Just like yours!" She held up a brand-new iPhone.

"Nice. Does your new phone have a new number?" I asked, and she nodded.

"Of course, silly. It's not like you can keep the same number," she said, chuckling at the thought. "I'm still trying to figure out how it works, so Rachel said she would text you the number." Her number could have easily stayed the same. Even I knew that. Who had changed it and why?

"I would love the chance to talk with Rachel," I said, and she grinned.

"She's due here any minute. I thought it was her when you knocked." She stopped at the sound of the big door in the foyer being opened, followed by a clattering of heels on the bare wood stairs. "That's her. She's taking me shopping so I can get everything I need for Jesse. My baby is coming home," she squealed and rushed to the door. Pulling it open, she cried out, "Look, Rach. Randi's back. How cool is that?" Rachel came to an abrupt stop at the top of the stairs. She went pale beneath a layer of blush, looking shocked to see me, as if I had returned from the dead.

"Hey there, Randi," she mumbled. "Good to see you." I smiled at her. How much did she know about her husband's gambling debts? How far had she gone to bail him out, even if it meant throwing her own sister under the bus? I was about to find out.

***

It only took a moment to break Rachel down. I asked her what the hell was going on and she sang like a bird. Her secondhand account of the last couple of weeks was twisted and, at times, she was almost incoherent. She swore she had known nothing until last night, when Eddie had confessed to her. He told her that soon after my first meeting with Becky; he had been approached by a guy who identified himself as a member of Kane's defense team. This guy said the word on the street was that there was a price on Eddie's head because he owed some bad guys a whole shitload of money. He wanted Eddie to do a few favors for him, just enough to get me and Becky to back off. No one would get hurt. To show his gratitude, he would settle Eddie's debts and give him a little something extra for his troubles.

I sat calmly through Rachel's story, eager to hear more while resisting the urge to scream at her. I had always felt there was something a bit off with Rachel, but had never believed her to be more than an opportunist looking for a payday. One glance at Becky revealed tears welling up in her eyes, her mouth hanging open in surprise.

According to Rachel, all the transactions were done over the phone. Each time Eddie completed an assigned task, an envelope of cash would be slipped under his door. The first job was the trashing of my home, followed by the vandalism of my car and the rock delivered to my front door. Rachel sobbed her way through her story, while Becky sat still as a stone, clearly in shock at her sister's betrayal. I have heard all kinds of things in my years as a prosecutor, but this was seriously messed up. I bided my time and let Rachel ramble on. She said Eddie had been on edge lately and seemed to be hiding something.

"Whenever I asked him if everything was all right, he told me to back off, to chill out. And to mind my own business," she said. Last night, Eddie had come home drunk and bragged about how he had gotten out of debt and still had a hefty sum to show for it. He told his wife he had taken Becky's phone earlier in the week, but had bought her a brand new one. He just needed Rachel to do a couple of little favors for him.

"Let me guess," I said. "He wanted you to cancel the appointment with Rick this morning and to send an email from Becky telling him the whole cover-up and disappearance three years ago was my idea. Am I close?" Rachel nodded miserably and looked pleadingly at Becky.

"I'm sorry Becky. I didn't know what else to do, you know? I figured the damage had already been done." Becky was not buying it.

"How could you do that to me? Your own sister? And Randi has been the best friend ever. What were you thinking?" Rachel's face was ashen, and she shivered almost uncontrollably.

"They were gonna kill him, Bex. He's my husband, Lucie's father. What was I supposed to do?"

"You should have told me or Randi. We could have figured something out together."

"No—no one was supposed to get hurt. Eddie swore no one would get hurt."

"What about the fake drugs, Rach? Did Eddie plant them? Get me arrested and make me lose custody of my baby?" Rachel nodded slowly, unable to make eye contact with her. Upset as I was, my heart broke for Becky at her sister's betrayal.

"I didn't know, I swear. I'm so sorry," she wailed as she hunched over, rocking back and forth. But Becky wouldn't let her continue, rushing towards her sister, her fists clenched and her breathing erratic.

"You need to leave. I mean it. Get out. You've turned what should have been the happiest day of my life into the worst possible day. How could you? I trusted you. I confided in you. I believed you, always. I thought you had my back." She swallowed back another burst of rage before she continued. "Jesse will be here soon and it will be better if he didn't see you here. He's confused and probably scared, and I don't want you anywhere near him. Ever." She stumbled over to the door and yanked it open. "Get the fuck out of my house."

Rachel looked at me, her eyes begging me to intercede on her behalf. I was disgusted, but held my tongue for now. I would have plenty to say to her in a courtroom. If I knew anything about anything, it was the law and I needed to make it work for Becky and me and against Terry Kane, Rachel, and Eddie.

Rachel left, after begging for just one more chance, which was denied by her sister. Seconds later, Becky suggested I get going too. She told me she was going to run to the bodega on the corner and get some milk, fruit, eggs, and cereal for Jesse's homecoming. I offered to go, but she turned me down.

"I've got to stand on my own two feet. I'll talk to you tomorrow. Don't worry," she said, brushing off my look of concern. "I've got this Randi." I kissed her on the cheek and told her I knew she did.

I drove home feeling lighter and somehow relieved. Adam might be a scumbag, but at least he had not been part of the vandalism and the planting of the drugs. I called Rick and left him a brief message about the DaSilva's involvement and requested an appointment to discuss Becky's upcoming testimony and to record her official denial of the charges against me.

It felt wonderful to get it out in the open. Shed some light on all the lies and deceit. Well, not all, but it was a start.

CHAPTER 27

I hurried into the crowded bar and quickly spotted Brian. He had called me while I was driving home from Becky's a couple of hours earlier and suggested getting together for dinner. I was feeling energized and offered to meet him halfway, like in Bridgeport, but he insisted he was already on the train heading to me and would see me around seven. His assistant had booked him a room at the Old Saybrook Inn, so I said I would meet him in the bar. His back was turned, but I recognized him from his erect posture and short brown hair. I had seen him just last week for the contract signing, but he looked different this evening. Casually dressed and seeming right at home in the nautically themed tavern. As I approached, he turned and saw me. He broke into a smile and just for a second, I remembered my dad asking me if Brian was on my radar for a relationship and how quickly I had told him no. Yeah, still a solid no. I grinned back and slipped onto the barstool next to him.

"Hey you," I said. "Welcome to the Connecticut shore." He looked around before focusing his attention back on me.

"Happy to be here," he said genially. "But I've got to be honest. This place is not at all like the Peyton Place from your recent adventures. Not a wronged wife or wanted felon in sight, unless, of course, you count the guy behind the bar." I glanced over at Pete, the shaggy-haired, heavily tattooed bartender who had worked at this place since I was underage and trying to get served. Pete saw me and came right over.

"What'll it be gorgeous?" he asked with an exaggerated drawl. Looking at Brian, he continued. "Why didn't you tell me you were waiting for this girl? I might have at least offered you some peanuts if I knew you were here to meet a certified celebrity and one of my favorite gals." He reached behind the bar and came up with a bowl of nuts in each hand. Brian raised a hand in protest and I knew he wouldn't be caught dead reaching into a communal bowl of salty snacks. I had no such qualms myself. I grabbed a handful and tossed a couple into my mouth.

"What's a girl got to do to get a drink around this place?" I asked. I looked over at Brian's drink. It looked like cranberry juice, so I assumed it was a Sea-Breeze or something like it and nodded. "I'll have what he's having," I said to Pete. He gave me a quizzical look before I turned to Brian. "So, what brings you out here to the boonies?"

Brian shrugged and took a long swallow of his drink. "I just thought we should talk. Get on the same page." Before I could respond, Pete set my drink down with a flourish. I took a sip and almost spit it out.

"Gahhh. What the hell?" Back in the day, Pete had a heavy hand for mixing drinks, even for me and my under-aged friends. "I can't even taste the vodka. Or gin?" I looked at Brian for affirmation, and he smiled ruefully.

"That's because there is no vodka or gin. I ordered a cranberry juice. I want to keep a clear head tonight. But don't let me stop you. I'm sure your friend would be more than glad to mix you something else."

"No, I'm good. This is fine." Over Brian's shoulder, I saw a couple gathering their things and exiting a booth in the corner. "Let's grab these and move over to the booth back there. I want to hear all about this same page of ours, and it'll be more private." Brian agreed and grabbed both of our drinks, following me to the booth. I slid into the seat and waited until he was facing me. I hoped that whatever was worth him coming out here to talk to me about was not something bad. Something that would affect my relationship with the Sterling Broadcast Group. "So, spill it, would you? What's so important we couldn't talk on the phone?" I asked with a touch of concern creeping into my voice. "Brian?" He steepled his hands and cleared his throat. *Damn, this would not be good.*

"Have you heard of E. Presley?"

"No, who is it?"

"E. Presley. He writes an entertainment column for the Times. *Prez Play*? E. Presley?"

"Brian, no matter how many times you say his name, I still don't know who he is or why I should." Brian reached into his leather satchel and withdrew a folded newspaper. He pushed it towards me so I could see the article at the top, above the fold. "Oh, crap." I read the headline, "Miranda Wrongs!" by E. Presley for *Prez Play*. The column featured an unflattering and dated photo of me he must have found on social media. The article began by describing how I had lost my job three years earlier because I screwed up an important case and allowed a violent criminal to go free. One who later may have attacked another young woman. It detailed Adam's recent arrest and referenced my alleged involvement in Becky's disappearance. E. Presley ended the attack on me with a question: "Can we believe a single thing that Miranda writes or says or does?"

Brian watched me as I tried to gather my thoughts. Technically, he hadn't lied about anything, so there was no actual crime committed. Even if I could get a retraction, the damage would have already been done.

"This is bad," I said simply. "I'm not sure what you want me to say, exactly."

"Can we get him for slander?"

"No way. Slander is verbal, libel is written. They are both defamatory statements, but in this case, technically, the statements are true." I ended with a shrug, which seemed to annoy Brian. He leaned forward, watching me closely.

"Miranda, I need to ask you this. As your agent and I hope as your friend, what the hell are you doing? Your recent behavior has the network more than a little anxious. You have to know how important your image is, don't you? The metrics are not good, I'm afraid." He paused, looking like what he had to say next caused him physical pain. "Are you really sure this show is what you want?"

I sat back, stunned. The show was precisely what I wanted, what I needed. It was the culmination of all my hard work. How could Brian doubt that? I struggled to keep my voice low and to speak slowly and clearly.

"Of course, I'm sure. I tried to explain this to you. I didn't know Adam was married. I didn't know he had been involved in the disappearance of my key witness back then. I was as shocked as anyone." I saw Brian's skeptical look and hurried on. "What do you want me to say? It's all just a big mistake, but none of it is my fault."

"Why were you fired?" I started to sputter my response, but Brian cut me off. "Whatever. Fired, let go, asked to resign, moved on to new opportunities ... You can call it whatever you like, but I need to know why. Did you really screw up a case? Is that why you are so intent on helping with this one?" I hated how all of this was making me feel. The guilt and shame I had borne back then. The anger I was experiencing now knowing I had been set up. How many times did I have to replay those terrible days over and over again? How many times could I be punished for a mistake as innocent as trusting my boyfriend?

"Why is it this important? I don't understand." Brian looked resigned as he squared his shoulders and faced me head on.

"I am hearing rumblings from the SBG folks. You were on thin ice before this column came out. And now ... I need to be prepared if I am going to help you."

"Help me do what?"

"To keep your job, Miranda. To spin all of this nonsense into something they can live with." I had to take a deep breath before I could speak.

"Am I out? Is that what you're trying to tell me?"

"You might be. Listen, whether or not it was your fault, look at it from their perspective."

"Whose side are you on?"

"I'm on your side, Miranda. Always. But they are investing a shitload of money into their new legal eagle. You're supposed to be the expert, the pro. A professional woman, beyond reproach. The recent headlines paint a different picture. They can't take a chance on someone who's less than credible, unreliable."

"Is that what you think? That I'm spoiled goods? That I'm tarnished?" I drew in a breath, waiting for his response. If my own agent no longer believed in me, I could probably kiss any future career plans goodbye.

He gave me a sad smile. "No, I don't. I think you're fabulous and I want everyone to see what I see, but you've got to level with me."

Here goes nothing, I thought. I told Brian everything. How I got assigned to the Kane case, the biggest of my career. How we had found Becky, how I had lost her. Adam's denials and his betrayal. Someone on Kane's defense team setting Becky up and vandalizing my home and car. The possibility of my being disbarred. The revelation that Becky's own sister and brother-in-law had been complicit. I didn't cry or try to hide anything. Brian watched me intently and when I was finished, he shook his head again.

"Jesus, you've really gotten a raw deal." I nodded glumly and slumped back in my seat. Now thoroughly exhausted, I struggled to speak.

"So, what do I do? Where do I go from here?"

"Where do we go from here?" Brian corrected me. "We need to flip all of this. Get that Kane bastard convicted, give Becky her day in court, allow Adam to be a stand-up guy and take full responsibility for the cover-up and have you come out smelling like a rose. Give SBG the chance to say 'look at this legal genius at work. Quinn is the real deal.'"

I nodded in full agreement, relief flooding through me at knowing he was still on my side. It was a tall order, a big job, but it had to be done. "Works for me," I assured him.

"So, here's a thought. Let's get out of here. All we need is one fan with a phone snapping a shot of you in another bar with yet another guy, albeit a devilishly handsome one. Let's quit while we're ahead tonight. We can go to your place, grab some food along the way, and figure out a plan. Then I can Uber back here and head back to the city first thing and get to work salvaging your reputation. What do you say?"

I was so tired I wasn't sure just how much I could contribute to a strategy session, but staying out of the public eye and eating something was probably wise.

"Sounds great. We can hit Nardelli's on the way to my place. It's only fair if you traveled all this way, the very least I can do is buy you the best Italian grinder you've ever had." Brian left a ten-dollar bill on the table and got to his feet.

"Let's do it, but a grinder? Please—it's a sub or a hoagie, for God's sake. A grinder sounds more than a little pornographic," he protested.

"Don't knock it till you try it," I said with a wink and he followed me out to my car.

**

We ate and talked and strategized as if my life depended upon it, and professionally speaking, it did. I was no longer worried about being disbarred, but in the blink of an eye, I could lose my TV show and I imagined a damaged reputation would not please my blog and podcast subscribers, either. *Epic fail.* Shades of three years ago. The common denominators were simple: Terry Kane, his defense team and the scumbag attorney who broke my heart. Fucking Adam Baxter.

"Motherfucker," I mumbled under my breath. I looked up to catch Brian's gaze. As he typed away on his laptop, he was watching me with something akin to what? Pity? Concern?

"The situation or the ex?" he asked me.

"Both," I replied with a frown. "It's just ... " Brian gave me his full attention now.

"Just what?"

"I'm just thinking. There's not a lot I can do about the past. Kane's acquittal, Becky's disappearance, Adam's fucking betrayal ... "

"But," Brian leaned forward. "Keep going."

"The only thing I can do is to move forward. I can't fix what's already happened, but maybe I can, I don't know, improve things going forward. I'm too close to Becky and that shit heel Adam, but Kane is a different story."

"We have to make sure Kane goes down for this crime."

"Yeah," I said. "But how?"

"You're the lawyer," Brian said with a sheepish grin. "I'm just an agent."

"And my friend," I insisted, realizing it for the very first time.

"Okay then. Let's get to work. It looks like Cooper is firmly on your side, you're square with Becky right now and the trial is not anything you can control. The key to your redemption is ... "

"Adam," we said in unison. "I have to talk to Adam," I added.

CHAPTER 28

I moved through the line for the metal detectors without incident, but inwardly, I was a nervous wreck. It wasn't every day I went to visit an ex-boyfriend in jail, so I took several deep breaths right before I reached the desk sergeant. I gave my name and told him I was here to see Adam Baxter. The officer, whose name tag identified him as Jim Crosby, gave me a quick appraisal before a flicker of recognition registered and he grinned at me.

"You're Dez's kid," he beamed, and I nodded. I got that a lot and honestly, it never got old. My dad was well respected by men and women on the job, as well as the community. When my mom died, hundreds of concerned residents came to mourn the loss of Dez Quinn's wife. It was a constant comfort to me, to be loved and welcomed in this place I had always called home. Many people I knew, former classmates and friends, couldn't wait to get out of this area, to escape to New York or Boston, anywhere but here. I had never wanted to leave.

Sure, I loved my adventures and traveling was fun. But I was always glad to return to the safe and familiar world I knew. The Sterling folks hinted regularly how it would be preferable if I were to live in Manhattan, or at least somewhere closer to the city. But I had yet to make that commitment. The idea of living in some quaint brownstone or a modern high-rise sounded interesting, but I just couldn't see it for myself. I was planning on commuting in most days and spending one or two nights a week in the corporate accommodations provided.

"That's me," I said, as I collected my visitor's lanyard and followed him through a set of double doors into the belly of the beast.

"Everyone is looking forward to your show," Officer Crosby said, and I flashed him my brightest smile.

"I'll tell my dad you were asking for him," I said as I showed my credentials to a uniformed officer who pointed towards a row of folding chairs placed in front of a glass wall. I took a seat and waited, trying to remain calm.

Eyes on the prize, Brian had texted me as I had walked into the station a few minutes earlier. The prize was not so simple, however, but if today's meeting went the way we had planned, we would be closer to it. All I needed to do was to convince Adam that it was in his best interests to tell the court that I had not been involved in Becky's disappearance and the ensuing cover-up. After learning how Eddie had been manipulated, I was more certain than ever that Adam had not acted alone. He needed to expose his former employers who had used him and bribed Eddie DaSilva.

I let out an involuntary gasp when the door opened and Adam appeared. While not the orange jumpsuit I had imagined, his tan scrubs with *New London County Correctional Facility* emblazoned across the chest hung loosely on him. Was it possible he had lost that much weight in just a few days? The last time I had seen him at the restaurant, it had appeared he had packed on a few pounds. All that success and the joys of married life, I assumed. But now he looked thin and unwell. Normally clean-shaven, his cheeks and chin were covered with dark stubble, accentuating his pale complexion. How have the mighty fallen, I thought without a touch of charity. This man had derailed my life and paid off a witness, resulting in a criminal being released onto the street and perpetrating yet another savage sexual assault.

"Randi," he croaked, then cleared his throat. "Sorry, I've barely spoken a word in two days. I guess ... " he trailed off, noting my total lack of sympathy for his situation. "I'm sorry. Truly, truly sorry for misleading you. I never meant—" I tried to be patient and let him speak his piece. But I needed answers. Big picture be damned.

"I just don't understand. Why would you do that to me?" My voice wavered on the last words. How long had I been dying to ask that question of this man, whom I had once thought of as the love of my life? "Why?"

He let out a long sigh and shook his head. "Let me try to explain how it all started." I watched him struggle as he spoke, describing the phone call he received three years earlier from John Houghton, a named partner at his law firm, asking him for help to get the case against Kane thrown out. Houghton told him he'd been college roommates with Kane's stepfather. That he had evidence Kane was not guilty of the crime, but that it was a sensitive situation, one that couldn't come out in court. He had asked Adam to use his relationship with me to find out more, anything to discredit any potential witnesses. He had sworn I would be fine, that Kane's acquittal wouldn't reflect on me.

Adam stopped and rubbed his eyes. "I swear I thought Kane was innocent and that you wouldn't be blamed, Randi." I choked back the bile that had lodged in my throat, not wanting to let him know just how much he had hurt me. I forced myself to stay calm, despite the butterflies that had taken up residence in my belly.

"What did he promise you?" I asked. "A fast track to being a partner?"

"Yeah, pretty much. Not in so many words, but he said anything I could do to get the charges dropped would be remembered when it came time for my annual performance review."

"And look how that turned out," I said with barely hidden scorn. "They threw you under the bus at the first sign of trouble." Adam hung his head and wouldn't meet my eyes.

"The trial was getting close, and I wasn't making any progress on my promise to John. Then I saw the name of the motel on the pad in your office and I figured that was where you had stashed Bec—her. I called him and told him what I knew. He told me to withdraw some cash to motivate her to disappear and that I would be reimbursed. So, I did and, well, you know the rest. I had no clue you would be blamed. Do you believe me?"

His voice was boyish, pleading. He looked hopeful, as if my opinion of him actually meant something. In my head, I could replay Brian's advice from last night. "Make him think you're on his side. He's got to confess in court that he took money to make Becky disappear." I drew in a long breath. I had the information I had set out to get, and it would be helpful if he would admit it in open court. But inwardly, I was still seething. If it were not for the plexiglass partition separating us, I might have smacked him right in the face. I couldn't let Adam know how I felt, so the best I could muster was a casual shrug, as I nodded reassuringly and got out what I needed to say.

"It's water under the bridge, Adam. I understand." The words caught in my throat, but I must have sounded convincing because he looked at me in amazement, his eyes wide and his mouth hanging slightly open. "Don't look so surprised," I chided him gently. He let out a breath he had been holding, and I watched in amazement as tears welled in his eyes.

"Thank you. You always believed in me. You were the best—" My patience ebbing, I couldn't hold in what I wanted to say to him any longer.

"What about your wife? Kimberly?" I asked. "I would have thought *she* was the best thing to happen to you."

"You know about her, huh?"

"Yes, your marriage is just one of the many facets of my current public relations debacle. Do you know what a shit storm you have caused me?" His eyes were clouded in misery. I had never seen him looking this sad.

"I know and I'm sorry, I am. I never meant for any of this to happen."

"Well, make this right then. You owe me that much." At his look of confusion, I said, "Admit to what you did. Tell them I had nothing to do with it." Adam nodded his agreement, but now he wouldn't meet my eyes.

"There's something else you should know. It's mine, Ran." It was my turn to be confused, but even as I heard myself asking what was his, I knew. I sat back in my seat and felt the little remaining energy drain from me. How much more could this man put me through? Emotionally spent, I waited for him to continue, and he did.

"The baby. Becky's baby. I'm fairly certain that it's mine." I drew in a breath and tried to remain calm. His words were no real surprise to me. Deep down, I had always suspected it. That first time I met Jesse, I had thought he had seemed familiar, that he reminded me of someone. *Damn.*

"That first night? The night before she was supposed to testify?" He shook his head, looking indignant.

"God, no. You and I were still together then. I never ... " he sputtered.

"Oh well, that's just ducky, isn't it? You waited until you forced me out of my job and my home before you started sleeping with my underage star witness. Why didn't you just say so?"

"She was nineteen," he replied. "It was a year later. She had been calling me, telling me she was out of money. I had been wiring her a couple hundred here and there and I was worried she would just show up one day, so I drove up to Portland to see how bad things were. Took a few days' worth of PTO and, well, you know ... "

"And sleeping with her was your brilliant way of solving the problem?"

"It just happened, okay? I got a hotel room for the week, figuring I could try to assess her situation. Find out where she was living, try to get her a better job, something more permanent, anything to keep her there. She was actually doing pretty well, from what I could tell. Had been renting a room, bussing tables in a cafe. She looked good."

"Yeah, she cleans up well," I acknowledged grudgingly.

"I took her to get something to eat. She was kind of wired. Uptight. She hadn't been using, she told me. But I wanted to get her to relax so I could convince her to stay put."

"And sleeping with her was your brilliant way of solving the problem?" I repeated.

"It wasn't planned. We were both single, unattached. So yeah, we spent a few days together. I left her some more money, and she sounded like she was planning on staying there. So I came home. Got back to work. Then I started seeing Kim. We had been flirting for a while, you know, just a little office romance, and we were both doing okay at the firm, so we met with Human Resources and disclosed our relationship status and—"

"You missed a step," I said.

"What's that?"

"You neglected to mention the fact that Becky got pregnant and had your baby."

"Oh yeah. Well, a couple of months later, she called me to tell me she was pregnant. She wasn't upset or anything. Told me it was mine. Said she hadn't been with anyone else. Said she needed money to get an abortion. She was very matter of fact, like it was just another financial transaction. Which I thought it was. So, I wired her another five thousand dollars, and that was it. I never gave her baby a second thought."

"Until now," I said, watching him closely.

"Until now," he repeated. "I did the math and yeah, it's probably mine."

"It's a boy. A darling little baby boy named Jesse." His total lack of enthusiasm for my news was apparent. His gaze was blank, and he shrugged noncommittally.

"So, what are you going to do?" I asked him.

"About?"

"About the fact you have a son. And it's not with your wife and you're in fucking jail. Do I have to spell it out for you?" I let him stew in his juices for a moment before I continued. "Adam, you need to get out ahead of this somehow. Arrange for bail. Admit you took a bribe. Tell the little woman at home you have a child to support." Silence. Still no response. "Adam," I shouted, causing the guard to put down his newspaper and glare at us. I smiled reassuringly at him and lowered my voice, turning my attention to Adam as he finally responded.

"I just can't believe I have a kid. Kim and I have talked about trying . . ." His words cut me to the quick. He already had a child, and now he was trying to have another one with his new wife?

"You're unbelievable. I always thought you didn't want kids."

"You're the one who said you didn't want kids." *Excuse me?*

"I never said that."

"Maybe not in so many words, but c'mon Ran. You know it as well as me. Kids were not part of your five-year plan." He stated the last part with just a touch of sarcasm. He had always chided me about my desire to raise within the ranks of the State system and my competitiveness with the assigning of cases within my department. Adam had been no less ambitious, but felt that, in his case, it was a given he would seek any chance to shine. Not because he was a man or anything like that. Adam was a lot of things, but he was never one to allow gender bias to filter in to his decisions. It was more that I worked for the State of Connecticut and I was merely a bureaucrat with job security galore. "Just keep your head down and toe the line," he had advised me back then. "Wait it out and you'll be next in line when old Coop steps down." How wrong he had been.

"Well, here we are," I stated flatly. "The window to make that choice for myself is closing rapidly, while you have all the options in the world and a young bride, to boot." Adam gazed around the sterile reception room and mumbled,

"Yeah, here we are."

We chatted for a few more minutes, discussing his bail arrangements which would be complete this afternoon, getting him home in time for dinner. Adam promised again to officially clear my name in court when his case went to trial, and I believed he would follow through with it. He swore he'd not known anything about the break-in to my home, the vandalism or Becky's arrest, but he wasn't surprised when I told him about Eddie's involvement.

"Yeah, it makes sense they got DaSilva on the hook. But I swear, I never would have gotten involved with that. I never meant you or Becky any harm and the thought of my kid in foster care? Oh, hell no!" His denials sounded credible, but with Becky and Jesse out of the picture, it was one less loose end to explain, especially to his adoring bride. Then I remembered something else.

"How did you know I would be at Nemo's the first time I saw you? And what about the restaurant the other night? Were you having me followed?" He reddened, but held my gaze.

"It wasn't me, but yeah, you were definitely being followed. I don't know and I didn't ask. Houghton called me both times and told me where to find you. He wanted me to put you on notice, to let you know you were being watched." There it was. I had been under surveillance. Probably still was. I wanted to run at that moment, to escape from this hellhole and this monster I used to love. But I was frozen, rooted to the spot and unable to move. Slowly, I forced myself to look him in the eyes, the same ones I had gotten lost in time and time again.

"And you did it. You threatened me, Adam. You're scaring the crap out of me right now. Jesus, who are you?" I broke off eye contact then, disgusted at the sight of him.

"I don't know," he mumbled. "But I'll make it right, you'll see," he said, and I wanted to believe him almost as much as I wanted to be rid of him. The tightness in my chest subsided and I let out a long breath.

He was silent after that, and a few minutes later, I watched as he was escorted back to his cell.

CHAPTER 29

I left the courthouse with a sense of clarity, as if some of the weight of this whole nasty mess had been taken off my shoulders. Seeing how far Adam had fallen was no consolation for my own troubles, but at least I finally knew what had happened. John Houghton, acting with or without the knowledge of his partners at SH&F, had bribed both Adam and Eddie to get me and Becky to back off, but he hadn't covered his tracks very well. And the truth shall set me free, I thought.

After buckling myself in to my minivan and starting towards home, I glanced at the time. As much as I wanted to share everything I knew, I decided not to call my best friend. It was snack time at her daycare center and she would be up to her elbows in graham crackers and milk cartons. I wasn't ready to talk with my dad yet. There were still too many questions to be answered, and he would want to know more than I was prepared to share. I left a message for Rick to call me, then I called Brian.

"How'd it go?" was his immediate greeting. "What happened with Adam?"

"Do you want the good news or the even better good news?" I asked.

"You're killing me, woman," he protested. "Start with the good and work your way up," he suggested.

"That's what he said," I quipped, and after allowing Brian to groan loudly in protest, I shared what Adam had told me.

"But he had to know how it would affect you," Brian said. "Did he actually view his success as some sort of consolation prize, or was your career just collateral damage?" I knew how cutthroat it could be for a junior associate trying to fast track their way to a partnership at a top tier law firm, but Brian was right. Adam had sacrificed me in his pursuit of career success.

"But at least he didn't break into my home or vandalize my car or plant drugs," I said.

"Yeah, he's a real stand-up guy, that one." I nodded sadly into the phone, suddenly feeling the need to move this conversation forward. Continually trashing Adam would serve no real purpose and besides, we had bigger fish to fry.

"So, Adam is going to clear me and expose the law firm. Jesse is back with Becky and she is keeping her distance from Rachel and Eddie. We're making some serious progress, don't you think?" A long pause followed, and I thought we had lost our connection. Then he spoke.

"It may not be enough. I'm sorry to tell you, but the optics are still not looking good. The network scheduled a couple of focus groups to determine just how badly your reputation has been damaged by all this. And before you tell me you weren't responsible for tanking the case back and that you did not know Baxter was a married prick and that Becky is not using drugs, you can—"

"Just tell me the truth, Brian. Am I done? Are they going to cancel my show?"

"I don't know. Honestly, it could go either way. But I want you to be prepared, okay? Focus on your blog, air your podcasts and keep your head down for now." He didn't add, 'and stay out of the press and no more disasters or shocking revelations,' but he didn't need to. He promised to stay in touch and we ended the call.

Well, that's that, I thought. I still needed to talk, to get some perspective on all of this. Since it was close to 5:00 p.m., I figured my dad would be home, so I drove to Old Lyme half in a daze. I parked on the street in front of my childhood home, crossed the yard and walked up the steps. The door was open, so I let myself in.

"Pop," I called out. A woman's voice answered me.

"Randi?" Sally emerged from the kitchen, wiping her hands on a dishtowel and looking concerned. "Your dad just went to pick up some creamer for my morning coffee." She added, "Is everything all right?" From the delicious aromas emanating from the kitchen, I knew Sally was making a wonderful home-cooked meal for my dad. Despite my grief, I felt grateful these two had found each other. I couldn't find my voice, but then Sally asked, "What's wrong, dear girl?" and I fell into her outstretched arms. She held on to me and let me cry, all the while patting my back and murmuring assurances into my ear.

"I bet you are a great mom, Sally," I said when I could finally speak, and she gave me a last squeeze. Before she could answer, my dad came into the room.

"Randi, I saw your car. Wait, what's burning?" he asked, and we all rushed into the kitchen. A large pan of what had started out as chicken piccata was smoking on the stove. Pop quickly turned off the burner and carried the charred remains of their dinner to the sink. "Who's up for pizza?" he asked with a grin.

***

Staying for dinner sounded like a good idea, so I took a quick shower to clear my head and changed into an old T-shirt and a pair of leggings I found in my dresser. By the time I was finished, a couple boxes of steaming hot pizza were on the counter and Sally was bustling around getting plates and napkins. The smell of scorched chicken still hung in the air and I suggested we carry our plates out to the back porch. It was a lovely evening, and we sat in silence as we ate. Sally nibbled delicately at her slice, while I literally jammed my first piece in my mouth and reached for another.

My dad had only taken a couple bites when he got up, asking, "Anything to drink, my girls?" My eyes blurred with tears at the words, the meaning. 'His girls' used to be me and Mom. Now it was me and Sally. And time marches on. I wiped my eyes and stopped chewing long enough to answer him.

"This girl's thirsty. How about you Sal?" She nodded, then turned to my dad.

"I'll take a soda. Thank you Dez," she said, and a couple of minutes later, he returned with a bottle of Diet Coke and three glasses full of ice. He poured and offered one to me, and I accepted it gratefully. I took a long gulp and swallowed my pizza, resisting the urge to belch loudly. I wiped my mouth and put down my napkin.

"If I'm not going to be on TV, I might as well eat whatever I like, yeah?" My dad started to protest, but Sally laid a hand on his to silence him.

"Let Randi talk, Dez. Let's listen to her, shall we?" He nodded slowly and turned his attention back to his pizza. Sally smiled at me, encouraging me to explain myself. I took a deep breath and told them everything; how Adam had admitted to bribing Becky, how he had fathered her child and was now married, unemployed, and probably out on bail. I told them of Eddie's actions and Rachel's deceit and their role in the disastrous last few weeks. I shared my conversation with Brian and admitted how bleak it was looking for my career in television. Pop seemed agitated throughout, but Sally's calm presence was enough to keep him from interrupting me. When I finished, they both sat and watched me, their faces etched with sadness. My appetite had deserted me, so I took a swig of soda.

"So I ask you? Could I be more of a screw up if I tried?" I tried to inject some levity into my tone, but from their somber expressions, I could see it hadn't worked. Sally spoke first. She leaned forward and grasped my hands in hers.

"Oh, you poor thing. I had no idea how much you've been carrying around. All you have had to deal with? You must be exhausted." I nodded, flooded with relief at finally opening up to those who clearly loved me.

"I am. I really am." Emotionally drained from the events of the past week and finally putting my thoughts into words, I felt I barely had the energy to stand up, let alone drive home. Sensing my thoughts, Sally suggested I stay with them tonight.

"Things will be brighter in the morning. You'll see. And we will have a nice breakfast and some coffee and figure out what to do next." My dad nodded mutely, and I saw a look pass between them. Sally would spend the night even with me in the house, and the thought made me smile.

"We'll clean up in here. You get some rest," Pop said gruffly, and I resisted the impulse to hug them both. It would only end in tears and I was honestly all cried out. So, I squeezed his shoulder, smiled gratefully at Sally, and trundled off to bed.

Whatever was going to happen next was out of my control, but I knew I could handle it better after a good night's sleep.

CHAPTER 30

The next day brought light rain and overcast skies, but no breakthroughs in the disaster film my life had become. Despite a sound sleep and a second helping of absolutely delicious French toast, I was no closer to knowing what to do next. Whatever it was, I had to get some work done. I changed back into the clothes I had left in a heap on the floor of my old bedroom and prepared to leave. I hugged my dad and turned to Sally.

"Thank you," I said. "For listening to me." She pulled me into her arms, smelling of cinnamon and coffee. I felt a powerful connection to this woman who loved my dad and apparently loved me, too. He deserved to be happy with her, and so did I.

"You got this, Randi," she whispered in my ear. "Everything will turn out fine." I straightened and started to walk away. Before I left, I turned to them.

"I love you both," I said, right before I raced down the steps in the rain towards my waiting minivan. My phone buzzed as I got on the highway and I answered without checking to see who was calling.

"Miranda? It's Rick Cooper."

"Hello, Rick. How are—What can I do for you?" I asked.

"I wanted to say thank you for all of your help. I got a call from Adam Baxter's attorney today. His client wants to formally absolve you of any wrongdoing regarding Becky Lewis. It sounds like he will name names of the partners at his law firm who were in on it. I understand you went to visit him before he got bail. I don't know what you said to him, but the bottom line is we should be in good shape to move forward with the Kane trial."

I was momentarily speechless. Adam had actually come through for me, and Rick Cooper was thanking me. I wanted to drink in this moment, to never forget how it felt when everything in my universe was in sync, even for just a moment.

"That is so good to hear, Rick," I said. "I'm glad I could help."

"And an arrest warrant has been filed on Eddie DaSilva," he said. "I'll keep you posted on any developments. Talk soon." I drove the rest of the way home with a big grin on my face, my windshield wipers working overtime to guide me through the familiar streets.

When I got home, I changed into dry clothes and made a list of the work deadlines that were approaching. I felt energetic and eager to make the most out of the day ahead. Rick's approval still meant so much to me, and the love I felt from Pop and Sally left me feeling warm and happy. I texted instructions to both of the Hansen kids telling them what I needed them to do and reminding them to submit their hours to me for the last two weeks so I could pay them, with thanks added to each. I was so grateful for the way both kids had stepped up. I texted Tracey just to say hello and then sent a text to Becky.

B- Celebration lunch tomorrow? Hug J for me. See you soon. R

I had not heard from her in a couple of days and, as always, I felt a ripple of fear when she didn't answer right away. If she hadn't responded by mid-afternoon, I would take a drive over and check on her myself. I held off checking in with Brian, praying no news was good news, and began outlining my next blog post. The topic was torts, or civil wrongs that cause one to suffer loss or harm, and I had been focusing on one particular type: intentional infliction of emotional distress. Reading through the court proceedings of some cases was gut-wrenching, but I needed to soldier on and be as well prepared as I could. As soon as we wrapped the Kane case up, I planned to file suit on Becky's behalf. John Houghton had possibly acted alone, but had represented himself as working on behalf of his firm. Regardless, the law firm had deep pockets, and I felt Becky deserved compensation for all they had put her through.

Engrossed, I quickly lost track of the time. I saved my work and stretched slowly. I had been hunched over for hours, a fact that my back and neck were now protesting loudly. I groaned and, not for the first time, regretted my decision to hold off on getting a hot tub for my deck. It had seemed like a needless extravagance not very long ago, and since the network deal had come through, I hadn't had the time to look into it. What if the TV show got cancelled? I would be okay financially for a while, as long as they didn't sue me for damages or anything. Was this the best time to spend so much money? I recalled Sally mentioned having one and on impulse; I texted her.

Thank you again for a lovely visit. Will you give me the name of your hot tub guy? R

I got her immediate response with a name and contact number. Plus, a smiley face emoji, a heart and what looked to be a tiny pool complete with bubbles. I sent back a thumbs up emoji and put down my phone. It immediately buzzed with an incoming text from Becky.

All good here. Yes to lunch! Hugs, B & J

Relieved, I grabbed a water bottle from the fridge and drained half of it, wiping my mouth with the hem of my shirt. The rain had finally stopped, so I stepped out to grab my mail, sorting through the pile of flyers and junk mail. I checked my phone again to see if I had any missed calls, but there were none. After the media circus and ensuing avalanche of texts, calls and emails, it seemed odd. Eerily silent. I checked my spam filter and found that I had not been totally forgotten. Apparently, a business executive from a foreign country with ties to an unnamed 'Royal Family' was trying to get in contact with me to share his newfound wealth. He just needed my money to make it happen. I could not believe the ridiculous scams I saw evidence of every day. An idea for a podcast interviewing actual victims of similar scams came to me, and I spent the rest of the evening doing research and taking notes. The episode would be a cautionary tale detailing the most prevalent cons and swindles, identifying those who were the most vulnerable and how to resolve the financial impact if you fell for one. I hoped I would find enough victims who were not too embarrassed to speak to me.

Around ten, I grabbed a slightly soft apple from the counter, turned off the lights, and headed for the shower. Not as good as a soak in a hot tub, but better than nothing. I vowed tomorrow I would toss the remaining fruit that had arrived in cellophane-wrapped baskets. The number of deliveries had dwindled off after news of my shenanigans had hit the airwaves. If they canceled my show, I would have to visit the local farmer's market each week, just like everyone else.

And honestly? That didn't sound half-bad.

CHAPTER 31

I woke to the sound of my phone buzzing and, without even checking to see who was calling, I answered.

"Hello," I croaked. "This is Miranda." I could hear my caller clearing his throat before he spoke.

"Miranda, it's Rick Cooper." I sat up in bed, glancing at the time. It was almost nine, and the sun was streaming in through my partially shut blinds.

"Hello. How are you?" I hurried to fill the silence that followed. "I mean, how can I help you?" More throat clearing. 'You called me,' I wanted to say, but held off. We had just spoken yesterday, so he must have something important to tell me. My patience was rewarded when his words came out in a rush.

"There have been some recent developments in our case against Terence Kane. Because of the seriousness of the charges and the threat to public safety if he were acquitted, we can't take any chances. We need to be doubly vigilant this time if we hope to be successful in his prosecution." What developments? I wondered. And why share them with me?

"Rick, I—"

"She died," he said. "His latest victim, nineteen-year-old Jennifer Ramos, died this morning in the hospital." I sat back, stunned.

"What happened? I don't understand."

"It appears to have been a brain aneurysm. Despite all their best efforts, they could not save her," he said.

"I am so sorry. That poor girl and her family." I would need to tell Becky today at lunch. "What is it exactly that you need me to do?"

"I would like you to consider sitting second chair on the trial. With me." My mouth hung open in shock. *What the hell?*

"I thought Steve Taylor was the lead. And I don't even ... I mean, how would that ... Why me?" I finally burst out.

"Taylor is a very competent prosecutor with an excellent conviction record. But the situation has changed. It's a capital murder case. We need to bring in the big guns. Me ... and you. You know more about Terence Kane than anyone in this office. Honestly, if the case hadn't fallen apart back then, you would have nailed him. You had everything going for you—"

"Until I didn't," I said flatly. "I blew it and everyone knows it." Suddenly restless, I hopped up and pulled on a robe with one hand, still holding the phone to my ear.

"I am going to be straight with you, Miranda. This case is weak. Very weak. The victim, who is also the primary witness, is dead. We need you. When the defense sees you in the courtroom, it will rattle them. That's what we need. They'll take one look at you and they'll be tripping over their ... well, let's just say they'll be left wondering what you know and why you're here?"

I smiled at the image of those sleazy bastards second guessing themselves. With Adam off the case, I wondered who might run lead. But the more immediate concern was on the prosecution side. Did I want to sit next to Rick for this entire case? What would the Sterling folks have to say? I pictured calling Brian. "Yes, that's right, I said murder. M-U-R-D-E-R! Thoughts?"

But, even more importantly, what did I want? Was this something I could do and feel confident about? I had thought my days in the courtroom were over. I was moving on, but could I lend my knowledge and skills to Rick and his team? See this through? I had years as a successful prosecutor with an enviable conviction record. I rocked in the courtroom. That had always been my happy place. I was Quinn for the Win, for God's sake. Yes, I thought. I can do this.

I told him I would schedule some time with him later in the week and disconnected the call. After a bathroom visit to ease my bursting bladder, I went in search of coffee. While it brewed, I took a quick shower and pulled on a T-shirt and khaki shorts. I poured the coffee into my travel mug, grabbed my laptop and my car keys, and headed out. I would go straight to my dad's and retrieve the flash drive. While he conjured up a breakfast sandwich exceeding even my wildest dreams, I would begin reviewing my three-year-old case files. The State of Connecticut vs. Terence Thomas Kane was back on track. While I wouldn't be the head conductor for this journey, I could do my best to ensure the sadistic bastard never drew a breath of free air again as long as he lived.

I wasn't certain that I would emerge with my broadcast TV career intact, but still I had to try.

CHAPTER 32

"Am I Olive Garden ready?" My dad eyed me suspiciously.

"Is that some sort of code? Some texting lingo?" he asked.

"No, I'm serious. I ran out of the house this morning and now I am supposed to meet Becky and Jesse at the mall. We're celebrating her getting Jesse back and Becky wants to eat at Olive Garden. I don't have any time to go home and change." I had spent the past two and a half hours reviewing the Kane files, and when Becky had texted earlier, a 1:00 p.m. lunch date had sounded reasonable. Now I had only a half hour left and the drive would take me at least twenty minutes, even with light traffic.

Pop looked me up and down and shook his head. "You look like you just finished cleaning out the garage," he said with a frown. *Aaarrgghh*. I already knew that. "And you're off to have lunch with Baxter's kid ferchrissakes." This wasn't helpful, and I wondered if there was a suitable dress code for when you were dining with your ex-boyfriend's love-child.

Maybe I could find something in my closet. As I hurried down the hall, he called out, "Sally leaves a few things here. Maybe you could ... " but I ignored him. Sally was half a foot shorter than me, and I doubted any of her clothes would fit me. I yanked my closet door open and found a polka dot sun dress hanging between a winter parka and a UCONN sweatshirt.

Good enough, I figured, and after stripping down to the basics, I rushed into the bathroom, applied deodorant and brushed my teeth. There was nothing I could do about the bags under my eyes, so I turned my back to the mirror and pulled the dress over my head. Grabbing my laptop, I blew Pop a kiss and hurried out the door.

"Lock up that flash drive again please," I called out and, after buckling up, I headed off to meet Becky.

***

Becky consumed a large bowl of salad and was enjoying a steaming serving of minestrone soup as the din in the restaurant grew louder. Nearby, there was a harried mom of three trying to get her children to eat while her clueless husband texted away on his phone, pausing only to swirl some linguini with his fork and shovel it in his mouth every couple of minutes. The dumbass would no doubt return to work shortly, feeling pleased with himself that he had taken time out of his busy day to join his family for lunch. *Ugh!*

I returned my attention to my own lunch and realized I had eaten very little of my pasta. I nibbled on a breadstick and watched as Becky urged her son to eat his 'ronis. Jesse appeared to need very little encouragement as he scooped up the noodles swimming in butter and parmesan cheese with his hands. What a good little eater. Just like his dad, I thought with a pang of sadness. This was the first time I had laid eyes on the little charmer since his father had been identified, and it amazed me I hadn't known immediately. The same chocolate brown eyes and springy brown curls no amount of combing could tame. But it was more than just their physical appearance. They both had an infectious laugh, Jesse's evident each time Becky tried to dab at his chin, dripping with butter. Father and son. *Freaking Adam.*

I turned my attention back to my pasta, but gave up after a couple more bites. This was harder than I had thought it would be, and I hadn't even gotten to the discussion I wanted to have with Becky. The one where I needed to ensure she would be set to testify in court as soon as next week. I wondered if I should address Eddie and Rachel's betrayal, but left that alone for now. Despite being close, I knew the sisters had weathered a lot of conflict between them, leading to long periods of estrangement, so it was possible that Becky was taking the whole thing in stride.

"Would you like a box for that, hon?" our server asked, indicating my dish of pasta with clam sauce. I was about to tell her not to bother when I caught Becky eyeing my lunch. My leftovers would provide her with one or two meals, and until we could figure out her next move, money was tight.

"You betcha," I said with a smile and minutes later, I pushed the container towards Becky and she smiled gratefully. "Who's up for dessert?" I asked, and they both answered with enthusiasm. An order of chocolate cheesecake with raspberry sauce appeared, along with two forks and a spoon. Becky and Jesse dove in and chattered away merrily as I sipped at a decaf cappuccino and bided my time for the right opportunity to begin what would be a tough conversation. Her appetite finally sated, Becky wiped her mouth with a napkin and turned to face me.

"I'm sorry," she said. "You must hate me." I was surprised by this. *Hate her?* I could never hate this girl. "I'm sure you figured out by now that Adam is the... well, you know." She hung her head, waiting for me to respond.

"I don't hate you," I began, but she hurried on.

"I wasn't in a good place when we got together, Adam and me. I was lonely and scared and bored out of my mind. I was trying not to use, but then I got laid off ... " At my look of concern, she went on. "I was working in the kitchen of a café down the street, but it was only a few shifts a week. So I got a job in housekeeping, but I missed a couple of shifts so they, well, they fired me. I don't know why I said laid off. I got fired. Then Adam shows up, and he's all, well, you know, handsome and full of fun. He took me out to dinner and bought me some new jeans and a sweater, and well, one thing led—" Now it was my turn to cut her off. *Stop, please,* I begged her silently.

"You don't owe me an explanation," I assured her. "Or an apology. Adam and I broke up long before then. You were both consenting adults ... " My voice trailed off, and I shrugged. "It's cool," I said. *Cool?* Seriously? What was I, twelve?

Becky dabbed at her eyes, which were brimming with unshed tears. "You're nice to say that, but even I know sleeping with a friend's ex is anything but cool. And we are friends, aren't we?" she asked, the hope clear in her worried gaze.

"Yes, we are," I said. "And we will get through this together." It was high time for me to shift into lawyer mode, so I faced her and spoke firmly. "You've got Jesse back and there are no charges pending. DCF will pop in for some unscheduled visits over the next few weeks. Lisa estimates they will probably stop after three or four. But you have to keep everything clean and tidy. Make sure you are always both dressed in clean clothes, and that there is healthy food in the fridge." I reached into my bag and withdrew three grocery store gift cards. "There is one hundred dollars on each of these. Buy lots of fruits and vegetables, go for organic. Get some chicken or fish, no processed foods, yeah? These will keep you going for a few weeks until we can sort out something more permanent." The tears now spilled over as Becky sobbed openly for a couple of minutes and I let her cry, hoping the tears would bring her relief.

"Thank you," she finally managed. "You have no idea—"

"You're welcome. So moving on, I can definitely see us bringing a case against Houghton and the law firm in the near future. They owe you big time for messing up your life. But for now, before I can help you find better housing and a job or daycare or whatever, I need your help." I kept my gaze on her and she sat up straight, wiping her face. She nodded in agreement.

"I'll do anything you say, Randi. Just tell me what you need from me." So, I told her she would need to be available to testify in court in only a little more than a week.

"And there's more. I'm sorry to tell you, Becky, but the victim? Jennifer Ramos died last night. A brain aneurysm. That makes this a murder trial." Becky's eyes filled with tears and I leaned forward and held her hand. She wiped her eyes with her napkin and tried to look brave.

"All the more reason to kick Kane's ass in court. What happens now?" Looking at her determined face, I was filled with a sense of pride. Oh Becky, I thought. You have come so far.

"You amaze me," I said, and her smile brightened. I explained how the defense attorney and I would interview potential jurors starting on Monday.

"It's called *voir dire*," I explained. "It means we get to interview prospective jurors to determine if they could be impartial in determining Kane's guilt or innocence."

"But we know he's—" I stopped her.

"Knowing something and being able to prove it beyond a reasonable doubt in court are two different things. Our job will be to identify potential jurors more likely to believe the state's claim that Kane is guilty of all charges. But the defense will try to do the opposite. To make you and whatever other witnesses are called appear less than credible, like you're lying or at least stretching the truth." Becky nodded her understanding.

"It's just like on *Law and Order*," she said. Well, not really, I thought, as not everything gets wrapped up nice and neatly in an hour in the real world.

"Yes. But honestly, there is a great deal of downtime waiting around. I'll need you at the courthouse every day once the jury has been seated. I won't know how soon we can call you up to testify until after both sides present our cases. It could be a few days of sitting around." Becky looked worried.

"What do I do about Jesse?" she asked. "I can't ask Rachel to help me out anymore."

"I'll think of someone," I promised. Would Tracey take him for a day or two? Or my dad? I groaned, thinking of enlisting his support to take care of Adam's child. I knew he would do it if I asked him, but surely it would not come to that. "Don't worry," I assured her. "I'll sort something out so you'll know he's well taken care of and you can relax."

Jesse was getting restless, and I knew it was time to go. Leaving money for our lunches on the table, including a generous tip, I hoisted my purse over my shoulder. Becky grabbed my leftovers, and we walked towards the door. I panicked suddenly, realizing we had not discussed the most important issue.

"You know Adam's out on bail and he won't be in the courtroom, right?" She shrugged.

"Yeah, I heard about Adam. I figured he wouldn't be allowed anywhere near the courtroom. But poor Jennifer. I feel responsible. If I had testified three years ago, none of this would have happened and she'd be—"

"You can't think like that. What happened was not your fault." She nodded, and we hugged goodbye. She had walked the few blocks from home with Jesse in his stroller and, as I did not have a car seat handy, she was going to walk back home as well.

"I should hurry," she said with a grin. "The cop squad will be watching for me." With a wave, she and Jesse set off, and I watched them head down the sidewalk and wait at the corner for the Walk signal. Becky turned and waved one more time and the two of them disappeared from my view.

I was so proud of her and the life she was building for her son. When I was her age, my only worries had been turning term papers in on time and wondering if my boyfriend Joey Turner was two-timing me with that skank Darlene from the bar. But I had just lost my mother and was concerned about my dad, so maybe it hadn't been all that easy for me either.

What doesn't kill us, I thought as I drove home.

CHAPTER 33

The next few days leading up to the trial flew by. My work day began at 7:00 a.m. when I chugged coffee and wrote and edited my blog posts for the next few weeks. Once the trial began, I knew I would have no time to work on anything else. I considered simply not posting any new content or finding a guest host for a week or two, but *Miranda Writes* readers and listeners still deserved my best efforts. So, I carved out a couple of hours a day to guarantee that would happen.

By nine, I would be in my car heading to meet with Rick to shore up our list of witnesses and strategize our case. We always worked through lunch and I would stagger home and scrounge up a meal around 4 p.m. One afternoon, I slipped away and took the train into the city in order to meet with the network execs. Brian had suggested I schedule in some face time to confirm my commitment to the show and to assure them that the trial I was involved in would not only be over quickly, but would also generate favorable publicity for the show.

"You are assuming the trial will be a slam dunk and that I'll be brilliant in court," I protested as I raced towards my track with only a few minutes to spare until my train was due to depart.

"I sure am," he responded. "Any idea how much is riding on this?" I thought of the young women who could walk freely, safe in knowing that a violent serial rapist was locked up, but I knew Brian was referring to the financial risk the network was taking on an unknown like me. Especially now that I was potentially less than one hundred percent engaged.

"I am about to board," I assured him. "I'll see you soon and we'll make sure they know I am ready, willing, and able to shoot the pilot episode in five weeks' time. My wardrobe is waiting, and the set has been designed, so unless you want me to get involved with the actual carpet installation," I teased, "which if I recall is a lovely shade of taupe, there is nothing else for me to do."

"Sounds like your to-do list is in great shape," Brian said. "But there are bigger issues at play. They are going to want to know about the case, the trial, and how it might affect your image."

"Yeah," I only half-joked. "God forbid, as a lawyer, I actually dabble in the law."

"I am merely the messenger, Miranda. Don't start with me. You knew right from the outset the network's stand on your getting involved with that witness and the late-night assignations with your married ex." I struggled to come up with a response, all the while thinking I would try to grab a peek at Brian's license to get his actual age. I had him pegged for mid-thirties, but at times, he sounded like someone twice that old. *Assignations.* Seriously? He must have taken my silence as some sort of tacit agreement. "So, be prepared, okay? That's what they are looking for. Assurances, tangible commitment, not some checked off to-do list a monkey could accomplish." *Ouch.*

"Don't sugarcoat it, pal. I'll be sure to address all of my dalliances and various and sundry peccadilloes with the powers that be when we meet. Got to go." I turned off the ringer on my phone and shoved it in my jacket pocket and spent the next twenty minutes trying to come up with some way of turning my involvement in the Kane trial into an asset, something the network would view as valuable, maybe for a future show? I finally gave up, closed my eyes and dozed until my train arrived at Penn Station. If I were to be fed to the lions, I might as well be well-rested.

***

After an hour and a half of groveling and two club sodas with lime, I was heading home on the last train stopping in Old Lyme tonight. It hadn't been all that bad; I had to admit. The "Miranda Wrongs" article was not mentioned, and I had shared how excited I was about the show and how I planned to use the likely conviction from the Kane case as an example of how justice would be served, even after a delay. How my role was a small, albeit important one in the trial. How perseverance always pays off. Truth, justice and the American way! I swear, if I had got my hands on either an American flag or an apple pie, I would have had the necessary props to make my argument even stronger. Before I could go full-on crazy for the ol' red, white and blue, Brian had kicked me under the table and changed the subject to the details of the upcoming pilot. I spoke enthusiastically about the topics I planned to cover and the two guests that had been lined up.

A short while later, following a round of hugs and handshakes, I had mouthed a silent thank you to my agent and rushed back to the train station. It seems as if I would live to fight another day. *Miranda Writes*, the TV series, was still in the works and I could breathe!

CHAPTER 34

"I'm not sure if it's the type of story ... " I twisted uncomfortably in my seat and blasted the AC. Not even 9:00 a.m. and the temperature was already an unseasonable ninety degrees. I focused on the heavy morning traffic and tried to keep calm.

"Paternity is trending right now," the associate producer assigned to *Miranda Writes* assured me. "After a fall from its heyday in the nineties, it's big again. Trust me." I gritted my teeth in response and tried not to explode. This was precisely the type of journalism that I did not want to celebrate on my show, complete with a pregnant woman and a trio of potential baby-daddies. *Ugh!* I thought I had been very clear on what types of legal topics I wanted to explore and what types were *verboten*. Perhaps my simpering and ass-kissing at the bar last night had been misinterpreted as weakness, like I would go along with anything just to keep the peace.

Overnight, however, I had grown a pair and this morning, I was in no mood to agree with this young woman. I was on my way to New London for a strategy session with Rick to discuss the Kane case. I considered blaming poor reception as a reason to disconnect, but I knew this type of conflict was unlikely to go away on its own. That it needed to be dealt with right away, but not necessarily by me. Wasn't that why I had hired an agent in the first place? To negotiate for me, to represent my best interests in order to earn his fifteen percent commission? I cleared my throat as I realized the caller had stopped talking.

"I'm sorry. I didn't catch your name," I said.

"It's Alexis. Alexis Whit—" I cut her off. I was pulling in to the parking garage next to the courthouse and wanted to concentrate on finding an open spot that wasn't up in the nosebleed section.

"Alexis, this all sounds like something I need to discuss with my agent, Brian Gagnon. I will have him call you shortly, okay?" Without waiting for a response, I told her to have a great day and ended the call. Good lord, was it going to be an uphill battle every step of the way with these people? That's why I loved my blog and my podcasts. I had total control over the content and the topics covered. I had known the network would not rubber-stamp everything I wanted, but I had assumed there would be some sort of honeymoon phase in the beginning. All the available evidence pointed to the fact I had been wrong. I hurried towards the elevator, furiously tapping out a message to Brian.

They want me to be the next Jerry Springer!!! Make it stop. R

I added a frowny face and hit send. I had more pressing issues to tend to and needed to focus one hundred percent of my attention on them.

Terence Kane had to be put away for good.

***

I sat back and stretched. My back made the appropriate creaking sounds, and I let out an enormous sigh of relief. Things were looking up. I smiled at Rick as he performed a similar stretch of his own from his seat across the large conference room table. I nodded happily at the very organized piles of files that had been scattered all over the table just a few hours earlier. He smiled back at me, a rare occurrence for sure.

"We're in good shape," he said. "I don't want to jinx it, but I'm feeling pretty good about our chances in court." I nodded enthusiastically and drained my water bottle. We had been at it for several hours, and despite mental fatigue and physical exhaustion, I was guardedly optimistic myself. The case we had built against Kane was solid, robust, even. I counted off the strengths in the case we had identified.

"We have excellent witnesses this time," I said, flipping through my notes. "The cops who found Jennifer and the staff from the emergency room can testify to the severity of her injuries. The doctors who treated her will confirm the cause of death was the injuries she sustained in Kane's vicious attack. And it looks like Kane's alibis are falling like dominoes. That should more than balance out any of the defense team's theatrics." Rick steepled his fingers and looked contemplative for a moment before he responded.

"Are you certain any feelings you have for the former lead defense attorney on the case will not present any issues? I understand your breakup was less than amicable."

"No, Rick. Seriously. That ship has sailed. It's water under the bridge," I said, perhaps a bit too emphatically. Thou dost protest too much, I warned myself. "We had a parting of the ways long before I found out what he had done to tank my case. Adam has promised to testify to the fact that Kane's lawyers would stop at nothing to prevent him from being convicted. And we can still call Eddie DaSilva in as a hostile witness if we need to. What lawyers would resort to all that if they had proof that their client was actually innocent?"

Rick nodded slowly, as if he still had some doubts, but I was feeling confident. The defense had screwed me royally both times Kane was charged, and any anger and resentment I still felt would actually strengthen my performance in the courtroom. "Anything else?" I asked as I got ready to leave.

"No. We're good. Thank you for your help today," Rick said. "I appreciate your jumping in to the case like this. Especially with all you have going on," he added. "You must be very excited about the show." I stood and buttoned my blazer, slipping the strap of my tote bag over my shoulder. I would no doubt remove the jacket for the drive home, but it was downright chilly in the conference room. I walked to where Rick was now standing and held out my hand.

"Let's get this bastard," I said with a grin and we shook on it. "Let me know if I can do anything over the weekend," I said. "I'm free as a bird. Seriously, anything at all."

"No Hollywood premieres or Grammy celebrations to attend?" Rick asked wryly. I grinned at his weak attempt at humor. The man had made a total turnaround this past week when it came to assessing my worth. Premieres and celebrations? *Hah!* I pictured the quiet weekend I had planned. Walking on the beach followed by binge watching whatever I could find on Netflix would be the highlights in between reviewing my notes and practicing my opening, that is. And maybe a meal with Pop and Sally.

"Not this weekend," I assured him. "But keep next year's Daytime Emmys in mind." What a coup that would be. I gave a last wave and left his office, heading for the elevator. It was nearly 2:00 p.m., and we had not taken a lunch break. I made a quick detour on my way home to Nardelli's. I chuckled, remembering Brian protesting that the term 'grinder' was mildly pornographic.

I enjoyed teasing him. It was just so easy.

CHAPTER 35

The next morning, I had arranged to meet Skip at the studio. I walked in and found myself face to face with a tall, good-looking man about my age. He was dressed casually in pressed chinos and a blue button-down, worn open over a vintage concert T-shirt. Talking Heads. Solid choice.

"Hello. Can I help you?" I asked.

"Sorry, I was looking for my nephew," he said. "You must be Miranda. He talks about you all the time." He grinned and offered his hand. "Nice to meet you. I'm Eric. Eric Hansen."

I shifted my tote bag and put my coffee cup on the file cabinet that served as an end table. I shook his hand and smiled back at him. "Hansen, as in Skip Hansen?" He nodded and let go of my hand.

"Yeah, Skip is my nephew."

"So that would make Sarah your niece," I said, watching as his lips twisted into a smile.

"That would be correct. Wow, everything they say about you is true. You're a sharp one all right," he said with a sly grin. A lock of his light brown hair fell over his right eyebrow and I resisted the urge to smooth it back. He was damn attractive, and I felt flustered as I grabbed my coffee and headed for the large table in the center of the room.

"That's me, Quinn for the Win," I quipped. I sucked at flirting, but still checked out his lack of a wedding ring. "Skip should be here any minute. Is there something I can do for you?" Eric walked over to where I was now sitting.

"He forgot his phone," he said, pulling one from his pocket and laying it on the table. I was about to assure him I would see that the phone was returned, when Skip hurried in to the room.

"Uncle Eric, what's up? Oh, you have my phone? Thanks man, I can't believe I forgot it." He grabbed it gratefully after tossing his backpack onto one of the folding chairs. "Oh, crap, I shoulda brought you a sandwich," he said as he placed a white paper bag already ringed in grease on the table. "I stopped at the place you like Randi." Digging into the bag, he pulled out two round sandwiches wrapped in aluminum foil. They smelled heavenly, but the thought of eating a greasy egg and linguica sausage sandwich in front of this well-groomed stranger was totally unappealing.

"Hey, Skip, don't worry about me. I promised your mom I would be right back. She is making her famous tater tot casserole," he said. Skip mumbled something totally unintelligible, having crammed half of the sandwich in his mouth.

"You can have mine," I told Eric, pushing the sandwich towards him. "I'm not very hungry," I lied, as my stomach growled, exposing the truth. "Well, maybe a little hungry," I said. Eric's grin was sincere.

"Your mom made me promise," he said. "And it sounded like you have a lot of work to catch up on." Turning back to me, he said, "Maybe the next time you're not very hungry, we can go out and not eat somewhere." I was suddenly aware of my army green cargo pants, pink T-shirt and black flip-flops. I tried to smooth back the strands of my hair that had escaped from my hastily styled messy bun. *A date?* With Skip's uncle? I had not seen that one coming. I swallowed and let out a breath.

"Umm, sure. I guess. When? I mean, are you, uh, local?" A very awkward line of questioning from a soon-to-be TV talk show host. *Ladies and gentleman, daytime TV's newest star, the tongue-tied and ever-so charming Miranda Quinn.* Eric was smooth. I had to give him that.

"I'll call you, if that's okay," he said with a twinkle in his blue, no green eyes. I nodded my assent, and he turned to Skip. "See you at home Skipper," he said and with a wave, he left the room. I looked around the dingy studio that suddenly felt vast and empty. I grabbed my sandwich and dug in. Grease dripping down my chin, I held off before grilling Skip on his fabulous uncle. As he chewed the last of his sandwich, Skip reached into his backpack and pulled out a Monster Energy drink and a cellophane package of powdered donuts. Breakfast of champions! Oh, to have the metabolism of an eighteen-year-old, I thought.

As Skip sipped and munched, I managed to eke out pertinent details about Eric Hansen, although some of them were a bit vague. Eric was indeed his father's younger brother. He was somewhere between late thirties to early forties, an architect living in New Rochelle, New York. He had arrived in town last night and was staying with Skip and his family for the next several days so the two brothers could enjoy some fishing on Long Island Sound. Today's trip had been canceled when John Hansen had to go into his office on some kind of personnel emergency. Eric was single, having gotten out of a long-term relationship with a woman who was a teacher or maybe a counselor, by the name of Molly, or possibly Polly.

"Some investigative reporter you'd make," I said as I gathered up the trash from our breakfast and snagged the last tiny donut. Popping it into my mouth, I motioned to Skip. "We should probably get some work done, yeah?" I dug in my bag and removed the folder with the script and my notes for today's podcast. I swallowed the last of my coffee and wiped my lips, imagining they were dusted with powdered sugar.

"He's a good guy, Randi," he said. "You'd really like him." Yeah, I bet I would.

"Sounds good, Skipper. Let's get to work."

***

If Skip noted my particularly chipper mood that morning, he didn't say, but I noticed his sly smile when I added some light-hearted commentary to my podcast on the less than lively topic of estate planning, trusts and wills. The morning flew by and I thought about how I had planned to spend the rest of the weekend. I mentally crossed things off my to-do list as I got in my car and headed home. I probably should have walked the few blocks this morning, but then I would have missed running into Eric Hansen. Day-dreaming over him would not get me anywhere today, so I shifted my attention to my most pressing responsibilities.

Becky was prepped and as ready for next week's court appearance as she would ever be, and Rick had told me to take the weekend to relax before the trial. Tracey would be knee-deep in cutting cheese sandwiches into fun shapes and pouring milk for her tiny humans and Pop had told me he and Sally were driving over to Newport, Rhode Island for the day to tour the mansions and gorge on the fabulous fried clams at Flo's Clam Shack. Brian was taking a long weekend and there was no one at the network who would need me today. Wow! I was footloose and fancy free and had the next two and a half days to do whatever I wanted. I couldn't remember the last time when that had been the case. Not since those dark days camped out on Pop's couch.

I pulled into my driveway and grabbed the mail before letting myself in. A few flyers and some junk mail and one, no two envelopes that could only be greeting cards. I didn't recognize either of the return addresses, so I figured they were from fans who had found my address online. I left them on the counter and tossed the rest of the mail into the recycling bin. I thought briefly of reaching out to Sarah to check on the mail she would have collected from my post office box, but I wanted to give her a couple of well-deserved days off, too. It was a beautiful day, so after scarfing down a pineapple yogurt, I headed to the beach. I left the mini-van in the driveway and walked the two blocks to the entrance. It was a private beach for residents only, and today, I had it all to myself. I stuffed my flip-flops in the pockets of my cargo capris and walked to the water's edge. I headed east along the shoreline, trying to clear my mind and 'be here now' as the bumper stickers advise.

Easier said than done, I knew and I found myself thinking about Adam. I had recognized his tendency to cut certain corners early in our relationship with, in his mind, the ends justifying the means. He could comfortably tell white lies, mainly about things that didn't really matter. Like if his mother called, he would tell her he had been just about to call her or when he got out of one social engagement in favor of another, with the excuse of needing to stay late at work. But I had ignored those things, telling myself he was essentially honest and ethical in his dealings with clients and colleagues ... and with me. But I had been wrong. Turns out he was more than capable of being corrupted and had no real compunction about destroying my career in favor of his own.

I had been happy during my time with him. I just always wanted what my folks had during their brief twenty years together. When my dad looked at my mom, it was a look of wonder, like how the hell did I get so lucky? And my mom, Nora, always blushed with pure joy when her husband entered the room. Like he was this amazing, larger-than-life miracle about to grace her presence. But maybe a fairy-tale romance like theirs was not in the cards for me. And that was fine. I had enough on my plate right now to keep me from pursuing any sort of personal life for the near future, but an image of Eric Hansen's handsome face caused me to smile. Where had he been hiding all this time?

I realized I had walked much further than I usually did, so I turned and headed back in the opposite direction. The sun was still almost directly overhead, and I felt my face burning under its glare. I had neglected to wear a hat and had forgotten to apply sunscreen. Based on previous experience, it was likely I would be sporting a beet-red nose just starting to peel on Monday, in time for the first day of the Kane trial.

Lovely!

CHAPTER 36

After taking a hot shower and slathering myself with lotion to minimize the peeling my freckled Irish skin would no doubt experience, I poured myself a glass of iced tea and took it out to the front porch. It had been a good day: productive, yet relaxing. I sipped at the tea and called my dad, just to check in. The trip to Newport had been a success, the mansions capturing their full attention before indulging in the best fried clams ever. The happy couple was about to watch a movie and I pictured them cuddling on the couch together.

"Netflix and chill," I teased. My dad was vocal in his confusion.

"What's that now?" he asked. I heard him telling Sally what I'd said. Being the hipper member of the couple, she laughed and told him it sounded good to her. I ended the call just in case they started kissing or something. Being glad your dad had a girlfriend was miles apart from actually witnessing their romance in action. Next, I called Tracey. We talked for a few minutes and I was about to tell her about meeting Skip's uncle when she interrupted me.

"The boys are having a sleepover at their friend Ben's house. Dale is dropping them off now, and he's picking up a bottle of wine. Oh wait, I think he's home. Crap, gotta shave my legs. Talk later. Byeeeee." I stared at my phone. Was everyone getting busy tonight or was it just my luck to call the two most in love people in the world? Before I had a chance to ponder that thought, my phone buzzed with a text from a phone number I didn't recognize.

Hey, it's Eric Hansen. Skip gave me your number.

I stared at the phone, thinking how to respond, when another text came in.

Are you home? I just wanted to see if maybe you weren't hungry, you would want to go out to not eat tomorrow night.

Hey Eric. I'm here.

Hi. So what do you think?

I could not eat.

Tomorrow?

Saturday? Saturday night?

Well, it's supposed to be all right for fighting, from what I hear.

And you can get a little action in. I was trading song lyrics with a guy I had just met. I waited for his response. Had I gone too far? Even to me, it sounded pervy.

Wow, I was just asking about not eating dinner. But I suppose if you're up for action, I can give it a try.

I didn't peg you for an Elton John guy. More David Byrne maybe.

??

Talking Heads? Your T-shirt?

Awww. You noticed what I was wearing. Yeah, big fan. How about you?

R.E.M., Counting Crows and Pearl Jam.

Nice. Can I ask you something?

OK.

Can I call you? Texting is really not my thing. I would really love to hear your voice.

Sure thing.

Seconds later, my phone rang and Eric and I talked for nearly an hour. He told me about his work as an architect and I filled him in on my upcoming show. He admitted he'd been following my podcast since the beginning, when his nephew started producing for me.

"You make the most complicated legal issues relatable to just about anyone. But you don't talk down to your audience or lecture them. It's like having a conversation with a friend who just happens to be a legal expert," he said.

"Wow, that was exactly what I was going for."

"Do you think the show will change things?" he asked.

"Well yeah, because it will be live with callers and special guests. And I won't be hiding behind a microphone. I'll be all up close and personal. And I'll be dressed up too. No more cargo pants and flip-flops."

"Damn. I mean ... I don't know. It just will be different. Like that favorite little hole-in-the-wall restaurant that you love. They buy the place next door and blow out some walls and suddenly it's not your favorite little hole in the wall anymore. There's a line at the door and the service sucks and the food is still good, but it's not as good." He paused. "Hey, I didn't mean anything by it. I'm sure it will be great. You'll be great." I was sitting there nodding when I realized he couldn't see me. "Randi?"

"I'm here," I said. "And I get it, I do. I know exactly what you mean. I'm afraid of that too." I let out a breath. "The Sterling folks want me to consider shows with paternity reveals and, um, stuff like that."

"Shades of Jerry Springer," Eric said. "Christ, I hope you told them to shove it." I chuckled.

"Um, that's not exactly how it works, I guess."

"That's not who you are, Randi. That's not *Miranda Writes*. Not by a long shot." I nodded in agreement, momentarily speechless. I could have hugged him, this man I barely knew who seemed to get me, the real me. It felt great. I quickly cleared my throat.

"Yeah, I know. I gave them a list of topics I wouldn't cover and I can probably veto certain things." I suddenly needed to change the subject. Enough about me and my brand. "So, is Molly or Polly a teacher or a counselor?" I asked. "Inquiring minds want to know." He laughed aloud at that.

"Leave it to Skipper," he said good-naturedly. "Okay, it's Molly. She teaches high school chemistry, and it's been a year since we broke up. And what about you? Was your ex really just arrested for bribing one of your witnesses?"

"Right to the point, yeah? Yes, turns out he's a total douchebag. Read all about it. But can we continue this discussion over not dinner tomorrow night? I'm suffering from sunstroke and I need to eat something, stat."

"We can talk about whatever you like," he said. "In between fighting and getting a little action in, I would love to hear more about you. What makes you tick."

"Pick me up at seven?" I suggested. He agreed, and we said goodnight. I started to put my phone down when a message from Becky arrived. It was a selfie with her and Jesse smiling and waving at me. Clearly, she had learned how to use her new phone! I send back a cascade of smiley faces and shuffled towards the kitchen. A bowl of cereal and a banana. Perfect to binge Netflix with.

And tomorrow night, I had a date with Eric!

CHAPTER 37

The next day I woke early to get a walk/run in before the sun came up, in the irrational belief I could somehow reverse yesterday's sunburn. I pulled on a pair of shorts and grabbed a sweatshirt on my way out the door. Living as close as I do to the ocean, I have found the early mornings are often overcast with a heavy mist that cools the air by at least ten degrees. It felt like even more this morning, as I crossed the street and headed towards the beach entrance. The tide was out and once again, I had the beach to myself. God, I loved this place.

I had grown up on the Connecticut shoreline and other than my college years, had not lived anywhere else. I never wanted to. But what if the show took off, and the network wanted to extend my contract? Living a four-hour train ride from the studio was tolerable when I was only going in once or twice a week. If I drove to New Haven and took the train from there, I could save an hour. But every day? I pictured myself getting up this time every morning, but instead of taking a walk on the beach, I would be elbow to elbow with all of those other commuters and tourists. I had yet to check out the accommodations that had been arranged for me. According to Brian, it was a tiny studio apartment, the kind that executives would stay in for the length of an out-of-town assignment. It was close to the studio and offered free-Wi-Fi and room service. I pictured it as clean, modern and very beige. Nothing like my cozy cottage just two blocks from the beach. But if I could stay there two or maybe three nights mid-week and spend the rest of my time here, that would be a reasonable compromise. It would have to be. I would make it work. It was a small price to pay for the perks of a daytime TV hosting gig. Suck it up, I told myself. It would truly be the best of both worlds.

By the time I had gone about a mile heading east, I was enjoying a gorgeous sunrise. The beach I had walked on during my recuperation period at my dad's was several miles away, but the comfort I felt from strolling on the hard-packed sand with the foamy waves sneaking up on me and the gulls looking for their morning meal was as familiar as anything I had ever known. I turned and headed towards home with the sun on my back and the tangy scent of the ocean filling my head. When the trial was over, I would invite Becky and Jesse to spend a weekend with me. I pictured the little guy playing on the beach, building sandcastles and splashing in the shallow water. What a cutie!

I held off on a shower for now, opting for coffee and some toast on the back porch. Once I was settled, I scrolled through my phone, checking for news alerts on the Kane trial, Adam's arrest, and any other shenanigans I might be linked to and was relieved I was no longer the news *du jour*. The CEO of a Fortune 500 company was the latest villain in the continuing #metoo saga and I scribbled a note to remind myself to look into a show featuring interviews with women who had come forward. Not the well-known survivors who'd called press conferences. I wanted to talk to the secretary at a manufacturing plant or the hostess at a local steakhouse. Their stories mattered too, and I hoped they would want to talk to me. And, just as importantly, that SBG would give me the green light to do such a show. I thought of Eric and his comments last night during our call. Was I indeed the local dive with the great service and mouthwatering food, striving to become a larger, blander version of myself?

I sure hoped not.

***

I kept busy all morning doing the kinds of tasks I rarely get to during the week: dry cleaners, bank, drugstore and grocery store. Naturally, since I hadn't showered after my walk, I ran into neighbors, old friends and well-wishers. I accepted their praise and congratulations, tried but failed to avoid any celebratory hugs and finally returned home in the early afternoon, determined to find some time to relax before my date with Eric. Tracey called me as I was digging around in my closet for something to wear and we chatted for a bit before I dropped the newsflash about my date.

"You'll never guess what I'm doing tonight," I said, and she let out a dramatic sigh.

"Gee, let me think. The network is dispatching a helicopter to whisk you away to some amazing getaway or maybe you'll be hopping on a corporate jet and getting whisked—"

"There'll be no whisking," I said. "Well, maybe a little whisking, but nothing like that. I've ... um, I've got a date."

"What? Oh my God, you're kidding me, right?" she shrieked. *Rude!* Was I hurt that it was more believable I would travel first class to some exotic locale this very evening than it was that I had an actual date? Yes, I was, but I ignored the slight. I waited until she calmed down. "Tell me. I want all the details."

"His name is Eric Hansen. He is Skip and Sarah's uncle. He is an architect from New Rochelle and we are going out for dinner. Tonight."

"That sounds great," my friend gushed. "I was hoping it wouldn't be Brian. He seems like a wonderful agent and all, but he's just not your type, you know?" Yes, I knew.

"So now my biggest challenge is my usual dilemma. What am I going to wear?" I moaned.

"I'm on my way," Tracey promised, and not fifteen minutes later, she came flying through my front door. "C'mon, we need to get you sorted," she said, and we headed to my bedroom. The process was painful, but over relatively quickly. After trying on and discarding several outfits one or both of us judged as "too conservative," "trying too hard" or "that's better suited for a trip to the mall," we agreed on a pair of dark wash jeans that made my butt look great, a silky navy top embedded with silver threading and black pumps. Classic, effortless and perfect for an evening out on the Connecticut shoreline, I decided while posing in front of a mirror.

"I've never actually worn this top," I said to Tracey, who was cutting the tags off with a pair of cuticle scissors. "I think Sally gave it to me last Christmas." Tracey studied me from head to toe, nodding her approval.

"It works and all I have to say is… Sally? You go, girl. You could learn a lot from her," she said. "Every time I have seen her, she is totally put together, you know?" I pictured my dad's girlfriend and smiled.

"After I shower and do my hair and makeup, I'll snap a selfie of me wearing the top and send it to her. I think she'll be pleased."

"You like her," Tracey teased. "You never used to talk about her without that little frown wrinkle popping up between your eyebrows. But you just smiled, no wrinkle. That's progress, my friend. Or did you get Botox?"

"Let's not get crazy," I warned her. "Yeah, she's a keeper and I'm glad my dad has her in his life. But back to business. Black wristlet or a purse with a pop of color?"

"Wristlet," said Tracey. "Keep your hands free, you know?" she asked, wriggling her fingers. "Jazz hands!" I laughed at her silliness, but dug around in my dresser to unearth a small black patent leather bag.

"Still with tags. I think it was from my last birthday. Thank you, Sally." It was nearly 4:00 p.m.

Just three more hours…

CHAPTER 38

After Tracey left with a reminder that I needed to shave my legs, I hopped into the shower and did just that. With my hair freshly washed, I wrapped myself up in a towel and took a personal inventory. Thanks to the largesse of the network, my recent haircut would make styling very simple, even for me. My eyebrows were well groomed and my mani/pedi was still in fine shape. I stretched out on my bed to rest my eyes for a few minutes. I considered heading to the fridge for some cucumber slices to reduce under-eye puffiness, but my bed felt so comfortable and I just ...

The buzzing was coming from somewhere close. Then I felt it under my right thigh. I was getting a call, and was just about to answer it when my doorbell rang and I heard someone pounding on my front door. What was going on?

"Randi," a male voice called out, and it hit me. I had a date with Eric and had fallen asleep. Now he was at my door and calling me on the phone as well. I answered the call, my voice still clogged with sleep, as I stumbled towards the front of the house.

"I'm sorry. I'm coming," I croaked and pulled the door open. Eric was standing there, slipping his phone into the pocket of his navy blazer. His look of concern morphed into one of unabashed delight right before my eyes. I beckoned him in and put my phone down on the entry table. He was no doubt wondering why I was wrapped in a towel instead of being dressed for dinner.

"I really am sorry. I fell asleep and guess I just ... " I stopped speaking as the smile on his face grew even wider.

"I'm over-dressed as usual," he mock complained. He gestured to his outfit of khakis, a yellow button down and a blazer. Boat shoes *sans* socks completed the look. "Damn, I thought I could pull this off, but what do I know?" He kicked off his shoes and made to take off his jacket. I grinned at him.

"What do I know?" I echoed him. "I figured terrycloth would work for tonight, but I can see I made a tactical error in judgement." He nodded agreeably.

"Well, clearly we got our signals crossed. I knew you were up for action. I mean, you came right out and told me you were. I was hoping to grab some dinner first, but if you insist." His blazer now lay on the floor, and he started to unbuckle his belt. I stopped him with a quick peck on the lips. Light at first, just to get his attention, but it quickly became a first-rate kiss, setting sparks off at every point of contact. I was gripping him around his waist and his hands were lightly grasping my face close to his. I probably could have helped him to drop trou and lose my towel if this kiss continued much longer, but cooler heads prevailed. His, not mine. He pulled back and studied me closely. With one finger, he tipped my chin up, so I was looking right into a pair of green eyes. Yesterday, they had sparkled like a sunny meadow, but tonight, they were dark and stormy. It was intoxicating, and all I knew was I wanted more. Much more. He cleared his throat. His voice was husky and deep.

"All kidding aside, I'm guessing you had every intention of greeting me at the door, all dressed and ready to go. I don't want to take advantage of the situation, so why don't you go get some clothes and we'll head to the Shrimp Shack. John says it's the best restaurant in the area and Sarah says you like seafood, so I made a reservation for eight. What do you say?" I grinned back at him and tugged my towel closer to my body.

"Sounds great. I'll be ready in a flash. Make yourself at home. Help yourself to water or iced tea ... whatever you like." Eric stood at the butcher block island separating my kitchen from the living room, surveying the mess. It was cluttered with the remnants of a dozen fruit baskets, reduced to a pile of wicker and colorful cellophane wrapping, dotted with foil-wrapped chocolates and small packages of mixed nuts and mints.

"Maybe I could find something here," he said. "Hell, why go out to dinner if there's all this loot just asking to be eaten?" He unwrapped a chocolate and popped it in his mouth. "Sea salt caramel, my favorite." He held up his hand as I approached him. "I called dibs, so get dressed while I forage a snack from your scraps." I leaned forward and kissed him on the cheek.

"Be back in ten," I said in a tone I hoped sounded full of promise of good things to come. Damn, now he smelled like chocolate and expensive cologne, lightly applied. I skedaddled down the hall to my room. I pulled on the clothes Tracey and I had chosen after locating the only somewhat sexy bra and panties I owned. A girl can't be too prepared, I told myself. I rushed into my bathroom and groaned. My hair was no longer soaking wet, but it had dried funny, so I pulled it into a messy bun and noticed a big comforter crease lining my cheek. You are a sight, I told myself and went to work with eyeliner, blush and lipstick before slicking on a couple of coats of mascara. I tried to remember how Belinda's magicians had done it and was reasonably pleased with the results as I checked myself out.

Slipping into my heels, I grabbed my wristlet. I had already packed it before my nap: lip gloss, mints, a credit card, driver's license and a twenty-dollar bill. I just needed to grab my phone, and I was good to go.

"I'm ready," I called out as I sashayed down the hall to where Eric stood, still contemplating the meager selection of snacks remaining. His eyes lit up when he saw me.

"You look amazing. I don't even miss the towel," he said, taking my hand. We were off.

***

We arrived at the restaurant just minutes before our reservation, but found we would still have a bit of a wait. Business was booming and the waiting area was teeming with hungry diners, so Eric took the little buzzer from the hostess and we made our way to the bar. Patrons were standing three deep, but we found an empty spot to stand in the corner.

"What can I get you?" Eric asked, gesturing towards the bar.

"I'm good. Maybe something with dinner."

He nodded in agreement, and we stood in comfortable silence for a moment before he spoke up.

"I haven't done this in a while," he said.

"What's that? Stand?" I quipped. Before he could respond, I added. "Yeah, me neither." He reached for my hand and squeezed it, and I squeezed back. For a second, it felt like we were the only two people in the room. We continued to stand there, holding hands and grinning at each other. A couple of minutes later, the buzzer went off. "That's us," I said, wishing we could remain in our little bubble for a bit longer.

We hustled up to the hostess stand and turned in our buzzer. Hand in hand, we followed the hostess towards the back of the restaurant. Seconds later, we sank into chairs facing each other at a tiny corner table.

"Your server will be right with you," she said and deposited two large menus in front of us. "The specials are listed inside. Enjoy your evening." Knees touching, we opened our menus.

The aforementioned specials list was front and center, so I checked them out first before diving into the extensive menu.

"I'm starved," I said as I read down the list. "Ooh…buffalo scallops? Could be amazing, yeah? I love to try new foods and I always order things I wouldn't make at home, which is actually a very long list." Eric asked if I liked to cook and I shook my head. "No, not really. It always seems like such a hassle for just one person, you know?" Eric nodded in agreement.

"I used to enjoy barbecuing burgers, ribs, fish. Then I started seeing Molly, and she was a vegetarian. Couldn't stand even the smell of meat or fish, so it was easier to do takeout. How many times can you grill eggplant or zucchini, I ask you?"

"What happened to Molly?" I asked as I folded my menu and placed it on the table, having decided the buffalo scallops and a side salad were in my immediate future. He shrugged.

"We grew apart, I guess. We wanted different things." He shook his head. "I love kids, really, I do. Spending time with Skipper and Sarah is the best. But I never saw myself as a dad. Too selfish, maybe? I don't know. I mean, right from the start, I told Molly I didn't want kids. She said she understood, that she didn't either. I thought we were happy. We were talking about getting married, buying a house."

"But things changed?" I guessed. "Turns out she did want children?" He nodded.

"At first it was little hints. One of her friends was pregnant or a co-worker was taking an extended maternity leave. I would just smile and say things like 'Oh, good for her,' but pretty quickly, it became a real issue between us."

"Can I take your order?" a young and very perky server asked as the busboy standing next to her filled our water glasses and deposited a basket of rolls on the table. We had already agreed to skip appetizers, so I ordered a sparkling water with my scallops and salad—oil and vinegar on the side—while Eric asked for a beer.

"I'll do the fisherman's platter," said Eric. "Fried, not broiled and extra cocktail sauce please." Turning to me, he asked, "You'll help me out with this, won't you?"

"You betcha," I said. The server gathered up the menus and left us, promising to get our orders right in.

"Alone at last," he said, and we smiled at each other. I still felt I needed closure on the baby issue.

"So ... that's what broke you and, um, Molly up then?" I asked. Eric stopped buttering a sourdough roll and nodded thoughtfully.

"Yeah, she was always so mad at me. Said I had wasted the best years of her life. Things dragged on for a couple of weeks, then I came home from a weekend visit with my brother and all of her stuff was gone. She had obviously been planning it for a while. No note. I called her but she wouldn't pick up, so I sent her a text saying I was sorry, but she never responded. That was a year ago." He said with a touch of wonder in his voice, "She's already married. Some guy from work. Their baby is due in four or five months."

"Wow," I said, nonplussed. "Well, good for her. I mean, she knew what she wanted, and she went for it." Eric nodded in agreement, chewing his bread and taking a sip of the beer that had just been placed in front of him. He swallowed before asking,

"What about you? Do you want kids?" His tone was casual, but his eyes revealed the importance of my answer. I shook my head.

"No, that ship has sailed," I said. "There was a time when I thought maybe, just maybe, but who am I kidding? I can't keep a plant alive. Can barely care for myself. And now with the show?" I took a sip of my water. "I'm hoping my dad's girlfriend's son has a baby soon, so my dad can be a grandfather. He would love that." Eric reached over and squeezed my hand. We smiled at each other; no further words were necessary.

Our meals arrived, and I turned all of my attention to the heaping pile of fresh scallops, glistening with a buffalo glaze and smelling better than anything I could imagine. We dove in; the only sounds for the next several minutes were from me as I moaned with pleasure after each bite.

"Try one," I encouraged Eric, who snagged a scallop and popped it in his mouth. He groaned happily. "So good, right?" He nodded, pushing his platter of fried seafood towards me.

"You promised you would help," he reminded me when I hesitated, so I helped myself to a couple of fried shrimp, dunking each in cocktail sauce before I ate them. We continued to enjoy our meals until I realized I had eaten my fill and couldn't take another bite.

"Enough," I announced as I pushed my plate away. Eric agreed, and we surveyed the amount of food left on our plates. "Doggie bags for sure," I said and just minutes later we were walking out to Eric's Jeep carrying a bag of still-warm seafood.

"Thank you for dinner," I said. "I am positively stuffed. I may never eat again."

"How about a walk on the beach to work off some of this food?" Eric suggested, and I agreed. We deposited the bag in the car and crossed the two-lane road to the beach. As we approached the sand, I slipped off my pumps and rolled up the bottoms of my jeans. Eric placed one of my shoes in each of his jacket pockets and we headed off hand-in-hand.

Despite my natural chattiness and inquisitive nature, I am better suited to asking the questions, not answering them. *Ergo*, my careers in law and now journalism. But tonight? I told Eric everything there was to tell about growing up, losing my beloved mother, my close relationships with Pop and Tracey, and finally, everything that had occurred in the three years since Becky went missing and how I lost it all.

Eric was a terrific listener. He nodded his understanding, squeezing my hand when he could hear the tears in my voice and occasionally murmuring sounds of encouragement or empathy. I ended by telling him Adam had fathered Becky's baby and it was only after hearing that did Eric let out a strangled expletive.

"Christ, what a douche-bag," he said. "That poor girl." I turned to face him. From the strategically placed streetlights and an almost full moon, I could see how upset he was. I leaned in and kissed him lightly on the lips.

"I agree with you. But all I can do right now is try to get a rapist off of the street. A killer rapist," I amended. "I can't waste any more energy on Adam or his firm. I just need to beat them in court." My tone was grim, but inside I felt a renewed sense of purpose. It had been a wild ride personally and professionally since all this began, and I was determined to put it all behind me with a conviction, followed by a huge cash settlement for Becky.

"And launch your TV show," Eric prompted me, and I nodded vigorously. Yeah, that too. I shivered suddenly, and Eric took off his jacket and slipped it over my shoulders.

"What a gentleman," I said, beaming at him. Eric's grin was contagious.

"If we're gonna get a little action in tonight, I can't have you freezing to death, can I?" I punched him playfully on the shoulder and we turned to walk back towards the lights of the restaurant.

***

Hours later, we devoured the leftovers while lounging comfortably in my bed. Guess I was wrong about not being able to eat again. Silly me!

CHAPTER 39

"You are a badass," I said to my reflection in the mirror. In the unforgiving fluorescent light of the New London District Courthouse second floor ladies' room, I looked tired and scared. And I was both. It was 8:00 a.m. on Thursday morning, the fourth day of the trial. *Voir dire* had gone relatively smoothly. The twelve jurors and two alternates had been chosen, and Rick had totally nailed his opening argument. He was somehow equally welcoming and intimidating, reflecting an attitude of 'if you're a law-abiding citizen, I will fight for you, but if you're a scumbag criminal, I will make you regret the day you were born.' I was proud to sit at the same table as him, making notes and jotting down my thoughts as he spoke.

Then it was lead defense attorney Andrea Barnes' turn. I had never met her while I dated Adam. In her seemingly identical collection of severe black suits, pulled back chignon, and stiletto heels, I thought she came across as cold and rather haughty, but it was the jury who mattered. The seven women and five men who would decide the fate of Terence T. Kane. Barnes had made a special point of telling the jury how her client had requested an expedited trial, that he wanted to clear his good name and get back to work and I had to stop myself from laughing out loud. As far as I could tell, the over-privileged little prick had never worked a day in his life. It was unclear if the defense would call him to testify. He was under no obligation to do so, but I made a note to remind Rick that if he had the chance, to ask just what sort of work Kane was planning to get back to. Nice try, Attorney Barnes.

I smoothed my hair, which was pulled back into a neat, low ponytail, and straightened the skirt of my navy suit. I had a powder blue shell under the jacket, and I could already feel myself sweating despite the near frigid temperature of the courthouse. "Badass," I whispered one last time, before I left the restroom and walked down the nearly empty hallway, my low heels click-clacking on the marble floor.

I was the first one in the courtroom and got settled at the table where Rick and I had spent the past several days. I sat facing the judge's bench but kept an eye on the entrance doors for Rick, the defense team, the press, and the expected gaggle of interested observers. I had been mostly silent all week, occasionally whispering something to Rick, but more often shoving my pad towards him with messages written in pen and circled for emphasis. Overall, we both felt the testimony elicited from the police and the ER staff had gone smoothly and would be viewed as credible and unbiased to the members of the jury. Despite the recurrent objections from the defense, that is.

But today it was my turn. I would call our next witness, Becky Lewis, so she could tell her story of being attacked by the defendant three years earlier. A story describing an assault that sounded exactly like the case that was being tried. The victim, a young woman, walking alone late at night. The attacker, a violent young man in a gray hoodie with icy blue eyes and a smirk pasted across his face. The recent victim's death, besides being sad and downright tragic, was ironically a plus for the defense. The account the witness had told the police before she died was not allowable in court as the defense could not cross-examine her (because the freaking defendant had killed her!!) but Rick had several strategies in mind to get the testimony heard by the jury. He told me he would watch for the right opportunity, then bam! I hoped he would find it, and soon.

Meanwhile, I would be the one leading Becky through her testimony. I expected Andrea would bark out her objections regularly and I reminded myself once again that it was not up to me to address her, but to wait for the judge to either sustain or overrule what she had to say. My job was to make Becky feel relaxed, valued, and respected. I had signed up for this three years ago and it was finally happening.

I sat quietly for several minutes, collecting my thoughts as the room filled and the low buzz of muted conversations grew louder. There was a palpable energy in the air, a level of excitement that was hard to define. It was something they never taught in law school, but I had never met a trial attorney who wasn't totally jazzed by those final quiet moments in the courtroom, as the judge and jury were seated right before the trial began. Rick slid into the chair next to me, a dour expression on his usually hard to read features. *Uh oh!*

"What's up? Is Becky a no-show?" I whispered. He signaled with his hand to silence me and I watched as he wrote on his pad, turning it so I could read his words. *Crap!*

She's here. Adam/Becky's baby is public knowledge. Defense wants to keep her off the stand. Woman scorned.

I read between the lines. They would try to argue that Becky was only testifying today to exact revenge on Adam, her former lover, after he cast her aside and married another woman. I scribbled furiously and shoved my pad under Rick's nose.

She was all set to testify 3 years ago, before she met Adam!!

Rick shrugged, and removing his eyeglasses, rubbed the bridge of his nose. It was going to be a long day. I watched the jury file in one by one and take their seats. Overall, I was pleased by the makeup of the jury. Not exactly a group of Kane's peers, *per se*, but they appeared to be a diverse group of open-minded individuals, mostly blue-collar workers or employees in the service sector as well as a couple of retired individuals. Two were school teachers, one was a new mother of a baby girl. I hoped they, in particular, would be sympathetic to the deceased victim and Becky, and not judge them or believe either of them was 'just asking for trouble' by walking alone at night.

The side door opened, and I watched Kane enter the courtroom, sandwiched between two guards. He was wearing a navy suit, expertly fitted, and a pair of horn-rimmed glasses that hid the glare of his ice-blue eyes. Smooth move, I thought, and scribbled a note to Rick.

Get those glasses off him!

Rick glanced at it and nodded. There had to be a way for the jurors to see what Kane's victims had experienced.

A hush fell over the courtroom as Hannah P. Stevens, the judge we had drawn for the case, swept into the room. A long, tall candlestick of a woman with a mane of fiery red hair made even more shocking by her matte black robe. She was mid-forties, fairly new to the court and had already developed a reputation as a straightforward, no-nonsense judge who frowned upon any type of theatrics or excessive drama in her courtroom. From the little I could tell from her rulings and comments to date, I felt we had drawn an excellent judge and Rick had seemed pleased when he had announced last week that she would oversee the case. I watched her as she sat and cleared her throat. We were about to begin: court was now in session.

***

After the opening drone of the guard and the judge's briefly worded instructions to the jury, I made my way to the center of the room. Nodding briefly to Judge Stevens, I introduced myself and addressed the jury.

"Earlier this week, you heard the defense tell you the defendant has a near spotless record with strong ties to the community. While it is true that the defendant has not served jail time, prior to his most recent arrest, he was charged with—"

"Objection, Your Honor. Mr. Kane's previous brush with the law is not relevant to the proceedings today," Andrea announced. "And furthermore—"

"I am trying to provide valuable context, Your Honor. In order to introduce my next witness, it is critical that the jury—"

"Overruled," the judge snapped. "I will decide what is relevant and what is not," she announced crisply. "You may proceed, Ms. Quinn, but please keep your focus on today's proceedings." I kept my expression neutral as I nodded again to the judge, resisting the urge to smirk at Andrea.

"Thank you, Your Honor. As I was saying, the defendant in this case has been previously charged with an attack very similar to the one he is currently facing charges on. We have a witness from that case with us, and she is prepared to recount her story to you today. The State calls Ms. Becky Lewis to the stand." I held my breath and turned to watch as the doors opened and the tiny figure of my long-lost witness entered the room and approached the bench. She was dressed simply in a lightweight dress and a cardigan sweater, both on loan from Sarah Hansen. After she was sworn in, I walked over to Becky. I would have liked to squeeze her hand in a show of solidarity, but had to settle for greeting her with a warm smile.

"Good morning, Becky," I began. "As you know, I am working with State's Attorney Richard Cooper on this case and on behalf of the State, I welcome you—"

"Objection, Your Honor," the defense attorney called out. The Judge looked a bit put out by the interruption.

"What is it this time, Ms. Barnes?" she asked, a hint of annoyance in her clipped words.

"The defense objects to this witness, Your Honor," said Barnes somewhat apologetically. "This witness is not relevant to the case. She has no knowledge directly related to these current charges against Mr. Kane."

"That is not true, Your Honor," I interjected. "This witness is well acquainted with the defendant and his pattern of behavior," I added with just a touch of emphasis on the word behavior.

"Overruled," announced the judge. "Your concerns will be duly noted, Ms. Barnes, but please, let's get back to the testimony that Ms. Quinn is trying to elicit from this witness." I smiled at both women, attempting to appear both wise and very patient.

"Thank you, Your Honor. As I was saying, welcome to the proceedings, Ms. Lewis. How are you enjoying your visit so far?" I quipped, eliciting frowns from Rick, the judge, and Andrea Barnes and a smile from Becky. She was used to my sarcasm, and it seemed to relax her a bit.

"It's been just fine, Miss Quinn. Thank you," she said with a butter-wouldn't-melt expression on her pretty face. I smiled back at her.

"Ms. Lewis, can you tell us about the first time you had the occasion to meet the defendant?" I asked.

Becky leaned forward and spoke directly into the microphone. "Certainly, Miss Quinn. It was on the night of May 5, 2018. It was warm for early May."

"And how do you remember those details so clearly, Ms. Lewis?" I asked.

"I will never forget anything about that night," replied Becky. "It was the night that Terry Kane viciously attacked me and tried to rape me," she said and sat back in her chair, looking both victorious and relieved to have voiced her accusation. I could have kissed her. Barnes leapt from her seat.

"Objection, Your Honor. I need to state most emphatically that the incident—"

"Goes to pattern of behavior," I interjected smoothly, right before the judge overruled the objection. Barnes couldn't control her response.

"This witness is biased against the defense team in this case," Barnes said. "We have it on good authority that—"

"Which is it, Ms. Barnes?" I asked sweetly, a confused look on my face. "Are you objecting to my witness because you believe her testimony is not germane to the case or because she is prejudiced against you and your firm? I'm confused," I said, a split second before the judge gave her gavel a resounding thud and practically bellowed, silencing the titters in response to my last statement.

"Counselors, approach the bench," Judge Stevens ordered, and I scampered towards her. Andrea trailed slightly behind me, no doubt aware that if there was to be a dressing down by the judge, it was likely she would get the lion's share. But Judge Stevens was balanced in her commentary. She told us both, in no uncertain terms, we were to quit the theatrics and only address the court, not each other. That last bit was meant more for me, I knew, and I nodded, before casting my eyes penitently downward. Addressing Andrea, the judge assured her she could examine the witness's motive during cross-examination, "should we actually get to that stage in this lifetime." Convinced that we were properly chastened, she asked us to return to our places, and I once again approached Becky and apologized for the delay.

I asked her to walk me through what had occurred that evening. With very little prompting from me, Becky described how she had been walking to a friend's house when she was grabbed from behind and pulled into the bushes. Her eyes wide, she shared how her assailant had ripped her shirt, grabbed her around the neck and forced his leg between hers to restrain her. She described her attacker clearly, describing his height and build, the color of his hair and the way she panicked the first time she made eye contact with him. As she stared into the bottomless pit of his cold blue eyes, she said that she realized she had to escape this man or die trying.

"I knew I was looking into the eyes of a killer," she said, and I frowned slightly. We had never discussed that, and I felt it lessened the impact of her testimony up until this point. I needed her to stick to the truth as I could not suborn perjury by allowing Becky to lie under oath. I looked over at the defense table and noted Becky had succeeded in getting Kane to remove his glasses. They lay on the table in front of him as he glared openly at Becky. His attorney nudged him and pointed to his glasses, but he pulled away and hissed at her. "Why don't you object?" he said loudly enough for half the courtroom to hear. "Get that lying bitch to shut the hell up!" Way to go, Becky, I thought. After the judge called for silence in the courtroom, I continued.

"Let's get back to that night, Ms. Lewis," I encouraged her with a look, intending to convey that she needed to stay on point. I have witnessed too many cases falter when a witness improvises their testimony, embellishing it for dramatic effect. "Tell me what was happening after you made eye contact with the accused."

Becky nodded in agreement and went back to recounting the facts of that evening. After ripping her shirt and backing her up against the wall, Kane had removed his grip around her neck. He had put his right hand over her mouth to silence her and with his left hand, he had tugged at the zipper of his jeans, all the while staring at her, "with that ice cold look of his," she said and shuddered. I glanced over at Kane and noted he was still openly glaring at her, his body rigid and his fists clenched. I let her last comment settle with the jury for an instant before I asked her to go on. She said she had continued to struggle when there had been a sudden sound like a car backfiring and just for a split second, Kane's attention was not entirely focused on her.

"I saw my chance, and I took it. I bit his hand, and I kneed him in the ba—um, privates. His, er, groin. He let go of me and doubled over. I took off running, and I didn't stop until I got to my friend Mandy's. I got away from him," she said, sitting up straight and beaming at me. "I got away from him."

I smiled at her, my friend who had been through so much in her young life. But now here she was, doing her civic duty and helping me to put away this monster.

"You did the only thing you needed to do that night, Becky." At her quizzical look, I leaned forward. "You survived," I said in a whisper loud enough to be heard by those in the balcony. But I had one more point to make before I would give up my place directly in front of her.

"You said you ran directly to your friend Mandy's. Why didn't you go to the police?" I asked. "You were brutally attacked. Why not report it to the police?" Becky's face contorted, and I thought she might cry. *We've discussed this, Becky. Remember how I told you it would be better if the question was asked by me, not the defense?* "Becky?" I added. She squeezed her eyes shut for a split second before sitting up even straighter in the chair that literally dwarfed her slight frame.

"I was afraid for my life, Miss Quinn. I didn't know that part of town. The only thing I knew was where Mandy lived and I just ran and ran till I got there." She sat back, exhausted from her ordeal. I would ask Rick to call a quick recess in order to give her a chance to collect herself before Andrea had her way with her. I hoped I could argue 'asked and answered' if the defense tried to delve further into what had happened after Becky ran away that night. I was fairly certain that I was the only one in the room who knew how she had smoked crystal meth and partied with Mandy and her friends well into the wee hours of the morning before crashing for twelve hours.

"Thank you, Ms. Lewis. The State appreciates how difficult today has been for you. No further questions." I said as I turned and gave Rick a look that I hoped he would interpret correctly, and he did.

"I call for a quick recess to confer with co-counsel, Your Honor," he called out, and it was granted. I sank into my chair for just a moment. Becky approached me and I squeezed her hand. I wanted to hug her, but I settled for a smile.

"You done good, kid."

CHAPTER 40

I held my breath as I watched the defense attorney approach Becky. It was like witnessing a wolf about to attack a baby fawn. I could tell Becky was scared, but I thought if she could survive what would undoubtedly be an initial barrage of questions designed to confuse and intimidate her, she would be fine. We had practiced several times with me posing the questions Barnes would no doubt ask. The impact of Becky's drug use and history of soliciting would pale in comparison with the grenade that would explode when it was revealed that Becky had a child with the defense attorney originally assigned to the case. C'mon Becky, I thought. You can do this.

Barnes greeted Becky cordially and introduced herself before diving in. "Miss Lewis, and it is Miss Lewis, am I right? You are single, unmarried. Is that correct?" It was a reasonable question, and I did not object, knowing there would be plenty of opportunities to do so. Pick your battles, I told myself. Becky nodded her assent and Barnes pounced.

"I need your verbal response, Miss Lewis. You are here of your own free will, are you not?" Okay, time to jump in.

"Objection, Your Honor. Miss Barnes is badgering my witness," I said. Before Barnes could respond, the judge made her ruling.

"The witness will answer the original question on her marital status and then you need to move on, Ms. Barnes."

"Yes, of course," Barnes said, and Becky leaned forward.

"Yes, I am single and yes, I am here of my own free will." Barnes ignored that last part and continued along, smooth and confident.

"You have a remarkable memory, Miss Lewis. Your account of what happened on that night three years ago is quite detailed, vivid even. I would like to back up a bit. You say that you met the defendant on the evening of May 5, 2018. What time was that encounter?" Becky's brow creased in confusion as she tried to recall.

"I'm not sure. Maybe around ten or eleven?" Becky responded in a tone lacking any shred of confidence. I was waiting for Barnes to respond, 'Are you asking me or telling me?'.

"I would think you would recall an important detail like this about the evening that was so traumatic for you." Barnes saw me start to object when she hurried on. "Well, let's just agree it was late in the evening, shall we? Let me ask a follow-up question. Where were you going that evening? Walking alone late at night? What was the reason?" I jumped up with my objection.

"Next thing you know, the defense will shame my witness for having the audacity to walk to a friend's house," I said. "Will her next question be 'what were you wearing?'" I asked with a smirk.

"Objection sustained," said the judge. "The witness may answer the question as to her destination that evening, but her attire will not be subject to questioning." I breathed a sigh of relief. I recalled Becky had told me she had been wearing a tank top and a short skirt that evening and a pair of Chucks. No bra. Uncertain as to panties. We had just dodged a bullet, I realized.

"I was going to my friend Mandy's," Becky said and Barnes nodded.

"Well, if I recall, the evening in question was a Tuesday. Kind of late to be out on a school night," she quipped. Becky looked confused again.

"Um, I wasn't in school," she said and Barnes frowned.

"But it was May, and you were only seventeen years old. Why wouldn't you have been a student?" she asked, a mixture of innocence and concern marring her features.

"I was almost eighteen," Becky said. "And I had dropped out of high school a year earlier," she added with a touch of defiance. I swallowed hard. *Damn.* I had not prepared Becky for the topic of her education, instead focusing on the attack and how she had been tricked into leaving town before she could testify. I objected, and the judge overruled Barnes' question.

"Please stick to the facts in evidence, Miss Barnes," she admonished her. "What the witness was wearing and what her educational status and what she ate for dinner are not relevant." Barnes flushed and nodded meekly.

"Of course, Your Honor." Turning back to Becky, she continued. "Please walk us through the events of the evening, Miss Lewis," and I sat back, breathing a sigh of relief. We were back on solid ground and I knew Becky had this down cold. Becky shared how Kane had grabbed her and pulled her into the bushes bordering the entrance to a park, before Barnes objected.

"Allegedly," she corrected Becky, who looked confused.

"I don't know what—"

"What allegedly means?"

"No, I mean, you want me to tell you what happened and I am trying to do that, but I'm telling the truth. It's what happened. There is nothing alleged about it." Barnes backtracked.

"My client Terence Kane has not been found guilty of these charges, so please keep his name out of your story. As of that evening, your assailant was unknown to you." Becky shook her head but continued with the details of the attack and how she escaped.

"And if it pleases the court, can you explain again why, after such a brutal attack, you did not go to the police for help?" asked Barnes.

"Objection. Already asked and answered," I said. "The witness was not obligated to report the incident to the authorities." The judge agreed and told Barnes to move it along.

"I understand, Miss Lewis. You were on your way to a party, isn't that right?" Before Becky could respond, Barnes continued.

"A party where drugs and alcohol were available. How long have you been addicted to drugs, Miss Lewis?" I exploded with my objection and before the judge could rule, Barnes said, "Goes to the character and reliability of the witness, Your Honor." Barnes shrugged. "She was recently arrested for drug possession, so I feel it's relevant.

"The jury will disregard this line of questioning," the judge said, but the damage had been done. I could see it in the jury's downcast eyes or outright glares. To them, Becky was no longer a victim, but a high school dropout who abused drugs, made questionable decisions and exercised poor judgement. Next to her, Kane looked like a choirboy or a member of his own defense team. He grinned widely before quickly covering his mouth with his hand. He had been coached and coached well. I looked back at Becky, silently willing her to stay strong. She looked positively miserable, and I had a bad feeling about where this line of questioning would go.

"Okay, Miss Lewis, we'll put aside any references to your issues with drugs and alcohol for the time being. Can you please tell the court why, after three years, you are just now appearing to testify in court? What happened three years ago when you were initially expected to testify?" Becky cleared her throat and sat up straight. This was a risky move by the defense as it opened the door for additional cross-examination of Kane's previous arrest. But I had thought it was likely, and we had discussed this. I hoped Becky would recall how I had encouraged her to respond. Becky's voice was strong and clear.

"Three years ago, I was prepared to testify about how Terry Kane had assaulted and tried to rape me. The night before I was to appear in court, a member of your defense team approached me. He told me he was engaged to the Assistant State's Attorney Miss Quinn, and that she feared for my safety. He put me on a bus to Portland, Maine, gave me money and a phone and told me to lie low until the danger had passed. He lied to me and tricked me into leaving town." There were more than a few gasps of surprise and now the jury appeared to be scrutinizing the male members of the defense team, apparently trying to identify the lawyer in question.

"That is quite a story, Miss Lewis," said Barnes with a shake of her head. "Can you identify this man who convinced you to leave town?"

"Yes, of course. It was Adam Baxter. He is also the father of my little boy, Jesse." This time, there were even more gasps and looks of shock and surprise. Barnes appeared shocked that Becky would offer such a juicy tidbit of information, but I had encouraged this revelation. In my experience, bombshells like this could be managed by controlling the narrative and its timing. Barnes recovered quickly.

"So Miss Lewis, are you saying you are testifying today to get back at SH&F for employing Mr. Baxter?"

"That is a ridiculous question, Ms. Barnes," said Becky, with a level of moxie that made even Rick blink in surprise. "And the answer is no. I was ready to testify in Terry Kane's previous rape case long before I even met Mr. Baxter. And besides, your firm fired his ass and had him sent to jail, so what is your point exactly?" The judge admonished Becky for her language choices and Becky apologized before Barnes continued.

"But you are aware Mr. Baxter is no longer engaged to Miss Quinn and that he is happily married to ... " I objected to the use of the term 'happily' and the judge overruled Barnes, but she continued unfazed.

"I stand corrected. Adam Baxter is married to a paralegal named Kimberly, although the exact emotional status of their union is unclear. Were you aware of that?" Becky nodded before being reminded to respond verbally.

"Yes, I knew that. But when we were together, Adam was neither engaged nor married. I would like to make that clear to the court." Becky sat back with a satisfied look on her face and I swallowed hard, trying to hide my surprise at the way Becky categorized her relationship with Adam. 'When we were together' made it sound like a long-term relationship instead of a brief hookup. I saw Barnes cast a look at me with a smirk obscuring her normally rigid expression.

"Can you describe the nature of your relationship with Mr. Baxter?" she asked. I objected, but was overruled and Becky was directed to answer the question.

"We were both single, and we enjoyed each other's company," she said a tad defensively. "I was lonely up in Maine. I didn't know anybody but the busboys and kitchen staff in the restaurant where I got a job, so it was nice to see Adam whenever he came to visit. He always stayed in a nice hotel and I would stay with him. We would order room service and well, you know ... " she said with a blush. Feeling flushed and suddenly anxious, I busied myself scribbling something illegible on my pad. I did not like where this line of questioning was going. I had assumed the physical relationship between them had only lasted a few days. Was Becky lying to make it sound like more of an actual relationship?

"Since you had a baby together, I'm sure we all know what you are referring to, Miss Lewis. No worries. And what was Mr. Baxter's reaction when you told him he was going to be a father?" Becky frowned and wouldn't meet her eyes.

"Um, he didn't really say," she admitted. "But he sent me money for an abortion." Barnes let out a loud tsk of disapproval before continuing.

"So even though your married lover deserted you and wanted you to terminate your pregnancy, you're telling this court you bear him no ill will and that you are not testifying today to get back at him?" Becky's eyes flashed with anger.

"When I knew Adam, he was single. I chose to have Jesse on my own without his help. I was prepared to testify against that rapist three years ago and if I had, he would not have murdered Jennifer Ramos." She pointed at Kane, who was now openly glaring at her. "He raped Chelsea. He tried to rape me and he raped and killed Jennifer. Who knows how many other women he has attacked or even killed?" As his attorney shouted her objection and the judge pounded her gavel and called for order in response to the clamor from the spectators, Kane burst out of his chair before the guards could contain him. Teeth bared and looking ready to attack, he shouted at Becky, practically spitting out an angry tirade.

"You little bitch. If I had wanted you that night, I would have had you. Why would I want to get with some skanky slut like you? I can have any woman I want. You did me a favor by kneeing me in the nuts." The guards had now grabbed him and were restraining him, but despite their best efforts, his lawyers had no luck at keeping him quiet. "You liked it rough," he sneered. "Same as that slut O'Hara and the Ramos broad, too. You're all the same, you fucking teases. Why can't you just relax and shut the fuck up? I only hit her till she finally shut the hell up." He flung his eyeglasses across the room and glared at the jury, his ice-cold blue eyes blazing with anger.

"Goddamn bitches. Why won't you all just shut up?"

CHAPTER 41

The courtroom was pure pandemonium after that. Kane was shackled and removed from the room while his defense attorneys spoke amongst themselves in hushed whispers. I could only imagine the sort of dressing down the entire team would receive when they returned to their office. Been there, done that, I thought. The judge tried unsuccessfully to quiet the room and finally admitted defeat. The jurors were thanked for their service and excused.

As spectators turned to leave and the members of the press raced off to phone in the latest developments, Becky came over to hug me. Tears in her eyes, she whispered,

"We did it, Randi. We did it," and I squeezed her tight.

"I am so proud of you. You were a superstar up there." She beamed at me, glowing with pride.

"I don't even know how to thank you for helping me to get my life back," she said.

"Wait till we sue those asshats and get you what you deserve," I said, and her smile grew even wider.

Rick shook hands with me and gathered up his files, stuffing them into his already full briefcase. He thanked us both and told me that as Kane had essentially admitted guilt in the charges against him; the next phase would be sentencing, a process I was not needed for.

My service to the State of Connecticut was complete.

"Thank you for including me, Rick. Working with you has been ... " I was about to say terrific, but went with rewarding instead. He raised an eyebrow, and I could see the gleam in his eyes behind his oversized glasses.

"Good luck Ms. Lewis," he said and turned to leave. "Knock 'em dead, counselor."

Becky and I turned and, arm in arm, walked toward the exit. I knew the press would be waiting on the courthouse steps for a comment from me, but I wanted to allow Rick his own well-deserved time in the spotlight first. I spotted Eric and he beamed at me. He had taken the day off to be in the courtroom again today, and I was so happy to see him. Standing next to him were Pop and Skip Hansen. I flashed them a V for victory, and then I saw Sally enter the room, struggling against the exiting throng of onlookers. She was holding a sleeping Jesse Lewis in her arms. Tracey had agreed to watch Jesse the last several days, with Sally providing transport back and forth. Becky rushed over and squealed with delight as she scooped him up.

"Proud of my girl," Pop said, and I burrowed into his arms. Eric squeezed my hand, and I felt myself relax. Winning a case like this produced a rush of adrenaline that warmed me to my core. I was elated. Becky had her day in court, I had redeemed myself with Rick, and Kane would spend the rest of his miserable life in prison courtesy of the State of Connecticut.

There was so much to celebrate!

***

I sent a quick text to Brian as I headed to my car. **We won! Talk tomorrow.**

Starting tomorrow, I was free to continue with the preparations needed to launch *Miranda Writes*, but tonight? I wanted to enjoy the win, surrounded by my family and close friends. After I rushed home to change into comfortable clothes not drenched in flop sweat, we all met up at Brennan's for happy hour. Pop and Eric, who had apparently become fast friends during the trial, commandeered an enormous table in the corner which was soon overflowing with an assortment of appetizers and pitchers of beer, delivered by Tracey and Sally. Skip had begged off, offering to drive Becky and Jesse home, but John and Tricia Hansen joined us, as did Dale, who crushed me with one of his bear hugs, leaving me breathless. I ended up happily squeezed into a corner between Tracey and Eric, basking in the glow of a job well done. There were toasts and many well wishes and congratulations. Hours later, the rest of the bar crowd had thinned out, but the Quinn party showed little sign of stopping.

"How're you holding up?" Eric asked. "Anytime you want to bail, just say the word." I looked around at the flushed faces of the revelers and guessed everyone had been drinking heavily. I had barely sipped at my first glass of wine and I knew Eric had switched to club soda earlier in the evening.

"Give it a half hour," I said. "I'll drive Pop and Sally. You take your family home and we'll call an Uber for Tracey and Dale. Then we'll meet at my place. Sound good?" He agreed, and an hour later, Eric and I were relaxing on my couch. REM's "Night Swimming" was playing on my iPod and I could not recall ever feeling so happy.

"God, you were incredible in there," said Eric. "I got the chance to experience Quinn for the Win firsthand."

"Do you think you can handle another firsthand experience?" I asked, and he kissed me, pulled me up off the couch, and led me to the bedroom.

I would just like to state for the record that I had no objection.

CHAPTER 42

After four long days in court and an incredible night in bed with Eric, I had a hard time getting going the next morning. He had left me with a kiss and a promise to call me that night. He had to return to his job and life in New Rochelle, and I needed to get back into my own reality. I had promised to meet Skip and Sarah for a combination staff meeting and team-building luncheon at the harbor at noon, so I wandered into the kitchen to find Eric had prepped a pot of coffee for me with a note to 'press here'. I did as I was instructed and trundled off to the shower, thinking about the topics I wanted to cover at lunch. I needed the Hansen kids to understand just how much I would need their help on the blog and podcast, since I knew I would need to spend a lot of time in New York going forward.

While my coffee was brewing, I scrolled through my phone. *Oh joy!* News of Kane's conviction was trending, but was running a close second behind the big news; how my ex-boyfriend and my missing witness had engaged in a yearlong affair and had a child together. This was going to go over like a lead balloon with the Sterling Broadcast Group. Perhaps I would not be spending much time in the city after all…

After properly caffeinating, I dressed hurriedly and ran out to my rented minivan. Was finding me a new car a reasonable job duty for my staff? God knows I didn't have the time to do it. As I drove, I called Brian, who answered the phone on the first ring.

"Congratulations," he said. I thanked him and he hurried on. "I am sending you a list of all the network affiliates. Familiarize yourself with the call letters and cities. They need you to go in and record a bunch of customized promos right away. It's probably too late today, but maybe Monday? Text your arrival time to Robin and let her know when to set you up in the studio. Wear something ... I don't know. Maybe ask her what she thinks," he added.

I wanted to tell Brian I could dress myself, that I wasn't prepared to head into the city on Monday and record promos, and that the only thing on my mind was whether the soup *du jour* at Nemo's would be shrimp and corn chowder, and if so, should I forgo my usual bowl of lobster bisque? I wanted to tell him I would rather spend the day in the dingy public access studio working on my podcast with Skip or in a coffee shop with Sarah coming up with social media content and a schedule of topics for my blog. But I couldn't tell him any of that.

"You betcha," I said, pulling into a parking spot. "Um, I hate to be the one to bring it up, but the press ... "

"Yeah, yeah. We're all over it. The baby daddy story was the topic of my first three calls from Sterling this morning."

"Sorry Brian. It'll die down soon, I'm sure. But right now, I gotta go. Meeting with my team to go over plans for my blog and the podcasts." Silence followed and for a second, I thought I had lost him.

"You mean plans to shut them down," said Brian. *Shut them down?*

"What are you talking about?" I asked.

"You signed an exclusive with the network. I thought you knew that. They own *Miranda Writes* and they want to concentrate on the show. So should you." I sat in shocked silence, not believing what I had heard, the lump in my throat rendering speech impossible. "Randi? Are you there? Say something," Brian said. I swallowed hard and tried to talk.

"It's just ... are you absolutely sure? Do I really have to give up my blog and the podcast?" He assured me I did, and I told him I would talk to him later. The thought of losing everything I had worked so hard to build was overwhelming. Did I care more about them than the show? Maybe I did. I wanted nothing more than to go home and pull the covers over my head. But I had two hard-working teenagers waiting inside for me. I locked my car and trudged towards the entrance of Nemo's Seafood, trying to psych myself up for what I had hoped would be an enjoyable meal with my staff.

Somehow, I got through our lunch and if either Skip or Sarah noticed that I barely spoke and only halfheartedly picked at my bowl of chowder and the cheddar bay biscuit on my plate; they didn't say a word. They were upbeat and lively and both had hearty appetites for their blackened cod tacos and glistening bowls of shrimp cocktail, as well as boundless enthusiasm for their job duties. Skip was lobbying for new equipment, which he said would revolutionize the sound quality of our podcasts, and Sarah marveled aloud about all the promos she envisioned executing.

"We could give tickets to your show tapings as prizes," she said, her eye shining. "That would be epic for cross-promotion and really strengthen your brand." I swallowed the bile that rose in my throat and put down my spoon. I suggested Skip send me the quotes for the equipment and that Sarah put together a social media calendar for me to review and begged off with a headache. I gave them my personal credit card and told them to stay, have fun and have some key lime pie for dessert.

Then I walked out, got in my car and cried all the way home.

CHAPTER 43

I slogged through the next couple of days as if I were on auto-pilot. I responded to calls from the SBG production team, which had seemed to double in size in the past week. Plans were made, deadlines were established, and we were officially in go mode. I agreed to everything, but the lump in my throat did not go away nor did the gaping hole in my heart. Nothing was said about my blog or podcast and I did not raise the subject either. That first afternoon, following on the heels of my less than motivating team-building lunch, I had dug out the contract I had signed just four weeks earlier. It didn't take long to find the language Brian had referred to. How the network owned *Miranda Writes*, had an exclusive to anything and everything I created. I had gone and signed away all of my rights for the duration of the agreement. The irony that I was a practicing attorney was not lost on me. That's the advice most commonly given when one is presented with a contract: to review it with an attorney prior to signing. Had I believed I was somehow immune? That I was safe from any sort of legal entanglements because I had gone to law school? I had been so caught up in my newfound fame, I had neglected to protect myself. That quote about having a fool for a client when you represent yourself came to mind.

I was a fool!

I had truly been naïve enough to think the network would allow me to divide my attention like that. I saw the three products as parts to a whole and believed in the concept of synergy, that the whole was greater than the sum of the parts. See that, Mr. Salvi? I was listening in tenth grade biology class after all. Why couldn't I have all three? If I was willing to put in the time and energy to regularly update my blog, produce a weekly podcast and tape daily versions of *Miranda Writes*, who was the network to tell me I couldn't? It was a rhetorical question, though I still felt it begged to be asked.

Besides figuring out how to cut ties with my blog and podcast, I needed to see what I could do to get Becky the compensation she deserved from the defense attorneys who had manipulated her and caused her to lose a whole week with her precious son. It was another addition to my plate while SBG ramped up my to-do list, and I couldn't help but feel all this was far from over.

I longed to talk about this latest development with someone I trusted. Someone who could help me to make sense of this new reality, and to deal with the fallout that would result from my further involvement with Becky. I had a kernel of an idea, the beginnings of a plan to work all of this out, but I always performed at my best when I could hash things out with someone else. I felt Brian would be sympathetic, but I knew he would urge me to be cautious and break ties with anything not related to the show. Tracey would understand and as my friend and a small business owner herself, she would no doubt rally against the power of the giant media conglomerate who was trying to control my business interests, as well as the big bad law firm for trampling over Becky's civil liberties. But other than tea and sympathy, there was not a lot she could really offer me. Ditto with Pop. Eric was terrific, but this relationship of ours was in its early stages; there was no way he could fully understand what all of this meant to me.

Strangely, my next thought was of Adam Baxter. Could he help me, despite his many misdeeds? He had successfully conspired to ruin my career in order to guarantee his rise to partner status, had seduced Becky and knocked her up, married a perky paralegal and was now out on bail. He would probably serve time for witness tampering, at the very least. But Adam was probably the smartest lawyer I had ever known, his crimes and misdemeanors of the past three years notwithstanding. He possessed the brainpower, drive and tenacity to take on a case and see it through to the end. What a waste of talent to get caught up in a push to become a partner!

I would call him and ask him to meet me somewhere out of the way. No members of the press, no colleagues, no interruptions. I would get him alone, share my plan, and ask him to play devil's advocate. I grabbed my phone, holding my breath as I waited for him to answer.

***

"I would have thought I'd be the last person you would ever want to talk to," Adam said as he slid into the booth across from me. I had been perusing the dogeared menu for the past fifteen minutes by that point.

"You're late," I said, and he checked his watch.

"Like five minutes maybe. What the hell? You call me yesterday, tell me it's urgent and that I have to drive to Rhode Island to meet you?"

"It's okay," I said. "I appreciate your coming out like this."

"I'm sorry. I had to stop for gas and it took me ... " I shook my head at him.

"Didn't Pop teach you anything? Never let your gas tank drop below a quarter full." It had been drummed into me since the day I got my driver's license. Something about possibly needing to get somewhere fast. Adam grinned, that same grin that always did me in. Not today.

"How is your dad?" he asked. "I miss him."

"He hates your guts, that's how he is," I said. "It was all I could do to stop him from going to your house to kick your ass. Oh, sorry. I meant you and your wife's house, silly me."

"You left me, Ran. You moved out and never gave me the chance to tell you my side of the story." I groaned in protest. We were wasting valuable time. I needed us to get past this. I had to get Adam to help me. He was the only person I knew I could count on right now. I forced a grin and pushed the menu towards him.

"Water under the bridge. I promised to buy you lunch so let's order, huh? Although, if memory serves, you'll want a patty melt medium rare on marble rye. How'd I do?" Adam returned my grin.

"Not bad," he said. "But I'm the easy one. You're the one who asks for something on the menu and turns it into something *not* on the menu. How'd I do, Sally?" he asked, and my cold, frozen heart melted just a tad. *When Harry Met Sally* was my all-time favorite film and that diner scene always had me in stitches. I pretended to discount what he said and turned to the server who had just joined us, pad and pencil in hand.

"I'll have the chef salad with oil and vinegar on the side." I started to say, 'with no onions and no ham, but double the turkey' but I stopped myself. From the smirk on my lunch companion's face, it was exactly what he was waiting for. "And a Diet Coke with lime, not lemon—or whatever," I quickly amended. "Lemon, lime, whatever you have back there is fine." I sat back and waited while Adam ordered, then I leaned forward as the server made her way to the next table.

"I need your help, and you're the only person I know who can make this happen. And besides, you owe me and you're probably already going to jail anyway, so what's one more tiny infraction, anyway?" Adam looked surprised that his straight arrow ex was looking to do something possibly illegal, or at least unethical. Then he leaned forward, eyes narrowed, and spoke in a conspiratorial whisper.

"What do you need me to do?" he asked.

So, I told him.

CHAPTER 44

With a renewed sense of purpose, I threw myself back into my work over the next several days. I went into the city for a couple of meetings with the network, which honestly could have been handled over the phone or on Skype, but I was a team player, was I not, and certainly not immune to the lure of an elegant lunch at a four-star restaurant. During my long train rides, I composed several blog posts to be published later in the month. Issues related to medical malpractice have always been fascinating to me and they almost wrote themselves.

Skip and I recorded this week's podcast, and he offered to pull together a 'best of' compilation tape for next week's show. Self-serving and a tad lazy, I'll give you that, but I honestly felt I had no choice. It was just one week and I could only guess that the shit was about to hit the proverbial fan. Or at least that was the rationalization I was going to stick with.

I had dinner at Brennan's with Pop and Sally and watched *The Bachelor* with Tracey. I also talked to Eric most nights, often for an hour or more, before I fell asleep. He, too, was busy with work, and we made plans to get together the following weekend to celebrate my birthday. There was so much I wanted to tell everyone, but I kept silent while I listened to more of what they had to say for a change.

Pop and Sally were planning a couple of midweek getaways up north to check out the fall foliage and had purchased a pasta maker together. Early attempts were less than successful, but they swore they would make a pasta meal we would all enjoy when we watched the pilot episode of *Miranda Writes* together.

Tracey's twins were becoming interested in girls and Tracey freaked when she found a very explicit note in the pocket of Logan's jeans before tossing them in the wash. Apparently, a ninth grader named Alisha was interested in hooking up with him and further, her parents were going to be returning home late the next couple of nights. My unsolicited advice was that both she and Dale needed to talk with both boys about respecting girls and to stress the need for condoms. I also suggested she tell the boys to do their own freakin' laundry as they were fourteen ferchrissakes and if they were mature enough to be thinking about sex, they were old enough to wash their own clothes. Problem solved. Tracey suggested I stick to giving legal advice going forward, and we agreed to disagree.

Eric was busy with several big jobs his company was handling, but he told me he was looking forward to taking some time off during the winter and suggested we get away somewhere warm. I told him it sounded wonderful. Sun, surf, sand and sex, lots of sex!

If any of them noticed how anxious I was, they would have probably attributed it to the show. The taping for the pilot was set for two weeks from now. I had been unusually complacent when the final roster of guests was lined up, none of whom had been on my dream guest list, but I was biding my time, picking my battles, yada, yada, yada. I had bigger fish to fry.

The news that Kane had been found guilty of all charges and sentenced to life in prison with no chance of parole was not exactly a surprise, but Becky, Jesse and I celebrated with hot fudge sundaes, anyway.

***

The following Monday, I filed a multimillion dollar lawsuit in New London District Court on behalf of my client Rebecca Lewis, who was seeking damages from the law firm of Schleyer, Houghton & Fogarty as well as named partner John Houghton. The suit claimed they had conspired to pressure her into not testifying against their client Terence T. Kane in two different cases, thereby preventing her from exercising her legal rights and causing her to be arrested and detained on trumped-up charges and to temporarily lose custody of her minor child. Our suit was especially robust as Adam had agreed to testify against his former employers in exchange for immunity and the State's dropping the charges against him. Rick had been agreeable to do anything he could to help Becky's case, as her testimony had been the last straw in Kane's shaky defense. Pending a reasonable outcome from the lawsuit, Becky agreed to not go after Adam for child support, which was good news for Adam. Facing certain disbarment, he and his wife were planning to move to Vermont, where his father-in-law had set him up with a supervisory position at the local Lowe's home improvement store. I spoke to him briefly the other day, and he sounded relieved he was being given a fresh start. I wished him well; what else could I do?

Despite an active arrest warrant, Eddie DaSilva had disappeared. Rachel and Becky were talking again and looking for a place to live together where Rachel could continue to work while Becky would stay home with the two children. I know

Rachel's actions had hurt Becky, but my resilient friend felt she would need her sister's support and was willing to forgive her.

As for me, I bided my time and waited for the inevitable ax to fall. And it did. Naturally, the media had a field day with headlines "Daytime TV Host Sues Ex-Lover's Partners" and "Homeless Teen Battles for Millions". Word of my involvement in this new lawsuit reached the network immediately. I received a phone call from Brian only an hour before I signed for a registered letter from the network. He had prepared me, so I knew what to expect. According to SBG, I had acted with woeful disregard to the clearly written expectations that had been agreed to by both parties and that I was in breach of the express terms of the contract. And further, that my actions would have a lasting negative impact on the network, which nullified the contract to produce my show. They sought my discretion in keeping the news from the press until they had a chance to do some damage control. In exchange for my silence, they would let me keep my blog and podcast and exclusive use of the name *Miranda Writes*. Although they did not state it directly, it appeared they had no plans to seek monetary damages from me for the show's considerable development and launch expenses. After I read it through twice, I called Brian back.

"You had to know this would happen," he told me. "The timing of this lawsuit of yours could not have been worse. What were you thinking?"

"I needed to see it through," I told him. "Becky had her day in court, but it cost her everything. If Adam hadn't been pressured to make her disappear, she wouldn't have had to spend three years alone in Maine. And they bribed her family to get her charged with drug possession and to lose custody of Jesse. Rachel was the only family she had, Brian, and yeah, it was really crappy of her to sell Becky out like that, but those lawyers were the ones who put all of this into motion. They have to pay for what they did."

"But you knew, didn't you? That they would pull your show?" he pressed.

"Yeah, I knew," I told him. Of course, I knew. I may have gambled and lost the chance to host a TV show, but I still had my blog and podcasts.

I would happily remain that little dive with great food and top-notch service.

EPILOGUE

One year later

The wedding was on my birthday. My fortieth. With all that had happened in the last year, it almost seemed anticlimactic. Almost. But honestly? It was a lovely ceremony, a beautiful day. I was dry-eyed as my dad and I walked down the makeshift aisle in the local Marriott ballroom, but when he let go of my hand, the enormity of it all hit me and I teared up. They were happy tears, though, and lasted only briefly. This marriage would no doubt change things, but I was ready. I kissed his cheek.

"I love you, Pop."

"Love you more, my girl."

***

One week later, I wiped the sweat off my damp brow with the hem of my T-shirt and looked around the nearly empty house. I surveyed the wall of moving boxes I had packed with a great deal of satisfaction. Only a small amount of the furniture and household items that had filled this place to the brim were going to the new home. The selection process had been a strict one. Only items seen as essential were packed up and anything that didn't bring joy or whatever it was supposed to bring was donated. I couldn't imagine a cupboard full of mismatched and warped Tupperware lids bringing joy to anyone, so I tossed them all. Ditto the chipped and mismatched china and serving platters. Out with the old, I had repeated to myself throughout the day. Everything that would be moved to the new house was carefully labeled with the room it would go to, including piles of infant clothes, books and toys. This baby would want for nothing!

It had been an exhausting process, but there was something liberating about it as well.

My phone buzzed, and I smiled. Tracey.

"Hey T," I said.

"How's the honeymoon going?" I snickered in response.

"Haven't you been following all the posts on social media? It's all fun in the sun, fireworks and drinks with little umbrellas."

"Well, that's good. I'm glad they are having a great time." I thought of my dad and Sally, beaming, waving goodbye from the back seat of a limo en route to the airport. They had flown to an all-inclusive resort in the Bahamas following a lovely wedding ceremony and a reception for family and close friends. Sally had been posting updates on their activities on social media daily.

"They are such a cute couple," Terry said, and I agreed. We talked for a few minutes about the wedding, the reception and the brand-new condo the newlyweds would move into upon their return. Pop's house had sold for well above asking price after only a couple of days on the market. Sally's son Jake had purchased Sally's house, as he wanted more space for his growing family. Fertility treatments had finally been successful and the new baby was due early in the new year. Desmond Quinn was going to get his shot at the role of grandpa at long last. I knew he would totally rock it. I would be an auntie and that was cool, too. I had gotten to know Sally and her kids really well in the past year and it was wonderful to enjoy holidays and build new family traditions with them.

My phone buzzed with an incoming call and a thrill shot through me as I saw the familiar face on my screen.

"Hey, got to go. I've got Eric on the line."

"Speaking of honeymoons ... "

"G' bye T."

I blushed, thinking about the whirlwind courtship culminating in our own beautiful wedding just three months earlier. We were building a new home that Eric had designed for us, just one block from the beach. The finished basement would feature a recording studio and a small reception area for guests of my weekly podcast. Eric was planning to work from home as well, setting up shop in a tricked-out shed in the backyard. We wanted to spend as much time together as our busy careers would allow.

"Hey babe," I greeted him as I pictured his handsome face.

"What're you wearing?" he asked, and now I pictured that face grinning at me.

"I'm cleaning out Pop's house, so naturally a thong and a pair of stilettos, duh."

"I can be there in fifteen minutes," he assured me.

"Sounds good, but hold that thought, yeah? I promised Becky that I would meet her at the accountant's office at two. It's not every day a twenty-one-year-old gets a seven-figure windfall settlement."

"Quinn for the Win strikes again," Eric said. "Hey did you ever look at those carpet samples I brought home? We're trying to finish up work on your studio and we need to lay the carpeting before we can install sound-proofing." I pictured the untouched stack of colored squares on the kitchen counter, right where he had left them. Evidently, I had as little interest in choosing carpet for my home studio as I'd had for my TV show.

"You pick. I trust you."

"You got it. I'll see you at home later."

"What sounds good? Burgers or Thai?"

"You pick," he said. "I trust you. But hey, I wasn't going to ask, but any word from Brian?"

"You know you'd be the first person I'd call. I think you're more excited about this than I am." It was a tiny white lie. I was actually thrilled at the prospect of a publishing contract and had been only partially successful at putting it out of my mind since my agent had first broached the subject earlier in the week. I heard Eric stifle a laugh. "No, seriously, but let's not jinx it, okay?"

"Sure thing, Quinn. Keep me posted. And by the way, I'm leaning towards burgers."

"Sounds like a plan. Love you," I said and ended the call. Life was good.

I went back to wrapping plates and coffee mugs in large sheets of paper. The repetitive nature of the task kept my hands busy, but my mind drifted. According to Brian, there had been quite the public outcry when Sterling had canceled my show. They had been inundated by calls, letters and social media posts defending me and demanding that SBG produce my show. So far, they were holding firm to their decision, but there was talk about "revisiting" my contract when things settled down. I wasn't holding my breath. My phone buzzed again, and I grabbed it.

"Hey Brian," I said, trying to sound casual. "What's up?"

"We got it, Randi. The advance, the royalties, the book tour. Everything we discussed. Initial print run of fifty thousand and guaranteed publication within six months after the manuscript is complete. Looks like *Miranda Writes: a consumer's guide to all things legal* will hit the shelves next summer." Tears streaming down my cheeks, I found myself unable to respond. Not with words, at least, but my squeals of joy told him what he needed to know. "I'll email you the draft of the contract as soon as we hang up. Let's talk tomorrow, first thing, okay?"

"Yes, yes, yes! That sounds terrific. You've stuck by me this whole time, through all the bumps and bruises. I'm so grateful for a friend like you."

"It's what I do. My job was simple," he said. "Now you've actually got to write the damn thing." I hung up, smiling.

I could write. It's what I do.

THE END

ABOUT THE AUTHOR

Gail Ward Olmsted was a marketing executive and a college professor before she began writing fiction on a full-time basis. A trip to Sedona, AZ inspired her first novel *Jeep Tour*. Three more novels followed before *Landscape of a Marriage*, a biographical work of fiction featuring landscape architect Frederick Law Olmsted, a distant cousin of her husband's, and his wife Mary. Her latest book *Miranda Writes* is a contemporary novel with a legal twist. She enjoys writing about quirky, wonderful women in search of a second chance at a happy ever after.

For more information, please visit her on Facebook and at GailOlmsted.com.

NOTE FROM THE AUTHOR

I hope you enjoyed *Miranda Writes*. I love to hear from readers and you can find me on Facebook at Gail Olmsted Author and on Twitter @gwolmsted or email me at gwolmsted@gmail.com. You can check out all of my other titles and get updates on new releases at www.GailOlmsted.com. I love writing about quirky, lovable women in search of a second chance at a happy ever after!

Please consider leaving a review for any of my books or even a quick rating. Word-of-mouth is crucial for any author to succeed. If you enjoyed *Miranda Writes*, please leave a review online—anywhere you are able. Even if it's just a sentence or two. It would make all the difference and would be very much appreciated.

Thanks!

Gail O

We hope you enjoyed reading this title from:

BLACK ROSE
writing™

www.blackrosewriting.com

Subscribe to our mailing list – *The Rosevine* – and receive **FREE** books, daily deals, and stay current with news about upcoming releases and our hottest authors.
Scan the QR code below to sign up.

Already a subscriber? Please accept a sincere thank you for being a fan of Black Rose Writing authors.

View other Black Rose Writing titles at www.blackrosewriting.com/books and use promo code **PRINT** to receive a **20% discount** when purchasing.

9 781685 130237